BREED

BY
M.H. SJOGREN

DENVER, COLORADO

Outskirts Press, Inc.
http://www.outskirtspress.com

ISBN: 978-1-4787-3364-5

Outskirts Press and the "OP" logo are trademarks belonging to Outskirts Press, Inc.

PRINTED IN THE UNITED STATES OF AMERICA

MANY THANKS TO:

W.L.S.

K.S.K.

G.S.K.

CELESTE LARRA

H.P. FORD

P. RYAN

CONTENTS

CONTENTS

❧ CHAPTER ONE ❧

BOSTON 1875

The morning sun warmed the study where the Reverend Mr. Josiah Potts sat reading a letter. Though still in early mid-life, Mr. Potts had developed a comfortable paunch and that, along with a premature baldness, gave him the appearance of a man much older. He was well thought of by townspeople and parishioners alike and much loved by his wife Lavinia.

As director of the "Cecilia Weathermorn Home for Orphaned Gentlewomen," he was often asked to aid one cause or another. Miss Weathermorn was a spinster of great wealth and awareness. Long before her death she had endowed and provided this home for Boston gentlewomen who were without family or means of support. Over the years she had provided not only a home but frequently a small dowry should one of the young ladies receive an offer of marriage. As a result, most of the recipients of her kindness stayed only a few years at the great red brick house. Some married, some under the tutelage of the Potts became school teachers and were able to support themselves. At present there were nine young women under the care of Mr. Potts, ranging in age from fifteen to twenty.

Lavinia Potts entered as her husband read the letter for the third time, a puzzled frown on his face. As she adjusted the drapes so the winter sun would not fade the Turkish carpet, Mr. Potts sighed and gave her the letter to read. Mrs. Potts was a tiny birdlike woman with a mass of wren-brown hair piled on top of her head in the hope of achieving a few more inches of height. Her good nature showed on her face, for her brow was unlined but there were deep creases at the corners of her mouth and dimples made by her frequent smiles.

Mrs. Potts put on her spectacles and proceeded to read the letter:

Dear Rev. Potts,

William Hawksbury, Esq., my agent and

man of law in Boston, will soon

contact you regarding the following:

Since my wife departed, our home is in

great need of a woman's hand and my

three young daughters of a mother's

care. I am not a man of great wealth,

but I do prosper and have high

expectations that it will continue.

I own land in the country and property

in the growing city of Los Angeles, California.

I propose and hope you will

consent to the marriage of one of your

young ladies and myself.

She could sail with my cousin

Captain Hugh Shepard on his vessel, the

Sara Blue, and we would be married

immediately upon her arrival here.

Perhaps your wife will kindly

remember my family as she and my late

mother were acquainted. In any case

I have instructed Mr. Hawksbury

to contribute the sum of five hundred

dollars to your very fine endeavor.

I remain your obedient servant,

> John Matthew Loughlan
> Rancho Dos Aliso
> Los Angeles, California
> July 17, 1875

Lavinia Potts put the letter down and looked at her husband, who stood, hands clasped behind him, in front of the small fire in the grate. "Well, my dear," he said, "what do you make of that?" When she did not answer, he continued, "It sounds very adventuresome to be sure, but perhaps might be very adventurous for one of our dear young ladies. I will, of course, investigate the gentleman thoroughly."

When he had ceased speaking, Lavinia said, "I do believe he must be Isabelle Loughlan's son. She was a neighbor of Mama's, a good and kind woman. She helped Mama when Papa had his last stroke." Lavinia paused as a small knock came at the door and the housemaid Breed entered. She carried a scuttle of coal and dusting cloths.

"Sure, Mrs. Potts, I'm sorry to disturb you and the Reverend, but Sassy Black was ill in the night and Cook let her sleep in. I'm doing her chores, so we are a bit behind." Both the Potts smiled at the young woman and made room for her. She was much taller than the Reverend and his wife. Her features were good, the chin perhaps a trifle too strong for a woman, but because of her height she carried it well. Her hair by her own telling was "as dull as ditch water," a nondescript blonde. Her complexion was clear but looked so pallid in the bright morning sunlight as to appear washed out. Breed's best feature was her eyes, large, very blue and fringed with thick dark lashes. She was twenty-seven years old and had lived with the Potts as a housemaid since she was thirteen.

As Breed dusted the study and mended the fire in the hearth, she gave only half an ear to the conversation between her employer and his wife. Her mind was on the afternoon ahead. Her monthly half a day off. She would leave as soon as luncheon was over and she had helped Cook clear up the kitchen. She hoped that Sassy was better by then so she could go.

Then it was down the hill to her Aunt Kate O'Brien and the stuffy little house that bulged with her seven cousins and their parents.

Breed's father had been a Swedish seaman and her mother the daughter of one of his shipmates. They met when the elder man had brought his friend home for a visit at the end of his last voyage.

Ellen and Lars Seastrum had a happy marriage. He was a large-boned giant of a man, much sought after as a mate. Hence, he spent more time at sea than at home. When he was ashore he would carry the young Breed high on his shoulders and walk down to the docks and point out the different ships. When his little son, Peter, was old enough to accompany them, Breed would walk beside him holding fast to his hand, so proud of him she could hardly speak. He was a quiet, gentle man with little formal education but great knowledge of the sea and his fellow man.

Ellen Seastrum was thirty-two when she married Lars. Her Irish ancestry was evident in her lovely blue eyes with their thick dark lashes. Other than that, she had only good teeth and health to offer in the way of beauty. She was very tall and her face had heavily scarred when she suffered from small pox at age twelve. Having long given up hopes of marriage, she was delighted and relieved when the big quiet Swede asked for her hand. She would have married him had he been half the man he was. To find him not only a gentle man but a thoughtful husband as well locked her love to him for the rest of her life.

When Lars was lost at sea during an early winter storm, Ellen was inconsolable. Neither the parish priest nor her sister Kate could make her realize that her deep mourning hurt the two young children. Breed was twelve and Peter eight.

Through the winter and into the spring young Breed ran the household, trying to make life a little less sad for her brother.

At night, in bed, she shed her own tears for the loss of her father.

With warm weather came two stark realities. The Seastrums'

small horde of savings had dwindled to almost nothing, and Boston was going to have an epidemic of typhoid fever.

When the fever flared up, Kate O'Brien packed her older children off to the country while keeping the youngest, still at her breast, home. Her husband's Aunt Sally lived in a ramshackle old farmhouse on the outskirts of Boston. Eighteen years a widow, Aunt Sally spent much of her time reading and wandering the countryside looking for herbs to use in her various potions and concoctions. She left the running of the farm to a family of black laborers who had come north after the Civil War. Fortunately they were hard, capable workers. With them and the occasional lucid streak, the old woman was able to foil both the banks and nature's attempts to take the farm from her.

Kate O'Brien approached her sister Ellen about letting Peter and Breed join her children in the country, saying, "I know, sister, you think Aunt Sally's crazy as a loon. But really it's just off and on and even when she is, it's harmless and old Ben and his family are there to keep her safe. Let the children go. It's going to be a bad time this summer."

Still dressed in deepest mourning, Ellen Seastrum sat in the kitchen of her small home drinking tea with her sister. "Kate, I don't think Sally's crazy. I know she is. Thank you but I'll not let my children leave me to go and run wild at Aunt Sally's!" She sighed deeply, poured them each more tea and continued, "They are all I have left, with my dearest Lars gone...."

Within ten days young Peter was ill with the fever and shortly his mother and sister also. Peter died first, giving as little trouble as he had in life. Ellen hung on but was too devastated to survive the blow of the boy's death. After a long time, Breed rallied and the fever went. It left her physically exhausted and emotionally drained when she learned of her mother's and brother's deaths.

And Kate O'Brien sent her off to "Poor daft Aunt Sally's" to recuperate. All the long summer Breed lay on the porch of the old house, too weak to even cry for her dear family. Her O'Brien cousins tried to cheer up the invalid, drifting in and out during the day, bringing her a cookie filched from the kitchen, or a jar full of polliwogs to keep her company. Aunt Sally, during her lucid moments, would read to the child long passages from the Bible or unintelligible poems written by long forgotten poets.

In mid-September, the first cold spell came early and Kate O'Brien felt it safe to bring her brood back to town. Breed was up and about by then, but nature had played a trick on her while she languished in bed. She had grown a full six inches, thin as a rail, awkward as a colt.

The good-natured O'Briens made room for the orphan and, as is the way with children, the pain of her loss faded and Breed became her usual good-natured self. She slept with their two youngest cousins in a trundle bed; perhaps that was the hardest adjustment she had to make. At home she and Peter had each had a bed to themselves. Times were hard and as the year wore on, Breed realized that her uncle's small salary could not stretch much further. So in May, when her oldest cousin, Coleen, went into service with one of the wealthy families, Breed asked her Aunt Kate to help her find a place also. She was thirteen years old and very tall for her age.

Two months later, Mrs. Goody, an old friend of Kate's and cook for the "Cecilia Weathermorn Home for Orphaned Gentlewomen," agreed to take Breed on as a kitchen maid.

Over the years Breed advanced from kitchen maid to parlor maid, and because she was willing and able often became lady's maid and even chaperone. Mrs. Potts, a kind woman, realized that Breed was not only cheerful but also intelligent and saw to it that she sat in on the lessons given to the younger girls during her care. Unfortunately for Breed, her many duties didn't allow much time. But over the intervening years she learned quite a bit of history, the ability to sew tolerably well and some useless etiquette. Mrs. Goody, the cook, enjoyed a reputation as somewhat of a gourmet and often had Breed help her prepare the meals.

Breed got along with the young ladies, often able to comfort the newcomers because she had lost her family. She stayed close to Aunt Kate and her growing family, visiting them every month on her one half day off. She grew quite tall and by the age of twenty-one stood five foot nine and a half inches—dwarfing everyone in the house! Her looks did not improve particularly, her features seemingly unfinished as though waiting for nature to decide what she would finally look like. Her figure, too, left much to be desired—wide shoulders that a young man would envy and long legs that were made for striding, rather than the more ladylike gait required of her.

When Breed was twenty-two, a young carpenter who had been called to put up new shelves in the kitchen pantry was much taken with her. He went to Reverend Potts with an offer of marriage. When Breed was approached on the subject, she wasted no time in assuring both Rev. and Mrs. Potts she was perfectly happy with them and had no desire to ally herself "to the wee many" as she referred to the unfortunately short, young carpenter. And so the years passed, if not particularly eventful, and she was at least contented. Breed loved the kind Lavinia Potts. As she matured, she unconsciously tried to emulate the elder woman.

As a result, Breed attained a polished manner that belied her true station and was often mistaken for one of the "young ladies." Frequently, Breed became friends with new members of the household. Lasting friendships would develop, and when a "young lady" left the shelter of the house she continued to write to Breed as well as the Potts. One such friendship was that of Elizabeth Staunton. She had been a sad and bewildered fifteen-year-old when her banker father had died, insolvent and leaving the motherless young girl to be cared for by the Weathermorn Home. Breed had taken the shy, timid Eliza under her wing and helped her through the worst of her adjustment and bereavement. Now, five years later, the two were close friends. Breed's more outgoing and independent personality bolstered the still shy and easily intimidated younger woman.

That evening, when Breed returned from her home visit full of news of the O'Brien doings, she found the house in gentle confusion. Mrs. Goody hurried about the kitchen, mixing up one of her well-known concoctions. The time-honored remedy varied with whatever fruit syrup happened to be available. It consisted of a squeeze of lemon, a bit of sugar, a dash of syrup (tonight she was using some of her cranberry syrup), hot water and a good stiff shot of brandy, (The latter being the secret ingredient since Reverend Potts was of the Methody persuasion and strictly abstinent). Sassy Black, the young kitchen maid, stood at the sink washing the dinner dishes and rolling her eyes in excitement.

"Lordy Breed, what did you miss 'tafternoon," she exclaimed.

"Hush you," spoke the cook. "Finish the dishes quick like, it's going to be a long night." Through with mixing the hot drink, she set it on a small tray. "Maybe you can do something with her!"

"Who?" asked the bewildered young woman, as she put aside her shawl and bonnet.

"Miss Eliza Staunton, that's who," piped up the irrepressible Sassy. "A big fat gentleman come asking for her hand this noon and she fainted dead away and been having 'sterics ever since!" Here she shivered at the sheer excitement of it all.

Breed looked at the cook for confirmation "It's the God's truth. He's a Mr. Carlton Smooty, Esq., a friend of her poor dead father's. Seems he's decided it's time to settle down and figured Miss Eliza would jump at the chance!"

Breed took the tray and hastened above stairs wondering where she would find the girl. One look as she reached the front hall told her. Several of the younger girls were clustered around the half-closed study door and she could hear sounds of the Reverend's voice trying to comfort the by now exhausted Eliza Staunton.

Breed cleared her throat and the little knot of girls and young women standing around the door guiltily moved aside. Breed knocked gently on the door and entered without waiting for an answer. Lavinia Potts was sitting beside the limp figure of Eliza Staunton, holding her hands comfortingly, while the poor Rev. Potts paced to and fro on the hearth rug. On seeing Breed he looked relieved. "Bless my soul. Here's our Breed with a hot toddy to settle your nerves, Miss Eliza," he said.

"Oh, Breed, thank God you're here," sobbed the distraught girl. Mr. Potts wiped his forehead with his handkerchief and excused himself, promising to return shortly.

Kneeling in front of the two women, Breed held the hot drink to Eliza's lips and coaxed her to drink a little. After a moment she asked Lavinia what all the commotion was about. Lavinia, with a worried look at Eliza, told the same story Breed had heard in the kitchen, if somewhat less luridly. At the end of her recital, Eliza broke in passionately, "I will not marry that awful man. He and Papa never planned for me to. He lied!" Breed sat back on her heels and looked at the pale, disheveled girl and wondered what would make her so upset about the appearance of Mr. Smooty.

Eliza Staunton's mother had died when she was seven. Her widowed father seemed to lose all sense of direction after his wife's death and began to let his successful banking business slide away. He spent most of this time with the little girl or sitting in morose silence in his library. Leo Staunton had been forty-eight when he married Anne Miles. She was a lovely young woman of only twenty-three, a mass of curling dark hair, huge grey eyes and weak lungs. Never strong but of a happy outgoing nature, she brought light and happiness to the middle-aged bachelor. As time passed, it became clear that his once prosperous business was failing. Too late he began to worry about the future. Mr. Staunton might still have been able to salvage enough for Eliza and him to live at least in comfort had one of his main creditors not demanded complete payment at once. The pressure and stress of trying to save something from his once-thriving concern began to show, and his health failed.

One afternoon, as Mr. Staunton sat laboring over papers in his library in a vain attempt to stall his bankruptcy, the maid announced a caller. Mr. Staunton rose from his desk, but as the visitor entered he sat back down, flushed with anger and surprise. Here was the man responsible for most of his troubles and he had the temerity to come unasked to the Staunton home. At first the older man felt a flicker of hope, his creditor had relented, but in a moment he realized it was not so. The creditor began to threaten his debtor, painting a picture of the dishonor and shame that awaited Mr. Staunton and his daughter.

"But wait. Perhaps there is a way out," the man said, pausing and then hurrying on. "If you were to give the hand of your daughter to me in marriage. One couldn't foreclose on one's father-in-law." The creditor had been standing at the window, gazing out at the garden as he spoke, but the sound of the old man rising from his chair made him cease speaking and turn. This final insult was too much for poor Mr. Staunton. He rose shakily to his feet, gasped and clutched at his neckcloths, making strangling noises. The younger man stood motionless, assessing the gasping man but making no attempt to go to his aid. At that moment Eliza Staunton, glowing and beautiful after a walk with school friends, entered her father's library. The young girl gave a little scream and rushed to her father's side. She noticed the other man still by the window and begged, "For the love of God, Mr. Smooty, have one of the servants call the doctor!"

Carlton Smooty snatched his hat from the table. With no word of farewell, he turned and nearly knocked down the house maid as he hurried out of the room. The old man suffered a stroke. He was paralyzed and unable to do more than mumble a few confused sentences. Eliza nursed him tenderly for six weeks but he did not last longer. The young girl was left practically destitute, with only a few of her own clothes and books after her father's creditors received their due. Of Carlton Smooty she saw nothing, thankfully, as she was sure he caused her father to have his initial seizure and his refusal to come to his aid proved he meant harm to the old man. Shortly before her fifteenth birthday, Eliza Staunton went to live at Weathermorn House and was befriended by the older girl, Breed Seastrum.

After much coaxing, Breed got the weeping girl to tell the tale of her last meeting with the loathsome Mr. Smooty. When she had finished, the tenderhearted Lavinia wiped tears from her eyes and announced that, of course, Eliza couldn't marry such a man "even though he is as rich as Croesus and very powerful. Mr. Potts will think of something, my dear. He's very good at 'arranging,' you know!"

Breed took the exhausted Eliza upstairs. She helped her into her nightgown and put a warming pan in the bed to pamper the younger girl. Cook's potion and the snug, warm bed began to work. Breed drew the curtains and was preparing to leave when Eliza said in a drowsy voice, "Breed, don't leave me. I'm so alone." The young housemaid sat on the edge of the bed and held the limp hand of the now sleeping girl. When she was sure Eliza was deeply asleep, Breed went quietly out, leaving the door ajar in case Eliza should call.

Breed had been up since half-past five in the morning, on her feet for much of that time, and was understandably weary. As Breed entered the kitchen, Mrs. Goody asked her about Miss Eliza and then told her to take the after-dinner coffee tray to the Potts, as they wanted to hear about the younger girl.

After washing her hands and putting on a fresh apron, Breed carried the tray into the study to her employers. Mr. Potts had assumed his usual stance in front of the grate with his hands held behind his back, while Lavinia sat with her basket of handwork in her lap. Lavinia patted the sofa beside her. "Breed, sit down with us," Reverend Potts said. "We must talk about Miss Eliza. It's plain to me that she simply cannot marry that Smooty man! The offensive behavior he displayed in approaching Miss Eliza before speaking first to me, her Guardian! Clearly, clearly he's no gentleman!" Here he stopped to draw breath and drink his coffee.

Breed assured them that the young girl was fast asleep, and that she agreed Mr. Carlton Smooty would not be a good choice as a bridegroom to the sensitive Eliza.

"The only problem is that Mr. Potts has asked about this Mr. Smooty and finds him to be very wealthy and influential here and about Boston," said Mrs. Potts.

"Sure, that could be awkward," Breed said quietly, for she sensed that the Rev. Potts was already planning what could be done to rescue her friend.

Mr. Potts cleared his throat and asked Breed if she had been listening to their conversation that morning. Breed truthfully told him she really hadn't paid much attention as she was thinking about her afternoon off, but wasn't it to do with a man in far-off California?

"Precisely," echoed the Reverend and Mrs. Potts, beaming. Then Mr. Potts took the letter from his desk and read it to Breed.

"Well?" he asked expectantly when he finished. "Do you think Miss Eliza would be willing to contract an alliance with Mr. Loughlan, should he prove suitable, that is? Truly, she must do something. We could tell Mr. Smooty she was previously spoken for and so have a perfectly legitimate excuse for not accepting his proposal."

The worried little man continued. Breed's head was reeling from all the happenings of the day and sheer exhaustion. But as she gathered the coffee cups and tray, she said, "From what Eliza has told me, she will be helping this California man's little girls. She must be agreeable. Ask her in the morning. Good night to ye both," and she left them.

Later, in the attic room she shared with Sassy Black, she was too tired to even think about what the next morning would bring. She fell sound asleep the moment her head sank into her pillow.

In the morning Eliza was calmer but adamant in her determination to refuse Carlton Smooty. Just before lunch, Mr. Potts returned from town, where he had gone to interview Lawyer Hawksbury.

Lavinia Potts asked Eliza to join them in the study and sent word to the kitchen for Breed to come also. When all were seated and giving their complete attention, Mr. Potts began to explain his maneuver to outwit the odious Mr. Smooty: "So there, Miss Eliza, it's agreed then. I'll inform Mr. Smooty that you have been previously betrothed to Mr. John Loughlan of Los Angeles, California. And as soon as passage can be arranged you will be leaving Boston."

Lavinia Potts sighed with relief and, patting Eliza's hand, told her, "There now, my dear. Mr. Potts has arranged everything and I'm sure Mr. Loughlan will be ever so nice. I remember his dear mother before they went to California. Such a kind person. He, of course, was just a boy but as I think back he did many thoughtful acts for my Mama—cutting wood, etc."

Eliza had visibly brightened, the thought of escaping the hateful Mr. Smooty cheering her immeasurably. "It will be such an adventure for us, Breed," she said. "But I shall not be one bit worried with you at my side."

"Breed?" said Mr. and Mrs. Potts in unison.

"Me?" squawked the startled Breed.

"You would not allow me to travel half around the world unaccompanied, surely," Eliza said. "And who is a better companion than our good Breed. Shall I be seasick, do you think, Breed?"

The Potts began to protest. "Breed has been with us these many years—why, she keeps us all together. Who will cook when Mrs. Goody is ill?" asked the good Reverend.

"And take you girls for walks and help me mend the linens?" asked Lavinia.

Breed, still not used to the idea of leaving the place where she had expected to grow old, thought to herself: "Sure. It's funny what people think is important, not a word say they of all the cleaning, dusting, bedmaking, marketing and such, ah well, the gentry are funny folk...."

The emotional Eliza began to weep again. "Please let Breed go with me. I could not leave all I hold dear and know and go alone.... Perhaps when Mr. Loughlan and I are settled, then Breed could return."

Mr. Potts, ever at the mercy of a weeping female, agreed hastily. "Very well, my dear, she must go but only to settle you, then back she must come to Boston. Now dry your tears."

Mrs. Potts sadly consented to the loss of her housemaid, wondering where she should ever find a replacement. So it was settled. Eliza Staunton would go to California and marry John Loughlan, and Breed would be her companion and maid. No one had yet asked Breed her feelings on the subject.

She was twenty-seven and had never been farther from Boston than Aunt Sally's farm. Her life had a settled routine that she had sunk into for want of any other, and here in the blink of an eye it was changing. Descended on both sides of her family from some of the world's greatest adventurers and mariners, she felt her brain begin to reel. To sail the high seas in a ship such as her father had, to see foreign ports and people, the thought was frightening but exhilarating. Breed was roused from her reverie by Mrs. Potts. "It will truly be a sacrifice," she said, "but if we must we must. Breed, advertise at once for a new girl to be trained before you go."

"Yes ma'am, but would you consider my Aunt Kate's youngest girl Maggy? She's a hard worker and a good girl." It was agreed that Maggy O'Brien should be given a try and that Breed must help Elizabeth go over her clothes so as to decide what items they must purchase.

Mr. Potts sent word to the lawyer Hawksbury that Mr. Loughlan's offer had been accepted by Miss Elizabeth Staunton and invited the man of law to dine the next night at Weathermorn House.

The whole house was abuzz with the news of Eliza's engagement and forthcoming journey. Privately, several of the older girls felt they would have been a better choice for the exciting Mr. Loughlan but held their peace, hopeful that their turn would come.

Mr. Hawksbury turned out to be an elderly gentleman with a somewhat stern expression that did not relent till well into the evening. Two helpings of Mrs. Goody's cherry nut cake with whipped cream mellowed him enough to admit that he was sure John Loughlan and Miss Eliza would do well together, Mr. Loughlan being partial to small dark-haired women. He explained the proposed agenda and gave John Loughlan's check for five hundred dollars to Reverend Potts.

In late April or early May, Captain Hugh Shepard, Mr. Loughlan's cousin and skipper of the sailing ship Sara Blue would return from his current voyage to California. After unloading his cargo and contracting for more, the Sara Blue would set sail again for California. Since the Sara Blue was a trading vessel, it would probably need three or four months to reach its destination as it must make many stops en route. Mr. Hawksbury approved of Breed's accompanying Eliza and reminded them to take both warm clothes and summer wear as it would be quite warm for a while. Then, as the Sara Blue approached the Cape of Storms, it would again be winter.

Eliza's sense of euphoria began to fade at the prospect of the long sea voyage, but when she felt too frightened she had only to think of her alternative, the detested Mr. Smooty, and her resolve strengthened. Breed, on the other hand, looked forward to the forthcoming passage and could hardly contain her buoyancy and excitement.

Christmas came and went in its usual flurry of decorations, church-going and gift-giving, but to the excited Breed it was just more time to be got through till they would be notified that the Sara Blue was loaded with cargo and ready for passengers to board her.

Mr. Potts had given some of John Loughlan's contribution to Mrs. Potts to buy Eliza a few things for her trousseau. Lavinia had generously given Breed a length of good grey wool to make herself a traveling suit.

The winter was severe and allowed little in the way of social life as the snow was very deep and the city street sweepers were hard put to keep the walks and roads cleared. Eliza and Breed's forthcoming adventure became an endless entertainment for all the young women of the house. Mr. Potts gave several classes on the geography of the sea and land they would visit, and Lavinia searched the public library for information she thought tasteful enough to impart to the soon-to-embark travelers. All the young girls got together and approached Mrs. Goody, asking her what they could give Breed as a going-away gift. She suggested a new portmanteau. She gave Mrs. Hibbs, the dressmaker who came twice a year to sew for the young ladies, money to make a lovely lawn shirtwaist for Breed to wear with her new suit. Mrs. Goody was very fond of Breed and would miss her too. The new girl, Maggy, was shaping up nicely.

As winter finally loosened its grip and spring arrived, Mrs. Potts sent Sassy Black and the handyman, Elmo, to fetch from the attic the traveling trunk Eliza was to use. The sight of the old humpbacked trunk in the corner of her bedroom brought home to Eliza that she would soon leave her old life behind. Never the bravest, she began to have second thoughts and once even suggested to Mrs. Potts, "Wouldn't it be easier if I just 'took the veil' instead of traveling half around the world to avoid Mr. Smooty?" But the distracted Lavinia chose not to hear her. When the worried Eliza suggested the same thing to Breed, busy polishing silver in the pantry, Breed answered off-handedly, "Take the veil where, Miss Eliza?" So Eliza concealed her anxiety as best she could and obediently did what she was told.

On the second Monday in April came a note from Mr. Hawksbury, announcing the arrival in port of Capt. Hugh Shepard and the Sara Blue. The note said it would take several weeks to refit and reload the ship and then all would be ready for the California voyage.

The Weathermorn House was in an uproar. Eliza became so agitated that she broke out in hives and had to be put to bed with a poultice. The doctor suggested she stay there for a day or two. Breed breathed a sigh of relief, for now she could get on with the preparations for their journey.

In the last week of April, Breed said goodbye to her aunt and uncle, promised to write her various cousins and paid a short visit to the graveyard where her family was buried. As she rose from her knees and said a final blessing, she noticed the elderly parish priest walking slowly along the churchyard wall reading his evening office. Fourteen years in the Methodist minister's home had dulled her never-too-fervent Catholicism, but she still said her Roman prayers and in moments of stress sought the saints' aid. Breed approached the old priest and was more than a little surprised when after a moment's conversation he said, "And you are Ellen Seastrum's daughter Bridget, aren't you?" She nodded and he continued, "I knew your mother well, and married her and your father, and baptized you and your little brother for all of that!"

He motioned Breed to sit down on the old stone bench under the linden tree. Gathering his cassock around him, he sat beside her. "Your Aunt Kate has kept me abreast of your doings these years and even if you have been lax in your duties to Mother Church I know you have been a good young woman. And soon now you go to a new land to a new life. I think we will not see Bridget Seastrum again in Boston....Remember your heritage, girl, and all will be well."

Breed sat with head bowed and work-roughened hands clasped tightly in her lap. The old man touched her arm and said, "Come now, daughter, and make a good confession and then receive Our Lord. His Grace will guard you on your journey."

Together they went into the stone church and Breed received the sacraments of her faith. Much later, as she walked rapidly home, she felt such elation and happiness that she could hardly keep from running. She was a new person going to a new land and a new exciting life. The chrysalis was beginning to open and make old Breed, the orphan housemaid, give way to the new.

Early on the 2nd of May an exotic-looking man knocked at the kitchen door of Weathermorn House and asked to see "the Missus." Sassy Black looked at his wild black beard, scarred cheek and single gold earring and slammed the door full in his face, bellowing to Breed, "There be a pirate at the door!" Breed wiped her hands on a dish towel and briskly put the frightened Sassy aside.

When she opened the door, carefully, to be sure, the seaman was still standing patiently on the back porch. When he saw Breed, he touched his cap and offered an envelope.

"If you please, Miss, Capt. Shepard sends his respects. Will you give this to the Mrs. Potts?" Breed thanked him and took the letter. Closing the door, she explained to the irrepressible Sassy that the seaman was not a pirate but one of the crew on the ship she and Eliza were to sail on.

Breed went at once to Mrs. Potts, who was sorting linens in the upstairs hall. When the young maid gave Lavinia the letter she took out her spectacles and sat reading on the window seat.

"Oh! Oh, my dear," said Mrs. Potts after a few moments of perusing the letter. "Captain Shepard asks Mr. Potts and me to escort you girls to dinner on board the Sara Blue tonight! And he plans to sail with the tide tomorrow!" Breed caught her breath and had difficulty subduing her excitement. Lavinia rose and, putting her spectacles and the captain's letter in her apron pocket, began issuing instructions like a general on the field of battle. "Breed, go tell Miss Eliza, then dear help her finish her packing. And tell Cook the four of us shall be out for dinner. And, oh, have Sassy press my good navy sarcenet ... run now, and I must go and tell Mr. Potts."

Breed gathered up her skirts and ran down the stairs to the music room where the music teacher was giving Eliza and Miss Horton voice lessons. She knocked gently on the door and let herself in. When Eliza saw the suppressed excitement on Breed's face, she knew the time had come. She gasped and sat down heavily on the piano bench. "It's come, hasn't it?" asked the younger woman. "We must go from here, from our own dear home....Oh, Breed, I'm so frightened!"

Breed took Eliza's hand. She pulled her to her feet, excused them both and left the gaping music teacher alone with his other student.

"Come you now, Eliza," Breed said. "No time for hysterics. Mrs. Potts says we must finish packing. Word has just come and we sail with the tide in the morning!"

The two young women spent the forenoon packing, putting their few remaining belongings in their portmanteaus and trying to find room for the various last-minute gifts they received. Ellen's friend, Miss Marion, with eyes full of tears, gave her the latest romance by Mrs. D. A. Comfy with instructions that Eliza should read it on the long voyage. Cook gave Breed an envelope full of her best recipes and several of her "potions" also. Even Sassy Black had an offering, two pennies' worth of lemon drops in a small bag. "To keep you from the scurvy," she announced triumphantly. Mr. Potts, in one of his dissertations on the forthcoming voyage, had mentioned the old use for lemons and limes to prevent the dreaded scurvy, and Sassy had assumed the lemon drops to be as efficacious as the less desirable, in her eyes, lemons and limes.

After Breed had helped Mrs. Goody with lunch and tidied the kitchen, she took her shawl from the hook on the kitchen door and let herself out quietly before anyone could claim her attention. Once out the garden gate she ran as fast as she could down the hill toward her Aunt Kate's. There were kisses and tears and promises of letters, but all the while Breed knew she would not see this little crowded house nor her aunt again. Kevin, one of the eldest cousins, a married man himself now, came in to see his Ma while Breed was there. He gave Breed a good punch in the arm and demanded, "Now you, Bridget me girl, don't forget all I taught about taking care of yourself," and he gave her a rib-cracking hug.

Breed gave them all a last goodbye, and with tears in her eyes hurried away to her future.

❧ CHAPTER THREE ❧

Hugh Shepard stood more than six feet tall and had broad shoulders. At thirty-eight, his black hair was thick and fell across his wide forehead, his skin permanently tanned by years of exposure to the sun and wind. His father and his uncle, John Loughlan Sr., were partners in a small shipping company when gold was discovered in California in 1849. They had been quick to realize the need for mining material, dry goods and food in the new gold fields and had bought a four-masted baroque in good repair, hired a crew, loaded the cargo and set sail for California before news of the gold strike was six months old.

In California, John Loughlan saw to the vending of their freight while a third partner, Frances Shepard, refilled the ship and obtained cargo for the homeward journey. Exposure to the excitement, danger and turbulence of the gold fields entranced the ship owner, and John Loughlan vowed he would return within the year. They had been men of means, living comfortable lives until then, but that first voyage and subsequent passages made them wealthy. Loughlan Sr. reluctantly left the gold fields and returned to Boston where he told his wife and young son, John, about the great new land. He arranged to take a leave of absence and provide for his family's welfare while he was gone, then made the return voyage with their company's ship.

Hugh Shepard went to sea at ten as a cabin boy and had worked his way up from the ranks. He was a man of courage and ability, and his crew had great confidence in his seamanship. The Sara Blue was a three-masted schooner-type vessel, built in Essex, Mass., about 1861, and was capable of high speed even when fully cargoed. Two weeks before the Confederates fired on Fort Sumter, Captain Shepard left for the Boston-to-San Pedro run, planning to be back in seven months. The ship sustained such damage in a storm that it took months of work to refit her. Captain Shepard and his crew were stranded in Valparaiso trying to get the vessel seaworthy. By the time they were able to set sail once more, it was 1863 and San Pedro was quarantined with an epidemic of the virulent small pox. San Pedro was the port of the city of Los Angeles, so being denied entry to one denied you both.

Hugh sent word to his aunt Loughlan and cousin John and sailed on to San Francisco. Disposing quite profitably of the cargo, he was engaged by a Far East trader to sail a load of tanned hides and machinery parts to China. The Sara Blue was gone three years. When she returned to the United States, the Civil War was over. The cargo from China—tea, colorful silks and beautiful porcelain crockery—was worth a half-million dollars. The Loughlans invested their profits in land in and around Los Angeles and Hugh Shepard spent his on the only female he would ever really love, Sara Blue. She became the most elegant sailing vessel in the trade, even the crews quarters were comfortable, which at that time was unheard of.

Everyone in Weathermorn House was gathered in the front hall of the huge old house to bid farewell to Elizabeth Staunton and Breed Seastrum. Tears flowed profusely, and Mr. Potts had his hands full getting the three ladies and the girls' baggage into the carriage. Finally they were on their way and both Mrs. Potts and Breed comforted the tearful Eliza, reassuring her all would be well.

As the carriage drew up to the wharf, Breed felt a lump in her throat that had nothing to do with farewells. She remembered her father and the story he told of the sea. For a few moments she was his little girl again, walking beside him, her hand in his. Mr. Potts had to speak to her twice when the carriage stopped, so far in the past had she gone.

"Look sharp now, my dears," said Mr. Potts as he climbed down from the carriage. "Give me your hand, Lavinia." Mrs. Potts gracefully maneuvered her cumbersome skirts and the two girls followed. Breed, unused to the fashionably full skirts, mumbled under her breath dire predictions of what would happen should she or Eliza have to run from a mad dog.

The early spring sunset lit the long sleek vessel as light catches a facet of a fine gem. Her brass fittings shone brightly and the fresh paint and varnish fairly glistened. Even the nervous Eliza breathed a little freer at the sight of the beautiful ship. Ezra Johnson as the first mate on the Sara Blue stood at the top of the gangplank to welcome the little party aboard. He saluted the ladies smartly and turning to the beaming Mr. Potts said, "The captain's compliments, sir. Will you and the ladies join him in the saloon?"

Mr. Potts herded the ladies ahead of him to the short flight of steep ladder stairs leading below deck. The saloon of the Sara Blue could have rivaled any in Boston for taste and comfort. Though it was not large, its sparse furnishings and uncluttered appearance gave the feeling of space. A long oak table was set with the finest linen and a set of beautiful china that Hugh Shepard had brought back during one of his voyages to the Orient. The saloon was lit with many candles in little wall sconces of burnished brass and one large candelabrum in the center of the dining table.

Hugh Shepard stood beside a small serving hutch cleverly built into the wall. Opened above his head was a cabinet containing the ship's private stock of wines and liqueurs, each set carefully in its own snug fitting. Just as the party from Weathermorn House entered, he finished pouring a glass of sherry for each guest. The captain and Mr. Potts shook hands and introductions were made. He was so gracious and gentlemanly that Elizabeth took heart and was able to raise her eyes and look around her. Breed had inspected the captain briefly and mentally assigned him the role of "a handsome boy and sure he knows it," then dismissed him. Her sole attention was the ship and while the others chatted she wandered around the small saloon, inspecting and marveling at its ingenious arrangements for comfort and safety. Nothing was allowed to stand free so that in the event of foul weather it could not be tossed about.

A young boy of thirteen or fourteen came in carrying a covered tureen of soup and announced, "Cookie says if you'll sit you down I'm to say dinner is served and give you your soup."

The party smiled at the youngster's serious expression and Captain Shepard said, "Very good, Harry, we will sit right down. Mrs. Potts if you will sit on my right...."

Mr. Potts held a chair for Eliza and the first mate, Mr. Johnson, stood behind one intended for Breed, but she hesitated. Her exact place had not been discussed. Was she the lady's maid, chaperone or friend? Was she to take meals with them?

Lavinia Potts noted her dilemma, smiled and nodded, saying, "Sit down, my dear. We must not keep dinner or the captain's cook waiting." Gratefully the young woman sat down at the table with her former employers, thankful that she had paid attention when Mrs. Potts taught the lessons on etiquette. The dinner was well prepared and the captain's wine ensured the success of the meal. He insisted each of the young ladies have a glass. Mr. Potts, usually abstemious, agreed that it was a time for celebration and toasted the Sara Blue and her passengers.

Breed ate slowly, keeping one eye toward Mrs. Potts to be sure she was using the right fork. The captain spoke easily of the forthcoming voyage and assured Miss Eliza she would find California every bit as desirable as Boston.

Eliza said, "Truly, sir, it would have to be a wondrous land to make me forget my dear home and friends."

Her eyes began to fill with tears and her voice quivered. Breed, afraid Eliza would dissolve into a fit of melancholia, spoke quickly to the captain: "Sir, your dishes are beautiful, did you bring them from China, sir?"

Hugh Shepard realized the need for a quick change of subject, took Breed's lead and in the next few minutes shared the exciting adventures of the Sara Blue among the Chinese. When dinner was finished, Captain Shepard suggested Mr. Johnson, the first mate, take the ladies and show them their accommodations while he and Mr. Potts smoked cigars on deck.

The narrow companionway that led from the saloon to the cabins had not been designed for use by three ladies in wide crinolines, so they were forced to walk single file behind Mr. Johnson to the cabin. When he proudly opened the door, it was more than evident that the room would never hold all three ladies at one time. Again, everything was built into the bulkhead of the ship, a bunk on either side and a multitude of cupboards, one of which folded out to a small table and again folded away when not in use. The cabin itself was freshly painted white, a concession to the gender of its new occupants was a large gold framed mirror and the two tiny portholes and curtains drawn across them.

Mr. Johnson proudly pointed them out, saying, "My wife, Mary Anne, made them and had the captain get the looking glass for you." Their baggage was piled in the middle of the floor and he assured them that what they hadn't room for could be stored in the ship's hold. He lit all the candles so the cabin would be ready later when the young ladies returned.

Up on deck the spring evening had turned chilly, so the Potts did not linger with the farewells. Also they were afraid Eliza would change her mind at the last minute and decide to stay in Boston. Both young women promised to write and Captain Shepard assured Mr. and Mrs. Potts he would take the very best care of the "fair maids."

One last embrace from Mrs. Potts and a firm pat on the shoulder from the Rev. Potts and they were gone down the gangplank into the waiting carriage and away. The young women stood a few moments until the carriage was out of sight, then Breed bade the captain good night and led the tearful Eliza below to their cabin. As they prepared for bed, Breed tried to cheer Eliza. However, the younger girl refused to take heart and spent so long at her night prayers that Breed thought she had fallen asleep on her knees!

When they were in their bunks and the candles had been put out, Breed lay for some time, exhausted by the excitement of the day, but with such a light heart that even Eliza's woebegone "good night" could not dull her high spirits. Soon the lapping of water on the hull of the Sara Blue and the creaking of wind in the riggings sent the girls to sleep.

Sometime after dawn Breed awoke, instantly as she usually did. She lay for a time remembering where she was, then quietly rose and dressed. She chose the brown serge dress she wore at Weathermorn House as housemaid without the apron. It was plain but preferable to the fashionable full skirt she had worn the previous night. After making her morning toilette she took her shawl and soundlessly let herself out of the cabin and went above deck. Breed gasped as she looked around. They were under almost full sail and land was only a misty green far to starboard!

As she stood gazing back, she heard the young boy Harry asking, "Miss, if you please, captain says to come up to the Wheelhouse and have some morning coffee." She turned to the boy and nodded. He quickly led her aft, up a short flight of stairs and presented her to the captain.

He was standing beside the black bearded seaman who had delivered his message. "Hold your course, helmsmen," he said, then motioned to Breed to join him at the rail. Hugh Shepard had changed his formal captain's uniform for a thick navy blue sweater and wore an old officer's cap cocked rakishly over one eye. He was used to being found irresistible by the ladies and was surprised when the young servant merely gave him a glance, then began to ply him with questions regarding their departure from Boston and how far they would travel. The captain answered all her questions as they drank the coffee Harry had brought.

When the excited Breed showed signs of running down, he said, "What kind of name is Breed?"

"It's the Irish for Bridget," she answered. "My Da was Swedish and me Ma Irish." Here she realized she was slipping into what her Aunt Kate had referred to as "Bog Irish" and hastily corrected herself. "They chose a name for me that was the same in both countries, only my grandfather spoke the Irish and called me Breed."

"And what should I call you?" he asked.

"Why, whatever you've a mind to, sir, as long as it's polite," she answered. Then, handing him her empty mug, she turned and made her way along the deck toward her cabin. Eliza had just awakened and Breed, her hair blown by the wind on deck, looked so contented that for the first time in months the younger woman began to feel a happy anticipation.

"Come now, Lala, get dressed. There's so much to see on deck. I'll go and ask Harry for our breakfast while you put your clothes on." Eliza smiled at Breed's use of her childhood name. Unable to say

Elizabeth as a toddler, she had told anyone who asked that her name was Lala, much to the amusement of her parents.

Harry brought the girls their breakfast in the saloon and though the cook had tried to make a dainty meal, it still seemed enough for a starving family of six so they insisted that Harry sit down and share with them, promising they would not tell the cook of whom he showed more awe than fear. "He do have a fine throwing arm when he be's mad," announced Harry proudly. As they ate they plied the boy with questions and were surprised by some of the answers. The captain was married to a lady who lived in Gloucester. There were pigs in a sty behind the "forecastle," three sheep, one lamb and even some chickens in a hutch by the galley. Also there were thirty crewmen on board, which surprised Breed because she had seen only a handful when she was on deck. And their next port would be Havana, Cuba.

On deck the wind was fresh and the sea smooth, and the great ship's sails caught the breeze as they raced toward Cuba. The passengers' first day was spent in exploration of the ship with Harry as their guide when he had time free from his galley duties. Eliza declared the lamb the dearest creature and wanted to ask the captain if he might become the ship's mascot. The cabin was a source of great interest because it contained so many cleverly hidden nooks and crannies, a bath cupboard held a bathtub of tin, another door opened to disclose at least a dozen drawers for storing personal clothing. "Truly," said Eliza, "we shall be quite comfortable."

They had dinner with Captain Shepard and Mr. Johnson and the captain teased and flirted outrageously with both young women to the amusement of Mr. Johnson. Eliza blushed at his compliments but Breed smiled tolerantly and continued to ask Mr. Johnson questions about the voyage, the ship and even his wife, Mary Anne, and their baby.

The fair weather lasted three days until they were off the coast of Georgia and the sea became demented. The sky overhead darkened and the wind, no longer a gentle breeze that drove the ship, turned on them. The Sara Blue sailed into the first tropical hurricane of the season. When the wind began to blow and it was evident the ship couldn't outrun the storm, the captain had heavy rope netting lashed up as high as six feet along the deck so none of the seamen would be washed overboard in the heavy seas. The animals were put below in the hold.

At first Breed found the wind exhilarating as the storm approached and the seas roughened. But she was glad when the captain insisted she join Eliza below in their cabin. Since their first morning on deck, the girls had smugly complimented one another on their freedom from seasickness. Now, as Breed made her way to the cabin, she realized she was going to be seasick. If she didn't quickly get to the chamber pot in the bath cupboard, she was going to disgrace herself by throwing up in the companion way!

As she reached the cabin door, young Harry appeared beside her. "Here, miss, let me help you." He deftly led her to her bunk and gave her the large bowl he had been carrying. "Captain says I'm to settle you in and take care of you if you be real sick," he said as he went over to Eliza's bunk. Eliza had already been through a bout of vomiting and lay gently moaning. Harry took extra blankets from one of the cupboards and tucked in each girl, then from somewhere he produced lengths of wood that attached to the bunks and turned them into a child's crib, so the bunks' occupants could not be thrown out of bed in rough weather. Breed saw him leave with the chamber pot and bowl she had used but felt too ill to call him back. He returned shortly, dressed in a southwester and oilcloth coat dripping wet. He carefully wiped each girl's face and put the clean bowl between them and the bunk wall for future use. "It be a big one, this old storm," he volunteered. "Mr. Hornby, the ship's carpenter, say it probably last a week." On that cheerful note, he left them again.

"A week? My God another day of this and I'll be dead," thought Breed. She could hear Eliza moaning but was too nauseous to do more than raise her head from the pillow.

The storm raged for several days and after the first twenty-four hours Breed's stomach began to settle and she was able to drink a cup of tea and nibble on a ship's biscuit. As Breed felt better, she noticed that the faithful Harry was beginning to look distinctly worn and told him that she felt he could take care solely of Miss Eliza now to save him some running. To herself she vowed to repay the boy for his kindly ministrations during their bouts of mal de mer.

Harry sat down a moment on her bunk. "If'n your sure, miss, it would be a help. Early this morning the cook was working on the foresheet, it be his 'sponsibility, only a gust of wind grabbed him and threw him against the galley bulkhead and captain thinks he's got both a broken arm and a broken shoulder!"

"Oh, how awful. Who will cook for the crew?" asked Breed.

"Me, I guess, miss, though there's not much eating going on with this storm. Cookie will just have to tell me how to do it...." He sat looking bleakly at his future. Cabin boy was hard work but he was up and down and in and out all day seeing everything and everyone while the cook spent most of the day in the galley. He shrugged his shoulders, took Breed's empty mug, and left. Breed lay for sometime waiting to see if the tea and biscuit would stay down. When she felt no ill effects, she put her feet over the side of the bunk and, holding fast to the wall, stood up. She was dreadfully weak and more than a little light-headed, but the wilding, tossing motion of the ship no longer seemed to cause her to feel ill. She glanced at herself in the mirror and was startled to see how pale and gaunt she looked. All the color three days on deck had given her was gone. She tottered over to Eliza's bunk but the younger woman was asleep, so Breed let her be and went about making herself presentable. By the time she had washed, combed and pinned up her hair she was so exhausted she crawled back in her bunk and fell asleep.

In the evening Harry brought more tea and a bit of soup for each of them. Breed ate hers and felt much better so she roused the still sleeping Eliza and insisted she at least try some of the hot soup. The soup she could not face, but she did drink a cup of tea that Breed had heavily sugared and was able to keep it down. Breed, feeling better every hour, freshened up Eliza, combing her hair and helping her put on a clean nightgown. She had asked Eliza if she would like her to read from one of the books, but Eliza had already dozed off. Breed gathered up the few dishes and, walking carefully, left their cabin and went down the short companionway to the captain's saloon. She heard several voices and so entered without knocking. The captain was sitting at the dining table, holding tight to his dish for the ship's rolling and pitching made it likely the meal would soon be in his lap. Harry was standing next to the captain and looked quite woebegone and Mr. Johnson seemed to be trying to soothe the captain. Everyone looked at Breed when she entered.

"Well, now at least one of our patients is up," said Mr. Johnson in a jovial tone.

"Damn it to hell," roared the captain. "She'll be back in her bunk soon enough if she has to eat this swill," and he shoved the plate away from him. Breed caught it as it slid nearly to the edge of the table and noted its contents did look unappetizing. What she assumed were fried potatoes were congealed in grease and the two fried eggs were charred and dried looking.

"I'm sorry, sir," said the dejected Harry. "I just ain't much of a cook."

Breed put her few dishes on the tray Harry was holding and added the rejected dish of dinner.

"Here now, Harry, take this back to the galley," she said. "Everything will be all right."

The boy brightened and, looking at the captain for permission, left the saloon as quickly as possible.

"For God sakes, Mr. Johnson, what are we going to do? None of us has had a proper meal since the cook was injured and we are still almost a week's sail from Havana, where we can hopefully engage another."

Mr. Johnson looked at the captain and then at Breed helplessly, but before he could say anything, Breed spoke up. "Calm down, captain, let me cook. Mrs. Goody trained me well and what help I need your cook can give me. He can sit right in the galley when he's up and around."

Hugh Shepard looked at her speculatively a moment, then slammed his fist on the table and cried, "Done!" Then, as a second thought, he added, "And I'll pay you the same wages as Cookie, but it had better be a whole lot better than Harry's muck."

Breed smiled and said, "Sure, I'll try, sir. Now, Mr. Johnson, would you show me the way to the galley?"

The next few days, Breed worked harder than ever before in her life. Cooking three meals a day for thirty-five people took every bit of her time. Even with Harry's help, she was hard-put to get it on the table at the right time. The cook developed a fever, was confined to his bunk and so was not able to help. Breed cooked everything three times, but after a day or so she picked up a few ideas from Harry and learned to just triple her recipes. The Sara Blue's galley was half the size of Mrs. Goody's kitchen at Weathermorn House, but even Mrs. Goody would have been impressed. There were the usual cupboard and drawers, but everything was secured against rough weather—a place for each item and that item was in it. There was a large marble slab for working pastry and dough on a large tin sink with water pumped right into it for washing and cleaning up. The huge iron stove was bolted to the bulkhead and had the largest ovens Breed had ever seen. Two huge grey tin coffee pots sat on the back burner, one always hot, and woe be to Harry, whose job it was to keep it hot, if the coffee ran out or was lukewarm.

A day or so after Breed had taken up her new duties, Eliza realized that if she planned to remain in her bunk for the rest of the voyage, she would be alone. So, tottering badly like an old, old lady, she crept up on deck intending to find Breed. Hugh Shepard saw her clinging to a hatch cover, looking for all the world like a drowned kitten, and took pity on the young girl.

"Here now, Miss Eliza, let me help you. Carlos, go quickly and get a chair from the saloon," he ordered a crewman nearby as he took Eliza by the elbow and led her to the poop deck. In moments, the seaman was back with the chair and had the forethought to bring a light shawl he found there. Captain Shepard settled Eliza comfortably and said, "I'm glad to see you up and about. I'll send for Breed and you and she shall have a quiet hour in the sun." He left her and returned to the wheel, first sending Carlos to the galley for Breed.

In a few minutes, Breed joined Eliza. She was wearing a large, white apron and wiping her hands on a towel. "It's good to see you up and about, Eliza," she said, kissing the younger woman on the forehead.

"A lot you care," snapped the invalid. "I could be dying down there and who would know? You're gone all the time, playing games in the kitchen. Really, Breed, do you think it's...it's quite 'ladylike'?"

Breed felt guilty at leaving her charge and said, "Truly, Eliza, Harry's been to see you were all right every little while—and it's not games I've been playing but making that soup that you ate this noon for lunch." She laughed as she ran out of breath. "And I'm no lady!"

Eliza refused to be mollified. "What would Mrs. Potts say?" she questioned.

But Breed would not argue. "We all must eat. You, to regain your strength, the crew if they are to remain well and sail us safely, and himself there, because he has a hollow leg and likes his vittles!" This last she said looking over her shoulder at the captain.

"Please, Eliza, don't fret me. It's a week to Havana and a new cook. I should be bored to tears just sitting here in our cabin. I'm used to being busy...and Groggens, he's the ship's carpenter, says I am turning into quite a 'seaworthy' cook!"

At this last information, Eliza sniffed, "Oh, very well, but if you are going to be down in that kitchen...."

Breed corrected her. "Galley."

"....Galley, then I'll just have to come and help you, for I will not be left alone!" So, it was that Eliza came as close to working in a kitchen as she would for the rest of her life. Breed, pleased at the turn of events, sent Harry down below for apples and knives, and she and Eliza spent a pleasant time on deck in the sun, peeling twenty pounds of apples for that night's apple cake dessert.

The injured cook, who had been delirious, lapsed into a coma late in the afternoon, and in the last hour of the late watch he died. The girls were upset when told the news at breakfast but insisted on being present as the crew and captain said the prayers for burial at sea. Breed wiped a few quiet tears, remembering her father's death at sea and wondering if he, too, had the benefit of prayers.

❧ CHAPTER FOUR ❧

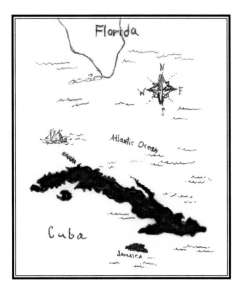

The weather continued clear and began to grow warmer as they went farther south. The captain had an awning erected on deck so the "ladies" would not get too much sun. Breed finally devised a menu that did not leave her exhausted, and the crew and captain seemed satisfied. One morning, they would all have great bowls of porridge, coffee and large sugar buns just out of the oven. The next, it would be eggs and slabs of salt pork. Lunch she kept just as simple, usually a bowl of chowder or cabbage soup, crackers and the remaining dessert from the evening before. Dinner was a challenge that the budding cook was hard-put to meet, but Harry, ever thankful to be relieved of his duties as cook, was more than helpful repeating past dishes that the deceased cook had prepared: roast mutton with potatoes, one of the smoked hams cooked with beans and applesauce, huge amounts of coffee and whatever dessert Breed decided.

After supper on the night before the Sara Blue was to make port in Havana, Breed stayed on deck awhile after Eliza had gone below. She stood by the rail, gazing dreamily out to sea, thinking of nothing much, just enjoying the soft, tropical air. Aft, toward the crew's quarters, one of the men began to play a guitar. Breed, still warm from the heat of the galley as she prepared the evening meal, took the pins from her hair and let it fall down her back, only to be gently lifted by the breeze. Farther down the deck, Hugh Shepard lounged, smoking an after-dinner cheroot and silently observing the young woman. On the horizon, the full moon rose so that Breed was silhouetted gracefully and enticingly to the man who watched her. The deserted deck was bathed in moonlight as Shepard, tossing his cheroot overboard, walked silently toward the young woman lost in reverie. He came up behind her and just as she heard him, he put his arms around her waist. Startled but not frightened, Breed reacted automatically. Lifting her right knee, she jammed her heel down with all her might onto Shepard's foot and, simultaneously, shot her right elbow back and jabbed the startled man in the stomach.

"Christ Almighty!" said the captain as he dropped his arms and stood back a pace.

"Oh! It's you, captain," said the unperturbed Breed as she turned toward him.

"Damn me, why did you do that? You could have broken my foot at the least," said Shepard as he nursed his bruised ribs and foot.

"For shame, captain, what would your good wife say if she saw how you just behaved!" said Breed. Taking the pins from her apron pocket, she wound her hair in its habitual knot.

"I meant only to be friendly, and leave my wife out of this. She's in Nantucket... where did you learn to be so... so unladylike?" demanded the captain.

"When I was still in short skirts, my cousins Kevin and Mike taught me, said t'was very important for a girl to be able to protect her virtue."

"Never mind my wife... no wonder you're still unmarried!" blustered the captain, nursing his wounded pride.

"Better single than sorry, my Aunt Kate says. Good night, captain," and she returned to her cabin.

Not long after breakfast the next morning, the ship reached Cuba and by midmorning was moored in Havana harbor. Captain Shepard, still irritable from his encounter with the virtuous Breed, was short with her and Eliza when they asked if they might go ashore when he did. So the two young women spent the day on deck looking longingly toward the teeming city. The great stone fort that towered over the harbor brought to mind some of Eliza's favorite novels, and she decided perhaps they were just as well off onboard. The captain did not return for dinner, but in the morning the ship was moored at the dock and Mr. Johnson told the girls that the consignment of rum from Santiago Province had not arrived and they must stay a day or so in Havana. Captain Shepard had made arrangements for them to stay at the Convent of the Sacred Heart with the nuns there. They were to take just enough luggage for a day or two.

Though only mid-May, the heat ashore was oppressive and both Breed and Eliza were glad the captain had ordered a carriage to take them to the convent. Harry was sent along to help. He spoke fluent Spanish, and after watching the young boy speak confidently to the driver of the coach Breed promised herself she too would learn the language. Eliza was wilting minute by minute, both from the heat and the experience of being a stranger in a foreign land, so Breed kept up a nonstop flow of cheerful chatter to distract her.

Havana was already an old city, its cobbled streets narrow and dark. The houses of the wealthy had high walls around them and only the tops of trees and bushes could be seen from the carriage. Here and there, a thick wooden door was set in a wall, or a window showed these buildings were occupied. Eliza was upset at the many beggars that chased after the carriage as they left the wharf, but even those fell away after a few well-put words in Spanish from Harry. Marveling at Harry's ability, Breed asked what he'd said. He announced smugly, "I just told them to be off, you were the Governor General's daughters home from Spain!"

The carriage finally arrived at the Convent of the Sacred Heart. Here too were high walls, painted white, and a small black iron gate set in the wall. Soon, a short, round nun in a white habit with black veil came to the door and, after a few words with Harry, opened the gate and gestured for the women to follow. Harry collected the portmanteaus, paid the driver and trailed after them.

The convent was large with beautiful grounds and gardens. Here and there, the visitors caught a glimpse of young females of varying ages dressed in white uniforms, walking arm in arm along the garden paths. A group of girls about Harry's age caught sight of him and there was much pointing and giggling till the nun spoke harshly to them and sent them on their way. The little party left the gardens and entered a cloistered walk, cool and dim after the bright sunlight and tropical garden. They walked for some time along the flagged stone floor and then abruptly the nun stopped, opened a louvered door, ushered them in and, closing the door again, scurried off.

The three young people stood close together in the large room. The walls were white and the high ceiling had great beams across the width of the room. The floor was of the same dark wood but polished to a mirror's gloss. Here and there were beautiful Turkish carpets.

The sparse furnishings consisted of heavy Spanish chests and several high-backed carved arm chairs. There was a beautifully carved crucifix on one wall, a large vase of roses on the shelf beneath it. Their heady fragrance, mixed with the smell of beeswax, was so strong that Breed felt giddy.

After a few moments, one of the inner doors opened and a nun almost as tall as Breed entered and, smiling at them, spoke to Harry for a moment. He turned to Breed and said, "This here lady is Sister Maria Cecile. She's the Mother Superior's secretary and she says you are to follow her to your rooms. I can't be here after sundown... it's the rule. So, I'll jes shove off now but be back in the morning." And, looking relieved to be rid of the convent, he left the way he had come.

Sr. Marie Cecile beckoned to Breed and Eliza to follow, so they each picked up their portmanteaus and hurried after her.

"Sure, she goes so fast, we may have to run so not to lose her," said Breed, only half joking, while traveling down several long halls and up two flights of stairs. The girls continued until they were completely lost. The nun stopped at a door and opened it, ushering them in.

It was a lovely room, high ceilinged, white walls again and bare floor, but there was a tiny balcony that opened off a French door. The room was at tree-top level, and a breeze rustled the leaves and found its way into the room. The huge, carved four-poster bed was draped with cotton netting and looked as soft as a cloud. The nun called the girls in from the balcony.

"Senoritas, el favor," and when she had their attention, she opened a door that Breed had thought a closet. Proudly, the nun displayed a truly marvelous convenience! A large, square-shaped bath, all lined in colorful Spanish tiles at least two and a half feet high. There was a pipe running from the roof that filled the tub and another that went through a wall to the outside. The nun turned a knob on the pipe and the bath began to fill with fresh rain water, warmed by the sun from the cistern on the convent roof. She produced large linen towels and, while pretending to eat something, she said, "Tomar la cena..." and held up six fingers. Breed, realizing she was telling them the time for supper, smiled and thanked the nun, nodding her head so she would know they understood.

The nun left them and in moments, their hot traveling clothes off, Breed helped Eliza into the bath. Later, while Breed soaked in the lovely warm water, Eliza sat on the balcony and combed her damp hair.

"It's surely not even six yet, Eliza, so why don't you take a little cat nap?" Breed suggested, for Eliza did look tired. "I'll join you after I wash my hair."

It had been a long day. Breed lay in the bath, submerged to her chin. It was the first time in her adult life she had ever been able to stretch out in a tub. The luxury of soaking in the warm water lulled her almost to sleep. Almost an hour passed before she washed her hair and, dripping, climbed out of the bath. Eliza was fast asleep, so Breed went out onto the balcony and combed her hair dry.

❧ CHAPTER FIVE ❧

There was a small knock at the door and Breed hurried to open it before it should wake Eliza. There stood two little girls, dressed in white, with huge brown eyes, dark curling hair and olive skin. They curtseyed to Breed and, giggling, presented her a note. "Please come down, as I must tell you of a change in plans," the note read, and it was signed by Captain Shepard.

Eliza had awakened and was looking worried, so Breed assured her everything was all right, but that they must hurry and dress as the captain was below and wanted to talk to them. As the two little messengers showed no inclination to depart, Breed offered them each a lemon drop from Sassy Black's gift bag. Shortly, all four descended and the two little girls led them to a parlor where Captain Shepard waited.

"And how do you like your taste of convent life, ladies?" he asked them. But before they could answer, he continued, "There's been a change. We must wait for a delivery of rum, so the carpenter thinks we should have some repairs done, which will take a week. So, there you are. I've spoken to the Mother Superior and she says you are welcome to stay."

Eliza looked relieved, as she had never really gotten her sea legs and felt better on dry land. Breed assured the captain they were very contented but asked him, "Captain, could I have my pay, and could we have Harry tomorrow take us shopping? Our Boston clothes are much too heavy for this heat, so we should purchase some lighter clothing, or at least material to make something."

The captain, pretending to be put-out, grumbled, "Women! They would find an excuse to go shopping in hell!" as he counted out some money for Breed. "Here is your pay, two gold pieces, but let Harry do the buying so you won't be cheated."

Breed was speechless at the fortune she now possessed and when she tried to thank the captain, he brushed her aside by saying, "You worked for it, and damn it, unless I can find a cook soon, you may have to do so again! Now, I must be off, as I have an engagement for dinner."

He was gone in a cloud of cheroot smoke, and to Breed's surprise, lavender water! After he had gone, Breed and Eliza put their heads together to decide just what they would buy on the morrow. Eliza still had the little purse Mrs. Potts had given her as a traveling gift from John Loughlan, so between them they were quite well off. Somewhere in the dim recesses of the convent a bell rang and the same two little girls appeared to guide them to dinner.

The dining room was long and opened into a patio. There were at least one hundred fifty young girls and perhaps thirty or so nuns. The girls sat by age, at tables of eight, and to one of these Breed and Eliza were escorted. Though the girls were all in their late teens, none spoke English. Two from the Island of Martinique spoke French. Eliza had a French governess until she was twelve, when her father's financial straits had made it necessary to dispense with her services. As a parting gift, Mr. Staunton gave her a small amount of money to use as a dowry. The thrifty young woman used it and her savings to open a hat shop in New York, where it was understood she was quite successful.

Each young girl introduced herself in Spanish, save the two from Martinique, who did so in French. Mme. Artois had been thorough in her teaching. After only a few halting phrases, Eliza was able to converse, if not fluently, at least with ease. There developed a three-way conversation, English to French to Spanish, and answers back the same route. When the girls discovered that Eliza was on her way to meet her bridegroom, she immediately became a heroine of such magnitude that for the remainder of their visit at the convent the older girls vied with one another for permission to dine at the visitors' table. Breed had Eliza ask one of the French girls, Lucy, where they could shop the next day. Lucy, after some thought and consultation with her classmates, told them to go first to the shops along the central plaza, then to look in at the open marketplace near the harbor. Breed was well-pleased with the information but decided to go first to the marketplace because it might be less expensive. The remainder of the evening was spent walking in the convent gardens before the long, tropical evening faded.

As the two Americans strolled through the gardens with the young ladies from Martinique, their paths crossed that of two nuns, intent on their evening prayers. When the little group halted to allow the nuns to pass, the elder woman paused and in fluent if formal English introduced herself and her companion to Breed and Eliza, asking if they were enjoying their stay. She was Sr. Juana Baptiste, the convent infirmarian, the other Sr. Maria Magdalena, the librarian. The girls were delighted to hear their own language spoken and the little group chatted a few moments, then parted as the bell rang for evening benediction. After benediction in the chapel, everyone retired for the night. There was a cool breeze blowing in the balcony door. The huge bed was comfortable and the single candle burning on the chest lit the room with a soft glow. Breed draped the mosquito netting around the bed and, in moments, both she and Eliza were sound asleep.

In the morning at breakfast, a note was brought to Breed from Harry. He was in the garden waiting and had a carriage to take them shopping.

The next few hours were some of the most exciting of Breed's life. She loved the hustle and bustle of the open market, the vibrant colors and pungent aromas of the food cooking at the outdoor stalls. Eliza stayed close to Breed. If Harry so much as left her sight, she began to call him, panic-stricken.

Breed was right. Their small hoard went much further at the market. Each girl bought a pair of the cool, open sandals everyone wore and several brightly colored, long cotton skirts, though privately Eliza wasn't sure they were what Mrs. Potts would approve of as "proper." A gauze peasant blouse for each and, since it was such a bargain, Breed insisted on buying several yards of white linen.

Harry was beginning to resemble a beast of burden with all their purchases. The young women pooled their last monies and purchased a handsome Panama hat for the cabin boy. He was delighted and took every opportunity to stop and gaze at himself. And this was their undoing.

Breed had held back her second gold piece, planning to buy herself something she had always longed for... a gold cross and chain. So when they had finished their shopping, they set out with Harry in tow to look for a jeweler. Harry had dismissed the carriage, but Breed, feeling the need to walk, insisted she had seen shops just a few moments away from the marketplace. They set out on foot, Harry stopping to adjust his new hat to a more rakish angle. This entailed depositing the recent purchases on a stone bench while basking in the admiring glances of two young girls sitting on it.

Breed, with Eliza in tow, hurried along the cobbled street unaware that their trusty guide was far behind. It took only a few moments, a turn here and a twist there and the girls were hopelessly lost. The hour of the afternoon siesta was approaching and the traffic began to thin out as people returned to their homes for lunch and a nap. Two facts dawned simultaneously on the young women: They were lost and, worse, they had lost Harry! They tried backtracking, but the maze of little alleyways and streets only confused them more. They were tired and hungry, and Eliza was fast approaching outright terror. The captain had warned them not to eat anything away from the convent, but when Breed saw the pushcart piled high with bananas, she approached the man standing beside it. Offering a few pennies, she pointed to a small bunch of the ripest. The man eagerly took the money and gave Breed four bananas. She then took Eliza's hand, leading her to a small fountain in the middle of the square. It was surrounded by a stone bench, hot from the noonday sun, but because the slight breeze sprayed a fine mist over them every once in a while they were not uncomfortable.

"Come you now, Eliza, eat up, then we will find Harry," Breed made her voice sound more confident than she really felt. She wasn't frightened, because she had money and knew once Harry alerted the captain they were lost, he would send searchers looking for them. Eliza ate her bananas, each bite flavored with tears she was so frightened. They finished their scant luncheon but still they sat, hand in hand, saying nothing. Eliza occasionally used her handkerchief to wipe a tear away.

The sun passed over the plaza and the shadows lengthened. The windows above them, shuttered against the noonday heat, were thrown open and the empty square began to fill with life again. Two young dandies, both handsome in a swarthy manner, strolled back and forth in front of the two unchaperoned young women, eyeing them. When the caballeros halted a few feet from them and looked as though they were preparing to address them, Breed made a decision. She jumped up, still holding the startled Eliza by the hand, and walked rapidly from the square, down the first cobbled street in sight. "It's best we keep on the move," she told Eliza, who had been unaware of the attention the young men had been ready to bestow on them.

Breed sailed along at a good clip, almost dragging the wilting Eliza over the dusty cobbled streets, now thronged with after-siesta crowds; mothers with young children clinging to them like fruit on a tree; farmers in from the country eager to sell the last of their produce and return home; beggars, soldiers and young men of every description lounging in the plaza, smoking, drinking wine or dicing in the dust. If she had not been worried about Eliza getting overwrought, Breed would have been in her element. Everything was so interesting, so new, there was so much to ask Harry and the captain about. There was a great deal of noise in the streets, no one seemed to speak in anything other than a yell, but it didn't bother Breed till Eliza happened to look over her shoulder.

"Oh, my God!" she gasped. "Breed, we're being followed!"

Breed came to a halt and turned to see a motley group of young street loungers parading behind them. The men clicked their tongues and rolled their dark eyes and, at the attention from the two young women, made loud calls of appreciation and colorful professions of love in Spanish! Poor Eliza, faint of heart at the best of times, burst into tears and sobbed. She begged Breed to take her home to Boston. Breed, with a stern glance over her shoulder at their admirers, told Eliza to wipe her tears.

"Look you, we are almost to the convent, I remember that climbing bush on the wall over there!" And taking the weeping girl in tow again, she hurried on. They entered another large plaza, again alive with people, but as they crossed the busy square their attention was caught by a group of men standing around an incredibly filthy little man. He held a riding crop in his hand and seemed to be extolling the merits of... "Good God in Heaven!" Breed whispered to herself. "That little Spaniard is trying to sell that poor woman." On a wooden platform, surrounded by piles of household goods, stood a tall, black woman. Her head was wrapped in a red scarf, and her body was covered by a long tattered and stained garment, not unlike a man's nightshirt. Her face glistened with sweat and her hands were roughly tied together by a stout rope.

Breed, half-dragging the exhausted Eliza, elbowed her way to the front of the small crowd. One of the men standing at the outer edges of the group was a Sr. Castillo, one of the head clerks at the rum merchants. He had heard Captain Shepard speak of the two young American women the day before. Recognizing them, he realized they were not escorted. Tossing a coin to a young boy standing close by, he told him to run "pronto" to the rum merchants' office, find the American sea captain Hugh Shepard and tell him his young senoritas were here alone. Then he moved closer to Breed, introducing himself to her in halting English.

The filthy little auctioneer was speaking again in rapid-fire Spanish. Try as she might, Breed could catch only a word or two that she understood. Then the auctioneer did something that made even Breed's cast-iron confidence slip and waver. As he spoke, he prodded the woman in the face with his riding crop. He forced her to open her mouth. Her tongue had been cut out, and recently too. Eliza let out a scream and fell to vomiting on herself and the bystanders.

The woman stood quietly, resigned but unbowed, maimed yet still imposing. Breed had been helping Eliza, when just for a moment she glanced at the woman. Their eyes locked, and Breed was engulfed by such a sense of despair and anguish that she could not look away. One mind spoke to the other, as easily as old friends chat and visit. "Help me!" came a silent cry. As if in a trance, Breed reached into her skirt pocket, where her remaining gold piece lay tied in her handkerchief.

Leaving the still retching Eliza in the care of Sr. Castillo, Breed shoved her way to the auctioneer and slowly, speaking very precisely, told the little man she would buy the black woman. He evidently understood her because he began to protest sneeringly that the woman was strong and worth much more than the gold piece Breed held up. Though she was maimed, he continued, she still had many good years ahead and "many men would consider a silent woman priceless!"

The laughing crowd, sensing the possibility of a drama, settled down to listen to a session of bargaining they were sure would be historic. But their enjoyment was shortened by the arrival of a coach in the square. The coachmen drew the horses up with a flourish, scattering children, stray chickens and dogs in all directions.

Even before the huge lumbering vehicle had drawn to a halt, the coach door was thrown open and Captain Shepard jumped down and walked rapidly into the crowd. Eliza was the first to see his arrival and in sheer relief fainted dead away. Leaving the embarrassed Sr. Castillo to hold the limp Eliza, Captain Shepard joined Breed. She turned to the captain and, in a tone of voice verging on hysteria, said, "Tell him she must come with us. Make him take my gold piece for her. For the love of God, Hugh, please...."

Shepard, realizing that Breed would not change her mind and that she too was close to the end of her rope, beckoned the wine clerk Castillo to take Eliza to the coach. He took Breed's elbow and guided her closer to the auctioneer. In Spanish, he told the man that the senorita had taken a fancy to the black woman and would buy her for one gold piece. The little man, conscious that his chances of making any more profit on the mutilated woman were fast decreasing, tried one last time to bargain for a higher price. But Hugh Shepard tossed the gold coin to him and in a quietly threatening voice told the auctioneer, "Have this woman pick up her bundle and be on her way to that coach in thirty seconds or I will speak to the Governor General about you." The man knew when he had met his match, caught the coin in mid-air and told the black woman to take her belongings and follow the captain.

Leading the way back through the crowd with Breed on his arm, the captain told the woman to climb up on the boot with the driver. But Breed, fast reviving, insisted she join them inside the coach. The captain spoke quietly to Sr. Castillo.

"Go quickly amongst the crowd and even to the auctioneer and learn what you can of this woman and her past," he said. "Report to me at the convent, where the senoritas are staying." Castillo nodded and faded into the rapidly thinning crowd. Inside the coach, Breed was rubbing the hands of the still faint Eliza. Hugh Shepard settled himself into his seat and signaled the coachman to move on.

At the convent, all was thrown into confusion with the arrival of the coach. Harry had returned sometime earlier, having failed to find the two girls in the market plaza. The good sisters were distraught at the thought of the young women, alone and unchaperoned, wandering the alleys and plazas of Havana.

Eliza was revived enough to climb down from the coach carefully with Captain Shepard's aid, and Breed and the black woman were helped by the amazed coachmen. The courtyard was alive with nuns and gardeners, who had been called in to join the hunt for the missing girls. A few of the older students lurked on the outskirts of the group, hoping to escape discovery by Mother Superior and share in the excitement.

❧ CHAPTER SIX ❧

W hen Breed saw Sr. Juana Baptiste, the convent infirmarian, standing to one side, she took hold of the black woman's arm and led her to the little nun. "Sister, here is a patient worthy of your skill. Can you help her? She is injured terribly and in great need of aid." The nun nodded briskly and motioned for the two women to follow her down the cool and shaded passageway. When they reached the infirmary, she had the black woman sit on a small stool and examined her mouth carefully. She put her hand on the woman's back. The woman winced in pain, so the nun gently cut away the sweat- and blood-stained shift.

Breed had steeled herself for the sight of the mouth, but it was all she could do to keep from disgracing herself in Eliza's manner.

First, by vomiting and then fainting! The sight of the straight and graceful back, the color of deepest brown crisscrossed with huge, open slashes and swollen welts was too much. Breed shut her eyes tightly to keep tears from overflowing. The nun stared in disbelief, wondering to herself what a human being could do that was so evil it warranted such cruel and barbarous punishment.

That the black woman was in shock was evident, otherwise she would be screaming in pain. Sr. Baptiste quickly mixed a cup of wine and laudanum and gave it to the woman to drink. "When the drug has begun to work, I will clean the wounds and put her to bed here," the nun said. "She is grievously injured but strong. With good care, she may live." The nun's English was heavily accented and slow from little use. "You, senorita, go and bathe your face and see that your little friend is well," she said to Breed. "Give her this powder with her dinner and it will help her to sleep tonight." The nun then called to one of the other lay sisters who helped in the infirmary. Between them, they began to take care of the injured woman.

In a daze, Breed left and walked through the passageways to that part of the convent where she and Eliza stayed. One part of her mind was numb from the sight of the woman's injuries and the thought of her pain, but another was busy planning strategy for she was sure of one thing: They would not leave the woman behind when they sailed.

Breed did not realize it, but more than an hour had passed since their return to the convent. The wine clerk, Sr. Castillo, had already come with his report to the captain and bowed to Breed as their paths crossed in the garden. She heard the Mother Superior speaking rapidly in Spanish to the captain but could only catch a word here and there, which only reinforced her determination to learn Spanish quickly. They were in the convent parlor, so she went to join them and tell them of the woman's condition.

Mother Superior sat in a huge carved wooden chair that had probably come from Spain a hundred years earlier. She was a small woman but held herself with such dignity and grace that one felt her to be of a more commanding stature. Her hands were folded under the scapular of her habit and only the flush on her cheeks showed she was agitated. Hugh Shepard stood by one of the louvered doors to the garden, his back to the room. When Breed entered, there was a pause in their conversation and the nun began to speak in precise and formal English.

"Captain Shepard, you must understand our position. All the better families of Havana, nay of Cuba and the whole Caribbean, send their daughters to us to be educated. To learn, not only academically, but morally, also. What will these same parents say when it is learned we are harboring a fallen woman?" The captain started to speak, but the nun held up her hand for silence and continued. "Because, you know, that is what she is. The head gardener has told me all and though her punishment has been cruel, she has brought it on herself!"

Shepard motioned for Breed to be seated, then asked Mother Superior's permission to light a cheroot, using the time to marshal his thoughts. After a puff or two, he began, "Sr. Castillo, at my bidding, spent the last hour inquiring about the black woman. As you say she is a fallen woman. She was bought from a slaver as a child of eight or nine by the Major Domo of a Dr. Enrique Costa-Nunez here in Havana. She was to be trained as a kitchen help. She was a bright little thing and soon caught the eye of the doctor's wife, a mean and difficult woman at best of times, who promoted her to helping Sra. Costa-Nunez's maid. Her name, by the way, is Lita.

"Sra. Costa-Nunez was twenty years younger than her husband. And though she did her duty and delivered a male heir, she spent more time enhancing her beauty and flirting with her many admirers than as a wife and companion to her husband. The doctor became interested in Lita. She was growing into a beautiful young girl. His son had been sent to Spain for schooling and the doctor was lonely. Lita was his companion for more than fifteen years, the last of them his eyes also after he went blind. Evidently, his wife was satisfied with the situation, since it left her to go her own way. Three days ago, Dr. Costa-Nunez died suddenly, no one is sure of what, but after all he was sixty-five. Lita was left to the mercy of Sra. Costa-Nunez, who accused her of theft and had her maimed, out of revenge, one would think, and sold her and the less desirable household effects from her husband's estate. Sra. Costa-Nunez and a Sr. Alfredo Miguel Ramos, reportedly her cousin, left Havana yesterday on the Sea Maid, bound for Rio."

When the captain paused, Breed rushed in. "Please, Mother Superior, let this poor woman stay till we leave—she is so badly hurt. I can take care of her aboard the Sara Blue, but right now she needs the expert treatment that only Sr. Juana Baptiste can provide."

Hugh Shepard realized what Breed intended to do with the black woman and started to deny any possibility of her joining them. But Breed gave him a look of such grim determination, mixed with pleading approval, that he said nothing. If she's as badly injured as the report says, she won't last the night anyway, he thought.

But Lita did last the night and the next and the next. Third day, she was well enough that the infirmary nun lessened her painkilling medication and allowed her to sit up for a few moments. Breed and the nervous Eliza had spent time each day visiting the infirmary and were glad to see their patient awake. Breed sat beside the narrow cot and with the nun to interpret told Lita of her plan. "It's glad I am to see you better, though know you have a long way to go. You must come with us to California. I haven't spoken to the captain yet, but he is a good man, so I know he will let you... that is, if you want to." Even though the woman's skin had an ashen hue and was still far

61

from well, her beauty was evident in the shape of her head with its close-cropped hair and the long neck that sat so gracefully on her tall, lithe body. Eliza, in one of her romantic flights of fancy, was sure Lita was the daughter of some faraway African chieftain. Her hands were beautiful, her long, narrow fingers and nails carefully tended.

"Our patient is doing well," announced Sr. Juana Baptiste as Breed and Eliza entered. "You know she can read and write in Spanish, do you not?" the nun asked. Their answers were interrupted by the arrival of one of the lay sisters, carrying the tattered shirt-like shift that Lita had worn when Breed and Eliza first saw her. "She insisted... I gave her a slate and chalk when she mimed writing on something... then she wrote, 'Please, may I have the clothes I came in, some shears and an old testament,' " continued the nun. Then, with the two young women and the nun standing beside her cot, Lita took the small scissors and carefully set to work destroying the large flower design worked into the material of the shift at the neck. In a few moments, she had cut away the threads on each of the two flowers, and Breed and Eliza gasped when they saw the embroidery had been a hiding place for four large and perfect diamonds!

Taking the slate, Lita wrote in Spanish, "They are mine. Doctor gave them to me two years ago and told me to keep them safe, so I should always have something." The effort had tired her. She sank back a moment, but when the two young women prepared to leave and let her rest, she reached out her arm to detain them. They stood before her, unsure of what she wanted, as she rifled through a copy of the old testament the nun had provided. When she had found what she wanted, she took Breed's right hand and gave the open Bible to the little nun. On the slate, she had written, "Please read this to the senorita."

The nun adjusted her spectacles and glanced over the text Lita had indicated. It took her a moment or two to translate the Spanish into English and then, as she began, Lita bowed her head and put Breed's hand over it.

The nun read, "It is from the Book of Ruth, Chapter 1, Verse 16: 'But Ruth said, Do not ask me to abandon or forsake you! For wherever you go I will go, wherever you lodge, I will lodge, your people shall be my people, and your God my God. Wherever you die I will die, and there be buried. May the Lord do so and so to me, and more besides, if ought but death separates me from you!' "

When the nun ceased, she cleared her throat and tried to blink back her tears. Both Breed and Eliza were openly weeping, tears streaming down their cheeks. For a moment, all was silence. Then Breed knelt beside the cot. She took the hand Lita had held over her head, moved it over the woman's heart and said, "You are the sister of my heart and we will go from here together. This is a promise." She kissed the brow of the now exhausted woman and helped her lay back as the nun translated her words. As Breed stood, Lita slipped the four diamonds into her hand and closed her eyes.

Breed tried to dissuade Lita, reminding her that Dr. Costa-Nunez had given them to her. But Eliza interrupted. "No, Breed," she said. "We can use some of them to pay her passage with Captain Shepard. That way, he can't deny her joining us!"

"Eliza, you are a marvel!" exclaimed Breed, "and soon as Lita can be up and about we will take them to a jeweler and sell them, then we can buy her some clothes!" Eliza nodded, though inwardly she vowed nothing on God's earth could again get her out of the convent on one of Breed's shopping expeditions.

Two more days passed languidly, the summer heat well under way. Though it was only June, Havana grew sultry. The siesta lasted well into the afternoon and the sweltering city only came alive as the evening trade winds swept across and cooled the island. Breed and Eliza spent mornings sewing a few light garments for themselves. In the afternoons, after the welcome siesta, they wrote letters to friends and relatives back in Boston. On the morning of the 4th of June, Harry arrived and announced that the Sara Blue was shipshape again, her storm damage repaired and the cargo of rum and sugar loaded so that the captain planned to sail with the tide in the morning. The ladies were to board at sunset.

Harry had two to three errands to run for the captain before he and the carriage would be at their disposal. Breed went in search of Sr. Baptiste to ask about Lita's continuing care. Eliza returned to their room to begin their packing.

Poor Eliza. This interlude was at an end and once more she was headed for California and a new, terrifying and unknown life. It was understandable that she had difficulty holding back her easy tears. Breed, however, was elated. Havana had been interesting, but to be at sea again! She could hardly walk down the long cloisters on her way to the infirmary, her feet wanted to run, even skip!

Sr. Baptiste was in her dispensary. It was a small room with shelves to the ceiling, each shelf packed with glass bottles or tin boxes, their contents written clearly across the front. Bunches of herbs hung from the ceiling to dry. At a small table, a nun worked with a mortar and pestle grinding something into a fine powder. The room had an aroma both pungent and pleasant. One moment it was wintergreen, the next the warm, spicy smell of clove. When Breed told the nun that they were to leave that evening, Sr. Baptiste went to one of the black tin boxes and set it on the table. "Our patient is better," she said, "but far from well. She will have good days and bad. Her back is healing nicely. I will give you a special salve and extra linen bandages to use. Now, as to the pain, this powder is laudanum. It is from the opium poppy, therefore dangerous. Mix this with a warm drink and it will help her sleep, as well as kill the misery. She must eat only soft foods or liquids till her mouth is healed. Only she can determine when that will be. She must rinse her mouth with warm salt water several times a day. There, that is all. Do you have any questions?"

Breed said no and thanked the nun for her kindness and help in restoring Lita. The two of them went into the room, where Lita was resting.

The young woman was sitting on the edge of her cot, dressed in the same shift she wore when Breed first saw her. The small slate Sr. Baptiste had given her was in her lap. Breed told her about their impending departure.

Lita listened with attention to Breed and then to Sr. Baptiste as she translated. When the nun finished, Lita wrote rapidly on the slate and handed it to her to read to Breed. Adjusting her spectacles, the nun read, "We must go first to Garcia & Fuca, the jewelers, and sell my diamonds, then to El Encanto. I must make a few purchases."

Sr. Baptiste cleared her throat and spoke to Lita. "You are not strong enough to go too long, keep your errands short. I will pray for you and your future. May the good God give you the grace to bear it." Lita rose from the cot and went to the little nun. She reached out and took hold of the crucifix at the end of the rosary that all the nuns wore attached to their belts. The regal, black woman knelt in front of the nun who had nursed her back to life and, raising the crucifix to her lips, kissed it fervently. She was still weak, so Breed helped her up. With many words of thanks, Breed and Lita bid Sr. Baptiste farewell, promising to write when they reached California.

Harry was waiting for them in the garden. He was regaling Eliza with tales of his time ashore and what a success even a fourteen-year-old cabin boy could be. When Eliza saw Breed and Lita, and realized they were determined to go with Harry, she quickly announced she would stay behind and finish their packing—and nothing Breed could do would budge her.

In moments, Harry had installed the two young women in the carriage and given the order as directed by Breed to take them to Garcia & Fuca, the jewelers in the prado. Harry was curious but too well trained to ask, so the time passed with Breed asking about the preparations being made to sail. She was particularly interested in the information that Captain Shepard had succeeded in signing on a new cook, one Busso Carp, a half-breed something or other who declared himself an expert cook. When the carriage drew up before the jewelry shop, Harry jumped down and helped the women alight. When he started to accompany them inside, Breed told him heartlessly to remain with the carriage and driver.

The shop was small. A single glass window displayed several lovely gold and coral cameos on a black velvet background. Before they even reached the door, it was thrown open by a young boy dressed in a red and black livery. His eyes opened wide when he saw Lita with Breed. As soon as the young women entered, he made a mad, if somewhat undignified, dash toward the rear of the shop.

The shop was so elegant, Breed was intimidated and could speak only in a low whisper. The carpet was deep and rich-looking, and the few display cases and chairs were in themselves works of art. They had only a moment alone before they were joined by a small, rotund man dressed in the height of fashion. His sallow skin became even more of a pallor when, upon entering from behind velvet curtains, he saw Lita. He approached her, wringing his hands and visibly shaken, and spoke, "Senorita Lita, I... we heard of your... of the outrageous behavior of Senora Costa-Nunez! God will punish her... I ... what can I do to help you?"

Breed was amazed at the air of consequence that Lita had assumed upon entering the shop and would have stood there gaping forever if Lita had not given her a nudge in the ribs. "Yes? Oh, yes, sir, my friend requests that you give her an estimate on the value of these two jewels." Breed produced two of the diamonds from a small box in her pocket.

It was almost comical, the speed with which Sr. Fuca's facial expression changed from friendly concern to one of consummate greed! His small eyes could hardly tear themselves from the beautiful stones. "Ah, si, si... Yes, one had heard that Dr. Costa-Nunez had purchased some of the most perfect blue-white diamonds available...." he trailed off, then said slyly, "Were there not four together?" Breed looked bewildered, so he spoke in Spanish to Lita, who shrugged and gave the impression of not knowing anything about any others. Sr. Fuca mumbled under his breath, "Perhaps the wife received the others... no matter."

Receiving another nudge from Lita, Breed spoke again, "Senor, we sail at dawn and desire to sell these jewels for as much as possible, as soon as possible." The jeweler nodded his head in understanding. He closed his eyes, as though contemplating what price he could offer, but really to hide his greed and desire. He coveted the diamonds and would have them made into earrings for his new mistress. She would be very appreciative.

He opened his eyes and said, "five hundred Yankee dollars." This seemed like a vast sum to Breed, who turned uncertainly to Lita. Sr. Fuca spoke to Lita, telling her his offer. Lita drew herself up to her full height and, eyes snapping, reached into the large straw bag Breed had brought along. She withdrew her little slate and a piece of chalk carefully wrapped in an old piece of cloth. Looking disdainfully at the jeweler, she wrote one word: "NO."

Sr. Fuca spread his hands. "I am not a wealthy man," he said to Breed. "Let us say seven hundred dollars for both. I really cannot do better than that. I have no more money available." He turned and repeated this to Lita, who fixed him with a stare so direct that he began to squirm and mop his brow. She wrote again on her slate, this time at greater length. When she had finished, she held it out to the jeweler. He read it, then licked his lips, again applied his handkerchief to his face and turned to Breed. She sensed that the bargaining had taken a new and more serious turn and wondered what Lita had written on the slate to frighten the little man so.

"It's true," he said. "I only have eight hundred dollars available, and the banks are closed for siesta. What am I to do?" He must have said the same to Lita, because she turned and went to one of the display cases, pointing at its contents, and motioned for Breed and Sr. Fuca to join her.

"Ah, si, si, you will take the remainder in merchandise," he said. "Very good." He looked relieved and took out a tray of gold earrings, pins and chains. Lita chose a pair of simple gold loops for her ears. Then she turned to Breed, pointing to the tray and then to Breed.

"Do you mean I'm to choose something?" Breed asked.

The jeweler nodded quickly, "Yes, for yourself and she writes the name Eliza." Breed was so excited that she was going to have a piece of jewelry, her very first. But first she must select something for Eliza. Lita, slate in hand, left her and went to the rear of the shop to complete the transaction. A few moments later, she was back with a large envelope that she carefully put in the bottom of the straw bag.

Breed had taken her time choosing Eliza's gift, a small cameo of coral set in gold filigree and surrounded by tiny seed pearls. For herself, it took but a moment, for she knew her heart's desire. There was a gold crucifix about one-and-a-half inches long. When she pointed to it, the jeweler nodded and quickly added it to a golden chain. Lita took the chain from Sr. Fuca and, standing behind Breed, secured the clasp. Breed was so delighted she could hardly contain herself. She put Eliza's cameo in the little box that had held the diamonds and took a firm hold on the straw bag containing Lita's passage money. Lita put out her hand to the jeweler and he took it quickly. She inclined her head and turned to leave. Breed hurriedly thanked the jeweler and followed Lita out the door.

❧ CHAPTER SEVEN ❧

Harry was nearly dead with curiosity, and Breed's order that they had to make a few purchases did little to relieve it. Lita wrote "Encanto Paree" on the slate and gave it to Harry to hand to the coachman. He evidently knew who or what El Encanto Paree was for in moments they had drawn up to another row of elegant shops and Harry again handed the girls down. Lita intimated by a nod that Harry was welcome to join them this time and he gallantly went ahead to open the door. Over his shoulder, he told Breed that El Encanto meant "the enchanted."

Upon entering the shop, they were again greeted with startled disbelief, this time by a heavyset middle-age mulatto woman. She was dressed in a beautifully embroidered linen shirtwaist and a black bombazine skirt. At the first sight of Lita, she gave a little cry of wonder and rushed from behind the counter and made as to embrace her. But Lita, beginning to feel tired and in discomfort from her various injuries, instead took the woman's hands in her own and leaned down and kissed her on each cheek. The woman, Sra. Alvarado, spoke no English, so again Harry translated. Lita wrote again on the slate. After a moment's thought, the woman smiled and went from shelf to shelf, taking a bottle here and a small pot there until finally she had assembled quite a number of items.

Breed was bewildered. The shop was filled with all sorts of bottles and jars, each more exotic-looking than the other, and the air was so fragrant one could imagine it a garden in full bloom. Finally, she asked Harry what manner of shop it was. He informed her it was a perfumery and that Lita was buying face creams and lotions. Breed marveled at the thought. The only cosmetic allowed at the Weathermorn Home had been a little rose water and a puff of powder on one's nose. Lita and the woman conferred for several moments over several beautifully shaped bottles. Finally, after trying each one on her wrists, Lita chose one for herself and two others for Breed and Eliza. Sra. Alvarado wrapped the purchases in silver tissue paper and tied it with silver twine. Lita signaled to Breed to pay the woman and they left.

In the carriage, it was evident that Lita was exhausted, so Breed told Harry to have the coachman drive them to the open-air market. The coachman and Lita could stay with the carriage while she and Harry finished their shopping. Breed, familiar now with the open-air stalls of the market, knew exactly where to go for her purchase. In less than an hour, she had purchased what she felt Lita would need for the remainder of their voyage: Linen and lawn for underwear; a nice shirtwaist; a woolly shawl; sandals; and a peasant skirt and blouse.

Mid-afternoon was upon them as they returned to the convent. Lita was resting against the carriage cushions with her eyes closed, so Breed took Harry with her to collect Eliza and the luggage. While Harry and the coachman stowed the various packages, boxes and small portmanteau, the girls sought out Mother Superior to thank her for the convent's hospitality. Harry had produced a sealed envelope addressed to the convent's head and told Breed to deliver it for the captain, a small gift to cover their lodgings.

Eliza and Breed found the Mother Superior in her austere office. They thanked her sincerely for all the thoughtful kindness and care those of the convent family had bestowed upon them, especially for the treatment of Lita. Breed then gave her the captain's letter and impulsively kissed the startled nun. Their new friends among the students were gathered in the garden and there was much weeping and sighing as the girls parted from one another. Finally, they were again settled in the carriage and on their way to the harbor.

As the carriage drove up the wharf, Hugh Shepard came out on deck. Harry and the coachman helped the three young women alight and then, as they went up the gangplank, began to unload the luggage.

Breed was nervous about approaching the captain regarding Lita's passage. She felt more confident when she remembered the money in her bag. Hugh stood at the head of the gangplank, hands on hips and glowering like a thunderstorm as the attractive trio approached. Breed whispered to Eliza, "Take Lita to our cabin and help her lie down on my bunk. I must beard the lion in his den." Eliza and Lita hurried past the captain, eyes lowered, and quickly went below.

"Well, Miss, what now?" growled the captain as Breed came and stood in front of him.

"No, Captain, before you say anything, what is the cost of a passage from here to the Californias?" she asked.

"And why do you wish to know that?" he asked. "And what is the black woman doing onboard? She looks like warmed over death!"

Breed rummaged around in her bag and produced the envelope stuffed with money. Holding it out to him, she asked, "How much, Captain?"

He took the envelope from her. Upon opening it, he had a hard time not showing his surprise at the large amount of money.

"Where did you get this?" he barked.

Breed explained about the diamonds, mentioning only the two Lita had sold. When she had finished, she again asked, "How much?"

Hugh Shepard knew when he had been bested, so he gave in as gracefully as he could. "Three hundred and fifty Yankee dollars, and she will have to share your cabin, as we have two new passengers that have joined us here in Havana."

Breed gave a great sigh of relief and quickly counted out the correct amount.

"Oh, Captain, thank you so much. You will not regret your kindness, truly."

She turned and nearly ran for the companion way to go below, stopping just long enough to call back, "Who are our new passengers?"

The captain said, "A Mr. Tiverton-West and his valet."

Edward Tiverton-West was twenty-four, English and third in line of succession to the barony of Holt-Tiverton. His uncle, Lord Holt of Tiverton, was the present baron. His cousin, Francis, the son and heir. Edward had been traveling for the past seven months. When his mother proposed he make the grand tour, he was delighted. He insisted, however, that he go to the Americas, rather than the usual expedition across Europe. His mother and his sister, Amelia, generally ran his life and he, being of a very lazy, easygoing nature, allowed them to. But this time they were unable to dissuade him from his plan. As is frequently the case, his good nature cloaked an iron will and determination when it was something he really desired.

Edward and his valet, Gobbs, had just concluded a month's stay in Havana. Tiverton-West had intended to remain longer, as he had made several congenial friends. But he suffered a relapse of fever he had developed in New Orleans and the attending physician suggested a sea voyage would be most effective in completing a cure. So, the young man and his valet were not seen for the first day or two of the voyage while he rested and gained his sea legs.

That night, the three young women dined with the captain and first mate. The new cook, Busso Carp, seemed adequate if insipid. He did have a light hand with the gravy, Breed reminded herself, as they excused themselves and left the two men to their brandy and cheroots.

In their absence at dinner, one of the seamen had brought into their cabin a thick floor mat about three feet wide and six feet long. It was on the floor at the end of the cabin, fresh linens and pillows placed on top. Breed insisted Lita sleep in her bunk, at least until her back was completely healed, and she would make her bed on the mat. Eliza unpacked their clothes and purchases while Breed attended to Lita's fresh bandages. Breed gave Lita one of the pills and a drop of the laudanum to help her sleep free of pain. Before the night watchman on the shore called the ninth hour, the three young women were deeply asleep. No one woke until long after dawn, when the Sara Blue was already far at sea.

The heat became oppressive as the ship sailed toward the equator and the women spent more and more time on deck under the brightly colored awning that Captain Shepard had ordered put up. Lita's health improved rapidly, as Breed insisted she rest.

After several days at sea, it became evident that the new cook was rather limited in his range of menus. In fact, it appeared he knew only three meals, which he alternated. Leek soup was one of his favorites. When he served it for breakfast, the crew rebelled and pleaded with the first mate that Breed do the cooking. The captain approached Breed and it was arranged that Busso would do the breakfasts, sans leek soup, and lunch. Breed would cook the evening meal with the cook assisting her. She was delighted. Boredom had set in after only a day or so of lounging on deck and she needed to be active.

Breed insisted Harry teach her Spanish and she tried to speak it whenever she found a willing listener. Since half the crew was either Spanish or Mexican, she had plenty of practice. Eliza was given the task of teaching English to Lita, which she did carefully, if somewhat reluctantly, while Lita gave her grave attention. Breed would speak to her in a mélange of English and pigeon Spanish, and Lita seemed to understand. If not, one of the crewmen who could read Spanish was brought forth and Lita would write her question on the little slate.

Mr. Tiverton-West finally appeared in the captain's saloon for dinner and was royally welcomed when it was learned he played whist. The Captain and the first mate, Mr. Johnson, were both confirmed card players and had more than once bemoaned the fact that they lacked a fourth player. Miss Eliza had already made it known that she too enjoyed playing cards. She and her father had spent many an evening at the small card table in his library.

Edward Tiverton-West was of a slight build and medium height. His hair was the color of ripe corn and fell boyishly across his high forehead. He had a small mustache and blue eyes.

"Such a beautiful blue," confided Eliza to Breed later in their cabin.

"Myself, I like his good nature, Eliza, for all his being an Englishman. He put on no airs or tried to impress us. Yes, he is a very nice young man," said Breed in her most Mrs. Pottsish manner. She caught Lita's eye over Eliza's head and the two exchanged a smile and a raised eyebrow at Eliza's unusual appreciation of the young man.

Late one afternoon, some days out of Havana, another ship was sighted. Usually when this happened, the vessels never approached closer than half a mile or so. On this occasion, the other ship fired a rocket into the air and continued to sail closer. When she was within hailing distance, the captain announced to Breed and Lita, who had been walking about the deck and stopped close by the ship's approach, "It's Shames McCarty and the Scottish Maid out of Glasgow! And he's asking for permission to send someone aboard."

Almost from the first evening they met, Eliza and Edward Tiverton-West had spent much time together. They walked the decks or, if it were time for Lita's lesson, sat under the awning together, teaching the woman. Occasionally, one or the other read aloud from a book. When Eliza and Edward were not together, she constantly found reason to bring him up in conversation or quote something he had said that she admired.

In the evening, the two young people played whist with the captain and the first mate, since both of the seamen were smokers and Eliza had given them permission to smoke during the card game. In what became habit at the conclusion of the play, Edward took Eliza on deck for a stroll to give her a breath of fresh air before retiring for the night. Breed was too inexperienced and too busy with cooking, tutoring Lita and trying to converse in passable Spanish to realize what was happening. The gentle young Eliza was falling in love and the young man was drawn to her too. She was the only woman he had ever known who had no desire to dictate or dominate him. He thought her at first acquaintance a pretty companion. But as time passed and they became friends, he realized she had character as well as beauty and her good taste was evident because she unconsciously revealed her admiration of him. The afternoon the Scottish Maid hailed the Sara Blue, they were strolling with Eliza's hand in the crook of Edward's arm and his other hand placed protectively over hers. As a long boat from the Scottish Maid drew alongside the Sara Blue, the young couple joined Breed and Lita.

The long boat was piled high with baggage and several large wicker trunks. She was manned by three stalwart Scotsmen who made quick time between the two vessels. "Who is that in the boat?" asked Eliza, but no one had any idea. One of the men was draped in an elegantly made traveling cape of the brightest peacock blue that must have been worn more for effect than need since the temperature was well into the eighties.

As the small boat nudged the hull of the Sara Blue, a rope ladder was lowered. In a moment, a young seaman scrambled up the ladder like a trained monkey. He saluted Captain Shepard and said, "If it pleases you, sir, Captain McCarty sends his respects. I'm to give you this letter from him and ask you to take this passenger aboard with you. He's a M. Armand Mornay... a Frenchy, sir!"

"And why, pray tell, must he change ships in mid-ocean?" barked the captain.

The young sailor, looking first at the captain and then at the three young ladies, blushed beet red and stammered, "It's in the letter, sir!" As the seaman spoke, several of the wicker trunks were hoisted aboard. As Captain Shepard opened the letter, the young man saluted and was over the side and out of sight.

Captain Shepard read the letter. As he finished, he looked up and caught Breed and Lita's eyes, storming, "By God, we'll not be saddled with this creature!"

Too late. Daintily, and with great care for his gorgeous traveling cape, a most bizarre personage climbed over the side of the ship.

His physical build was slight, his complexion fair and his hair, golden ringlets! Eliza gasped when she realized he was rouged and had powdered his face, perhaps to hide that he was no longer in his first youth. With much twittering and fluttering and sweeping of his cape, the colorful apparition bowed low and introduced himself.

"Ah, Mon Captain, it is too kind of you to allow me to continue my journey on your so beautiful ship...."

Captain Shepard spluttered a moment, then rushed to the rail of the ship. Seeing the Scottish Maid's longboat already halfway back to the ship, he bellowed, "Come back here, you bloody sea dog! You will not leave this misbegotten son of a...." Eliza winced at the captain's language and Edward tightened his arm protectively around her.

Realizing that the longboat was ignoring him, Hugh Shepard whirled around and glared at the new passenger. "Mr. Mornay, it looks like we are stuck with you, but by God you behave yourself or I'll keel haul ye and then feed ye to the sharks!"

The new passenger fell back a space in agitation at the captain's harsh words and threatening expression. However, he quickly regained his composure. Bowing elegantly to Mr. Tiverton-West and the ladies, he said, "Mon Dieu, I will be an angel, mon Captain! Allow me to introduce myself: Armand Mornay, photographer extraordinaire." The other passengers stood awkwardly together, not knowing exactly what to make of the newcomer. Finally, Breed introduced Mr. Tiverton-West and simply explained that she and the other ladies were "Eliza, Lita and Breed, myself, traveling together to California."

Before she could go into further detail, the captain roared, "Mr. Johnson!" The first mate appeared in seconds and was given the duty of finding accommodations for M. Mornay.

As the little Frenchman followed the first mate below, Captain Shepard tore Captain McCarty's letter into shreds and threw it overboard. The wind picked up and Breed watched the pieces until they fell from sight into the sea.

Eliza, with Edward at her side, returned to the awning with Lita and took up the book she was using to teach English to Lita.

"Captain, why did Captain McCarty not want M. Mornay aboard his ship?" questioned Breed.

"Ah, don't ask. I'll get even with him, though, the yellow livered...sticking the Sara Blue with that perversion of a man!"

His last words gave Breed a hint of the problem. "Sure, Captain," she said. "Is it that he's a 'pretty boy' like Chauncey Gilroy at home? He used to wear his sister Maeve's petticoats and gear?"

Captain Shepard looked at Breed. She frequently surprised him with her knowledge and perception. "Yes, he's one of those," Captain Shepard said. "He prefers his own kind to women. If he leaves my men alone, he can stay aboard, but the first misstep and I'll set him adrift in an open boat!" So saying, he lit a cheroot and stomped off.

❧ CHAPTER EIGHT ❧

The languid summer days followed one upon another as the Sara Blue sailed farther South. After settling below in his cabin, the irrepressible M. Mornay came on deck lugging one of his large wicker trunks. He approached the awning where the three women sat. Eliza was sewing on a linen shift and Breed sat beside Lita, who was teaching her how to braid her long blonde hair into a single herringbone-patterned rope.

The Frenchman stood a few moments, observing the tableau. "Mademoiselles, you must allow me to photograph you!" he said. "I shall commit you to history! Oui, it will be a modern representation of the 'Three Graces'!"

The young women allowed the photographer to pose them this way and that, watching with interest as he unpacked a large field camera from the wicker trunk. Even Edward Tiverton-West was drawn to the forward deck, his curiosity aroused. He had imposed exile on himself and spent much of the morning with first the captain and then Mr. Johnson. His feelings for Eliza were beginning to worry him. He found it hard to be content out of her company and was jealous of any attention she paid to even the other women.

M. Mornay spent the rest of the afternoon posing and reposing the young women and when in the course of the conversation it was revealed that Eliza was a bride-to-be, he insisted on a photograph of her alone.

The next day, the Frenchman presented the girls with his finished pictures and stood by expectantly as they looked through the result of the previous afternoon's work. It was more than evident that he was an artist in this new field. The photographs, if somewhat stiff from the necessity of sitting posed so long, were exquisite studies of the young women, catching something of each one's personality.

When Hugh Shepard glanced at them, he was forced to agree that the "Little Twit is talented...." The photo of Breed standing alone, looking out to sea, had a quality that made him think of some long ago Viking maiden. He realized that these weeks at sea had turned the young woman into a completely different person. The sun had bleached her drab hair almost white, her undistinguished complexion had taken on a golden tan that caused her blue eyes to sparkle like pools of cool water. Even her figure had trimmed down. "By Gad, I'm waxing poetic," he mused to himself, handing the photos back to M. Mornay.

M. Mornay approached Edward Tiverton-West and presented him with the "Bridal Portrait" of Eliza, with his best wishes for their happy life together. Edward flushed and Eliza gasped in embarrassment at the Frenchman's misconception. Breed quickly spoke, "It's a mistake you've made, sir. Mr. Edward is just a friend we have made on our voyage. Eliza is betrothed to Mr. John Loughlan of Los Angeles, California, where we are bound!" The Frenchman excused himself profusely and at such length that poor Eliza was nearly in tears. Finally, to calm her, Lita took her arm and drew the young girl below deck to their cabin. Breed could have shaken the little man for causing the embarrassment. But she held her tongue, only thanking him nicely for the picture he had given her of the "Three Graces." Seeing that Edward was still uncomfortable, she excused herself on the pretext of having to start dinner preparations.

That night, as they all sat at dinner enjoying the poached fish in wine sauce that Breed had concocted from one of the crew's catch, Captain Shepard announced that the next day should bring them to Buenos Aires on the coast of Argentina. Lita's English was still minimal, but she recognized the name of the city and on her small slate wrote in Spanish, "I have been there with Dr. Costa-Nunez. It is a most beautiful city. May we go ashore?"

Harry haltingly translated and the captain, in an expansive mood brought on by the excellent dinner, said jocularly, "Aye, you may all go ashore, but only if Mr. Tiverton-West and Harry put you in a baby's leading strings so Breed doesn't wander off and get you into trouble. Come to think of it, she'd probably start a revolution."

Mr. Tiverton-West said he would be happy to escort the ladies ashore. He added, "If you will kindly go with me to the British Counsel, I am hoping to find my mail from home has caught up with me. It's been over three months since I heard how all was going!" Later in the evening, after the gentlemen and Eliza had completed their game of cards and she and Edward had gone on deck for their evening stroll, Breed spoke to the captain.

"Sir, I wish to buy a guitar when we make port. Harry spoke to Lita for me and she says she knows where the street of the fiddle makers is, so could we three go there while Eliza and Mr. Edward go to the Consulate?"

Hugh Shepard pondered the tip of his cheroot a moment, then said, "By God, Breed, if you get lost or arrive back here with any more problems...." Here, he pointed his chin in Lita's direction and continued, "I'll set sail without you!"

Breed thanked him and assured him they would be back on deck at the appointed time. The conversation was interrupted when Eliza and Edward entered. They both were flushed, and Eliza began to talk of the chill in the air the moment she joined the rest of the passengers. "Yes, now that we have passed the equator, we will be going into winter again, the farther south we go," offered Mr. Johnson.

The women bid the gentlemen good night and retired to their cabin. Eliza was quiet as they prepared for bed, but Breed failed to notice because she was so excited at the forthcoming visit to Buenos Aires and the purchase of a guitar.

During the night, the clear weather broke and a thunderstorm accompanied by chill winds tossed the ship to and fro on choppy seas. Breed opened her eyes in the chill darkness of the cabin. She was cold, but that wasn't what awakened her. The ship's creaking and rocking no longer bothered her and the sound of thunder was muffled below deck. She was sure the cabin door was locked and she heard no sound from above. Deciding she had imagined it, she decided to get up and put more blankets on all their bunks. And then she heard it again. One of her cabin mates was crying, trying to muffle the sound in her pillows.

Even in her deepest pain, Lita had not shed a tear or even moaned, so Breed knew it was not her. "Eliza, what is the matter? Are you ill?" she whispered.

"Oh Breed, I am so sorry. Truly, I tried not to wake you," said the now openly sobbing girl. Breed stood up and carefully made her way to her friend.

"Eliza, what is the matter?" she asked as she perched on the edge of the bunk.

"Oh Breed, I'm so ashamed...." stammered the distraught girl.

"About what, Lala? Did you and Mr. Edward have a spat?" The older girl's question sent Eliza again into tears.

"Oh, Breed, Edward and I must get married. I'm pregnant!" she blurted.

Breed sat in stunned silence a moment before saying, "Impossible. You've not been out of my sight long enough to catch cold, much less lift your skirts!"

Eliza was shocked, but nevertheless assured Breed that it was so. "It happened last night!" she said.

"Eliza, how in the name of God could you get pregnant? You were in full sight of both the captain, Lita and me, save for the few moments you and Edward strolled on deck!"

"That's when it happened," sobbed Eliza, a little less unhappily, remembering the event.

Exasperated, Breed nearly shouted, "What happened?"

"Edward kissed me! And now I'm going to have his child!" she said defiantly.

Breed didn't know whether to hit the girl or laugh. She took a deep breath and said, "Eliza, kissing does not make babies!"

"Are you quite sure?" asked the relieved girl.

Breed shook her head in the darkness at the thought of such a child being sent blindly into a marriage bed with a complete stranger. "Didn't Mrs. Potts tell you anything about being married?" she asked.

Eliza used a corner of the sheet to dry her eyes, then said, "Mrs. Potts told me that when I was a married lady, I must do whatever my husband wanted me to. And that it would seem undignified and even boring, but sometimes it would be quite nice...."

"And that's all?" prompted Breed. The younger girl nodded.

Breed took a deep breath and said, "One day, when I was thirteen, I went looking for range eggs in the hay field at Aunt Sally's. And there behind a haystack was Jany, the hired girl, and Sam Pierce, the Carters' boy from town, laying together in the hay. Him, with his pants down and her with her skirts up, and both of them thrashing about something awful. Later, when I told my Aunt Kate, she laughed and said Sam Pierce wasn't the first but if he wasn't careful, he'd be the last as she had heard Jany had a "loaf in the oven" and needed a baker quick-like!"

"But, Breed," sniffled Eliza, "what does that mean?"

"That's what I'm trying to tell you, Eliza, that's how you get pregnant. Like when Reverend Potts sent Emily the cow to see Farmer Jestro's bull."

"Never!" gasped the shocked Eliza.

"Yes, that's how it happens," countered Breed.

Once, several of the young ladies had gone out for a walk

along country lanes behind the Weathermorn property with Breed as chaperone. Their walk took them past Farmer Jestro's stock pen, where they came upon the Potts' cow, Emily, being vigorously serviced by Black Dan, the farmer's prize bull. The small group stood transfixed with interest at the spectacle until Breed remembered this was a less than seemly diversion for young ladies and shepherded them off.

Breed's explanation of the marriage act, thanks to Aunt Kate's earthy vocabulary, left little to be imagined by the wilted young girl. "So now Edward and I shant have to get married?" questioned the girl, a little disappointedly.

"Not if that's the only reason you had for doing it," said Breed. "Besides, you're promised to that Mr. Loughlan." She tucked one of the extra blankets around Eliza.

Eliza took her hand, gave it a squeeze and said, "Thank you for explaining it all, Breed." Then, as she settled herself more comfortably she murmured, "I should really like to be Edward's wife. I did so enjoy his kiss, and I even think the rest would be pleasant." Breed smiled to herself, put another blanket over Lita and padded back to her own pallet, where she lay down and fell instantly asleep, not realizing the seed of passion she had planted in the young girl's mind.

❧ CHAPTER NINE ❧

The Sara Blue sailed on and in due course reached the harbor of Buenos Aires. The three young women, dressed more warmly than they had in some time, waited on deck for Harry and Edward Tiverton-West. It was arranged that Tiverton-West would go first to the British Counsel to collect any mail from England. The women in Harry's care would go to the street of the fiddle makers to purchase Breed's desired guitar. Eliza was not looking forward to the shopping expedition, remembering all too clearly the last one. So when at the final moment Edward suggested she accompany him to the counsel she was as relieved as she was delighted. When Breed hesitated, wondering at the propriety of a young lady going off with a gentleman not related to her, Eliza looked downcast and her lower lip began to quiver. Breed forgot Mrs. Potts' admonitions regarding the duty of a chaperone and agreed. The two parties were to meet at eleven o'clock at the Church of San Ignacio, which Captain Shepard had told them was much worth seeing.

M. Mornay at first planned to join the shoppers. But after dithering undecidedly, he announced he would go ashore alone as he must find a supplier of photographic chemicals and did not wish to detain the whole group. Mr. Johnson, the first mate, reminded them to be back by three as they planned to sail on evening tide. The small shipment they were delivering was a piano ordered from Boston by the Governor General and should not take overlong to unload.

In a holiday mood, the two parties set off, each contented with the arrangements. Using her small slate, Lita wrote directions for the driver of their coach so he should not assume they were innocents abroad to be cheated.

"The street of the fiddle makers was cobbled and picturesque, the buildings in the colonial Spanish style," quoted Breed from the guidebook that Tiverton-West had lent them.

Harry translated to Lita what Breed read, but Lita merely sniffed and wrote in Spanish on her slate, "Be that as it may, their drains must have been laid down by the Romans!" Breed laughed at Harry's translation of her friend's words but agreed. Away from the damp, cold wind off the harbor, the city was cold and smelly. She was glad when the carriage drew up to a small shop with a sign in the shape of a guitar hung above the door.

It was warm inside the shop and the air smelled of sawdust and glue. Sr. Polivoces, the guitar maker, was a cripple confined to his workbench, but he had several apprentices who worked beside him or darted here and there to do his bidding. Much intrigued by Breed's appearance, he listened patiently to Harry's explanation regarding Breed's desire to learn to play a guitar. After a moment, he barked an order to one of the gaping apprentices. He chatted pleasantly with Harry and Lita, never taking his eyes off the "Golden One," as he referred to Breed.

Shortly, the young boy hurried from the rear of the shop with a large package carefully wrapped in yards of muslin. He cleared a space on his workbench and with a dramatic flourish removed the wrappings from the instrument. It was a work of art. The long, fretted neck was of a golden wood, polished so that it almost glowed with its own light. It was inlaid with pieces of dark wood and tiny chips of mother pearl. Breed reverently stroked the instrument and without even plucking a string told Harry she would have it and to ask Sr. Polivoces the price.

The guitar-maker was pleased at the appreciation of his art but not humbled in the least and asked an exorbitant amount. Lita, who had remained in the background, at once came forward. She put her hand on Breed's arm and drew her toward the door. Sr. Polivoces realized his greed had gotten the better of his judgment. He spoke quickly to Harry, assuring him that the price he quoted was, of course, for the common patron and that he was sure they could come to an understanding so that his noble instrument and the aristocratic senorita could be brought together. As the bargaining went on between Harry and the guitar-maker, Lita allowed Breed to return to the counter where the instrument lay. Finally, Lita wrote on her slate the amount Breed would pay, mentioning also that Sr. Polivoces realized she still must purchase a case to store the guitar. The haggling continued a moment or two longer before Polivoces conceded. He had made a comfortable profit and it pleased his vanity that his creation should be in the hands of the beautiful gringa.

The bargain was struck. Breed gave him the amount he desired and Sr. Polivoces told Harry that in the open market, close by the Calle Florida, they could find a seller of hide cases for the guitar.

Triumphantly, Breed carried her new treasure out to the carriage, refusing even Harry's offer of help. The stall that sold leather and hide goods was quickly found and Breed purchased a sturdy case in which she at once put the guitar. Back in the carriage, Harry directed the driver to take them to the Plaza de San Ignacio, where they were to join Eliza and Edward Tiverton-West. They had made good time in their shopping and would be early.

As they drove into the crowded square, Breed's attention was wholly taken by the beautiful old church. She did not see Tiverton-West's carriage until Lita touched her on the arm and pointed. At once, she realized something was greatly wrong. Eliza was weeping openly and Tiverton-West sat next to her, as still and stiff as stone with his face turned from them. Without waiting for Harry to hop down and give her his hand, Breed gathered her skirts and jumped from the carriage the moment it came to a halt behind the other carriage.

Nearly running, she rushed to Eliza and asked, "For the love of God, Eliza, what has happened?"

Tiverton-West never moved or turned to greet the new arrivals. But Eliza stretched out her arms to Breed and practically threw herself from the carriage. "Oh, Breed! It's so terrible, so sad. Word was waiting for Edward at the consulate that his cousin Francis had died in a hunting accident. And when they brought him home, his father, Edward's Uncle Lord Holt-Tiverton, had a stroke and...." Here, she ran out of breath and looked sadly at the still figure of the young man, before continuing, "And after lingering a few days, he also died. So, now Edward is Lord Holt and he must go home at once to England!" Here, she dissolved into fresh tears. Breed signaled for Harry and Lita to stay in their carriage. Handing Eliza back into her carriage, she went around to Edward's side. The young man was holding himself under tight control but it was evident to Breed it would not last.

She reached up, put her hand over Edward's hand, and spoke. "Sure, we know how you are feeling, for have we not also lost a dear one? We will all pray for you and your family, Edward." Then, remembering Eliza's words regarding Edward's accession to his uncle's title, she added, "Sir".

In a distant tone, he answered, "Yes, yes, good of you. Sorry to spoil the outing, but I must return to the ship and speak to Captain Shepard."

"Of course, we will all return," Eliza said. "Breed, I'll join you and Lita in your carriage."

But as she made to climb down, Tiverton-West roused himself. "No, Eliza," he said. "Stay with me, I... I do not wish to be alone." So she dried her tears and regained her seat across from the young man. Breed returned to Harry and Lita and quickly told them of Edward's recent bereavement. She signaled the driver to follow after Tiverton-West's vehicle.

All was confusion with the arrival of two more carriages at the wharf. Another huge, private traveling coach was pulled up alongside the Sara Blue and M. Mornay could be seen wrapped in his beautiful blue cloak, directing the crew in removing his many pieces of luggage and wicker baskets of equipment. Catching sight of Breed, he waved gaily and beckoned her to come and join him. Breed saw Edward assist Eliza aboard, then parted from her and walked toward Hugh Shepard, who could be seen going through a bill of lading. She signaled to Lita that she would join her below. Then she went to the little Frenchman and asked the meaning of the removal of his possessions. "I thought you said you were bound for California?" she asked.

"Mademoiselle, a most auspicious happening," he said. "Whom should I encounter at the chemists, but my very dear old friend Henri, whom I have not, how do you say, lain my eyes on since we were both in Madrid, simply years ago. Dear Henri has begged me to stay awhile here in Buenos Aires. So what could I say? I'm sure we will meet again soon in California, Mme. Breed, and you can introduce me to your new husband!" Before Breed could correct his mistaken idea that she was to be married, the little popinjay bowed low, kissed her hand and tripped daintily down the gangplank after the last of his luggage.

Edward Tiverton-West was deep in conversation with the captain. They had been joined by Mr. Johnson, so Breed retrieved her guitar in its new case and went in search of Rudy Navarro, the crewman she had so often heard playing his guitar. Rudy was short and slight of build and his hands were roughened by his work as an able-bodied seaman. But during the long evenings of the voyage south, he had spent his free time playing for himself and the crew with as much virtuosity as one might find in a concert hall. Breed approached him to be her teacher, promising to pay him for lessons when she received her cook's wages from the captain. Breed displayed her new treasure with pride. Rudy admired the guitar, assuring her that the great amount she paid for it would be worth it. He took the instrument and, sitting on a forward hatch, tuned it and taught Breed how as he went along. Before he was called to help lower the gangplank, he gave Breed some simple movements to practice.

❧ CHAPTER TEN ❧

It was too cold now to sit long on deck. The sun had given way to dark clouds promising rain, so Breed went below. In the cabin, she found Eliza pacing to and fro in the small space, wringing her hands and occasionally wiping away a tear. Lita sat well back in her bunk pretending to read, watching the young girl compassionately.

"Edward is speaking to the captain now," Breed said as she entered. "I know there's a ship on its way to the Falkland Islands with the new governor, and if Edward can get there he can return home on the Nelson.

"Come now, Lala, it is very sad about Edward's loss and it will be dull when he leaves us. But you have known all along that it would be so when we reached the Californias." Breed put her arms around the unhappy girl and coaxed her to lay down on her bunk. "I'll send Harry with tea for you both. I'm going to start dinner. Try to cheer up. Edward has enough to think about without seeing you downcast."

At dinner that night, Hugh Shepard announced he had agreed to convey the new Lord Holt-Tiverton to the Port of Stanley, on the East Falkland Island, in hopes of overtaking the Nelson. It would delay them only a few days in their own journey and perhaps they would pick up extra cargo for the rest of their voyage. Conversation was subdued and the men abstained from their usual card game when Edward excused himself. He asked Eliza to join him topside for a stroll.

"Yes, you best go now," said Mr. Johnson. "It's getting on for a blow and should rain soon!" Breed and Lita remained awhile in the captain's saloon talking with Hugh and Mr. Johnson, but it had been a long day and they soon said good night and went to their cabin.

As Breed and Lita prepared for bed, they heard the rain begin. In moments, it was lashing at their porthole, a full-blown squall. "This will be just the first of many, now that we are nearing Cape Horn," Breed said, quoting the captain. She kept glancing at the cabin door, wondering what was keeping Eliza. Finally, just as she had made up her mind to put on some clothes and go looking for the girl, the door opened and Eliza entered.

She looked slightly damp. Her hair, which had a tendency to curl, had blown free of its clasp and was a mass of ringlets around her face. Her cheeks were flushed, her eyes bright. She looked thoroughly happy. "Eliza, come you and get warm and dry. Whatever kept you so long?" said Breed, though privately she was sure the two young people had been saying their "goodbyes."

Eliza could not contain her happiness any longer. "Oh! Breed, Edward said he loves me!" she blurted.

Not wanting to spoil the happy moment for the girl but knowing it was important to bring her down to earth, Breed spoke briskly. "Come now and put on your nightgown," she said. "Soon, Edward will be aboard the Nelson on his way home and you will be once again on your way to Mr. Loughlan and your marriage."

Eliza was properly subdued, but as she began to undress, she said, "How can I marry a perfect stranger when I know Edward and love him?"

Breed refused to be drawn into any discussion on the subject. She helped the girl settle herself in her bunk and tucked the blankets in around her. Bidding her cabin mates good night, she blew out the candles and climbed into her own pallet. She said her prayers and added as an afterthought, "Please Lord, don't let Eliza be hurt too badly when Edward leaves." Having consigned Eliza to the Almighty, she turned on her side and slept.

It was still overcast the next morning but the rain had passed and, though the weather was cool, the sun was trying to break through. The women spent most of the day below decks. After lunch, however, they appeared on deck. Edward at once sought out Eliza and they strolled toward the bow of the ship. Lita had brought some sewing with her and she set to work. Breed, with her new guitar in hand, went in search of Rudy Navarro, her music teacher-to-be. In a few moments, she was engrossed in her first lesson and it was evident that Navarro was a qualified and skilled teacher.

Eliza watched, agitated, as Breed and the deck hand talked and worked together. When Captain Shepard appeared, she rose from the cushions she and Edward were sharing and went to him. "Please, captain, you must speak to Breed. She is trying to get that sailor to teach her to play her guitar."

He glanced toward Breed and the deck hand, then back to Eliza and said, "Calm yourself, Miss Eliza. If Breed thinks she must play the guitar, nothing I say will change her mind."

Eliza, looking distraught, blushed and spoke again. "Captain, it's not... seemly and it's not very safe encouraging a common seaman, a foreigner too!"

Hugh Shepard had come out for a breath of fresh air and was tired of Eliza's hectoring. "Miss Eliza," he said brusquely, "Breed could take on the whole crew. She's at least a head taller than Rudy and twenty pounds heavier. Set your mind at ease. Breed could probably keelhaul any man aboard, myself included, should she so desire." So saying, he lit a cheroot and walked toward the helm.

Later, when her lesson was over, Breed joined Eliza and Lita under the awning. Eliza took up her refrain but before she was truly launched verbally Breed raised her hand and laughingly said, "Eliza, for the love of God, give over and stop trying to make a silk purse from a cow's ear! I'm no lady and not likely to ever become one." Eliza's lower lip quivered and she looked on the verge of tears, so Breed put her arm around her and spoke again. "Truly, Lala, you must not worry so. A few more weeks and we will be safe in California...." Before she could finish, Eliza drew a quick breath that ended in a sob. She looked distractedly at Edward, seated across from her, and then rose and went below to their cabin. Breed, at a loss to explain Eliza's behavior, started to follow but Lita touched her arm and shook her head. Instead of following the unhappy girl, Breed went to the galley and made tea. She sent a tray with Harry to Eliza, hoping a good cup would calm the upset girl.

Dinner that night in the captain's saloon was quite festive. Breed had outdone herself with the entrée and even Eliza was again her cheerful self. She has finally admitted to herself that Edward must go and she must stay, thought Breed as she watched Eliza and the three men playing one last game of cards. Just before the ladies returned, one of the seamen on watch shouted, "Land Ho" and everyone went on deck to catch their first glimpse of the Falkland Islands. That night, the Sara Blue anchored in the harbor of Stanley on East Falkland Island.

In the morning, it was decided that Breed and Lita would go with Harry to the wool market to purchase cloth for a winter dress for Lita. Eliza would go with Edward to see about his passage with the Navy ship, Nelson. Breed had qualms about Eliza gallivanting around the island with Edward, but Eliza was being so brave and even cheerful that Breed felt the young girl deserved to spend the last few hours with her friend. As their carriage pulled away from the quay where Harry and the two other women stood, Edward called, "If the captain asks us, we shall stay to dine, so do not worry if you return before Eliza." Assured that Eliza would be occupied for the morning at least, the three intrepid shoppers set off to see the sights of the small town and make their purchases. At the wool merchants, Lita chose a wine and black tartan and Breed bought herself a new shawl, knit by one of the island women for export. Burdened with their purchases, the three found a tea shop on the street leading back to the harbor and settled in for a leisurely lunch. The young waitress was intrigued by Lita, having never seen a black person. Harry flirted outrageously with her and told her Lita must be served first as she was the daughter of an African chief on her way to visit her uncle in San Francisco. The three spent a happy hour in the little shop and Breed was sorry to see the outing end. As they approached the quay, Lita touched Breed's arm and pointed toward the mouth of the harbor. There, under sail and headed seaward, was the Nelson. Breed felt guilty. She realized that while they had been enjoying themselves ashore, poor Eliza must be watching Edward Tiverton-West sail out of her life forever. Standing by the gangplank was a young boy about Harry's age. As the three drew closer to the Sara Blue, he walked up to Breed and, touching his cap, said, "Be ye Miss Seastrum?" When she nodded, he handed her an envelope and walked quickly away.

"What in the world?" said Breed, opening the letter. For that is what it was. And it began:

My Dearest Friend,

Please do not be angry with me. I'm only doing what my heart tells me I must. The "Nelson" sails with the tide at noon, and Edward and I with it. We will be married by Captain Horton as soon as we are at sea.

After you and Lita went on deck this morning, I packed my small portmanteau with a few articles and a change of clothing and gave it to Edward's valet. We will shop in London before we go to Tiverton to meet his family. I am a little frightened of the encounter, but my dearest Edward assured me they will be very pleased.

I beg you make my excuses to the captain and thank him for his kindness. I am so very happy and Edward says I will be a beautiful Lady Holt-Tiverton.

Dearest Breed, forgive my selfishness and know I will always hold your friendship precious. Tell Lita I marked out the next six lessons in her book and for her to take care of you.

Sincerely your loving friend,
Elizabeth Staunton

"Oh, my God!" gasped the stunned Breed. She thrust the missive at Harry, telling him to read and translate it for Lita. Gathering up her skirts, she ran up the gangplank and along the deck in search of Hugh Shepard. She found him on the afterdeck, with Mr. Johnson, pouring over charts. But even as she called his name she looked once more toward the harbor only to realize that the Nelson was well underway and heading rapidly for the distant horizon! Breathlessly, she told the captain all that had transpired and the contents of Eliza's letter.

"God blast it women! Every petticoated one of yea are more trouble than you're worth!" he bellowed, bringing the anxious Breed to the verge of tears.

"Captain, what will you say to Mr. Loughlan?" she asked, biting back tears of worry and guilt.

Viciously jamming the rolled charts into their case, he growled, "Damn it to hell! He's expecting two women. Well, I'm bringing him two women. He can choose between you!" He put a cheroot in his mouth. Lighting it, he looked at Lita, who had just joined Breed, and stomped off.

Late in the afternoon, the Sara Blue herself was underway, only she was headed in an opposite direction from the Nelson. The fresh South East trade winds would take them shortly to the Straits of Magellan and Cape Horn.

Dinner that night was a gloomy affair and the first mate tried his best to lighten the company. "Well, ladies, sometime tomorrow morning, we shall be approaching the Cape of Storms and once round it, we will be on the last leg of our voyage!" Breed tried to smile at the well-meaning man, but it was all she could do to keep the lump in her throat from welling into tears.

As the silent meal drew to a close, Captain Shepard spoke of the subject that had been on all their minds. "You could have knocked me over with a feather when you told me that Miss Eliza had jumped ship," he said. "I'd never have given her credit for having the gut... gumption to go with Tiverton-West." Glancing at Breed, he continued, "You are not to blame yourself. There was nothing you could have done, once he had convinced her. I'm sure he will take good care of your little friend."

Breed, still upset, could only nod her head when he had finished speaking. Tiring of the subject, the captain said, "I hope you ladies have got your sea legs ready because the next few days may be rather rough sailing. Chances are, we will run into really stormy weather as we round the Horn. Stay below, and Breed, don't think about cooking till we reach calm water beyond the Cape."

Since the other players in their nightly card game were missing, the captain and Mr. Johnson thanked the ladies for their company at dinner and went on deck.

The young women helped Harry clear away the meal and then set about cutting out Lita's new wool dress. The two worked in companionable silence and the task took Breed's mind off the happenings of the day. But by nine o'clock they both were tired and decided to retire. Breed was afraid she would not be able to sleep. However, the long day and its excitements took their toll and both were asleep in moments.

The Sara Blue sailed on through the night, sails billowing like the wings of a giant white bird. The cold, crisp night soon gave way to a biting wind straight from the barren polar lands to the south. By dawn, the great ship was caught tight in the grip of a raging storm. Sleet pounded the decks and the wind lashed out at the rigging like a mad animal. Breed awakened when the motion of the ship became so sharp she was nearly thrown from her bunk.

One look across the cabin at Lita informed her that the other woman was feeling the effects of the storm. Indeed, Breed felt a bit queasy herself but decided she felt better on her feet. Harry stumbled in with a pot of tea and biscuits and information from the captain.

"This is a granddaddy of a storm," he said, "and you are to keep your life belts at hand, just in case!" The boy seemed to be relishing the tossing and turning and the rampaging elements around them. He delivered the captain's message as though he were promising the ladies a great treat.

❧ CHAPTER ELEVEN ❧

Breed helped Lita drink a little tea, had some herself, then dressed warmly with the intention of going topside. She climbed the steps leading from the companionway to the deck, twice nearly losing her hold on the rail. The hatch cover had been securely battened from the outside and, had not one of the crew appeared behind her, she would have had to return to her cabin. When the man opened the cover, she was right behind.

The cold was paralyzing. Sleet dashed against the deck and made drifts against the ship's rail. During the night, heavy rope netting had been lashed to the bulwarks to keep from washing overboard any of the men who must be exposed. The nets and the ship's rigging were draped with huge icicles. As Breed tugged at the companionway hatch, trying to get below again, a great wave struck the Sara Blue with such force the ship shook and rattled as though possessed.

Breed was soaked by the freezing water and so frightened by the awesome violence of the storm that she was close to hysteria by the time she forced entry to the safety of the companionway. She struggled to shut the hatch securely, then stumbled to the cabin. She undressed, wrapped herself in blankets and huddled in her bunk, alternately praying for safe delivery from the hurricane and thinking of her father, lost at sea in just such a storm.

The hurricane lasted three days. The two young women never left their cabin. Indeed, in her first attempt at English, Lita wrote on her slate, "I am died." Though Breed felt fairly well, she was so worried about the ship's floundering that she could only give a weak smile and commend Lita's attempt.

Harry plied them with constant cups of tea in the belief that it would keep them calm as the captain had ordered. Unfortunately, he was deeply devoted to Hugh Shepard. Given his captive audience, he spent part of each visit telling them tales of other voyages and storms and their alarming outcomes. He would finish a harrowing story by assuring them that Captain Shepard was a man of great courage and ability, and that rounding the Horn with him at the helm was no more dangerous than "rounding" Cape Hatteras.

Nevertheless, Breed and Lita breathed a collective sigh of relief when, on the morning of the fourth day, the wind abated and the sun broke through the clouds. It was still freezing cold, but Mr. Johnson assured them it would begin to warm up again in a day or so as they were now sailing north up the western coast of South America.

True to the first mate's words, the stormy weather was over and the Sara Blue, all her canvas unfurled and full, sailed north. In Valparaiso, they went ashore for a few hours while cargos of Cuban sugar and rum, and cotton cloth from the mills of New England were unloaded and the ship was reloaded with a shipment of guano for farmers in California.

Breed had lost interest in sightseeing since Eliza left, so after only a cursory walk through the central plaza and open market of the city she and Lita returned to the ship. Though sunny, the weather was still cool and Breed asked the captain if that was why the country was called "Chilly"? He laughed and explained that is was a native Indian word and it meant, "Where the land ends." That evening, they weighed anchor and set sail again, headed ever north with Lima, Peru, their next landfall.

Several days later, they reached their destination, but as they waited at the mouth of the harbor for a pilot to guide them in, it was evident to all aboard that something was wrong on shore. The docks and buildings along the harbor were shrouded by heavy smoke. The quay, which should have been crowded with ships and cargo being loaded and unloaded, was deserted. Captain Shepard spent some time with his telescope, trying to unravel the mystery to no avail. A fire of large proportions was evident but the smoke hid the answer. After an hour, a single man rowed out in a small skiff and hailed the Sara Blue. He climbed aboard, speaking rapidly in Spanish to the captain and the first mate.

After a few minutes' consultation, Mr. Smith hurried aft to where the crew was lounging and began shouting orders to sail within the hour. Captain Shepard spoke a while longer with the man from the skiff, then gave him two gold pieces for his time and information and saw him over the side to his little boat. The deck was alive again with the crew preparing to raise anchor and unfurl the sails. The captain gave a few orders and joined the two young women. "What's amiss, captain?" Breed asked.

"Earthquake early this morning and a pretty bad one, from what the harbor clerk says," he related. "Somehow, a fire started, which has devastated the whole city." He paused to shout instructions to one of the crew aloft in the rigging.

Breed broke in, "Are we leaving? Perhaps we could help? We have medical supplies and..."

Captain Shepard glared at her. "Hush!" he said. "We must leave as quickly as possible. A quake this strong is frequently followed within twenty-four hours by a tidal wave, and if we get caught in one of those while we are anchored here in the harbor, it could toss us right ashore and leave the Sara Blue smashed like kindling across the jetties." With that, he turned and went aft to take the helm as the ship was again under sail. Harry came up a few moments later with the captain's telescope. "Here ye are, Miss. The captain says to use this and look landward." She took the scope and after a moment's adjusting was able to see what was left of the city of Lima. The sight was frightening. Fire and smoke obscured the harbor area, but the part of the city still visible showed such destruction and devastation that Breed was horrified. "Good God, Lita, look you," she said. "Could there be anyone left after such an awful happening?" She handed the scope to Lita, blessed herself and prayed for the people of the city. Soon, the Sara Blue had cleared the harbor and again was sailing north.

The days were drawing out and the heat drove the young women on deck again. Harry set up the awning and brought out their cushions so that they might be comfortable. The sun beat down on the Sara Blue, leaving crew and passengers listless and short-tempered. The captain and Mr. Johnson consulted their charts and maps and at length announced that they would take on fresh water and supplies at Guayaquil, Ecuador. From Santa Elena, they would sail straight to Los Angeles. "Well, Miss, does that suit you?" the captain asked teasingly of Breed.

In no mood for his heavy-handed humor, she retaliated by asking, "And are you ready to tell how you lost your cousin's bride-to-be in mid-ocean?" So saying, she threw down her mending. She began to pace the ship's decks and walked, for miles, or so it seemed to the watchful Lita. This nervous energy lasted all afternoon until Harry, at Mr. Johnson's bidding, told her they were approaching the coast of Ecuador and would anchor off Guayaquil by evening. As they spoke, a crewman up in the rigging let out a shout, "Man adrift!" All those not actively engaged in operating the ship rushed to the side and beheld a truly remarkable sight: A man of burly build and swarthy complexion sitting astride a huge log of eight or ten feet in length. His wrists and ankles were manacled to rings of iron driven into the log. As they watched, the captain ordered a boat be lowered with a seaman and tools aboard.

After several attempts to remove the wrist and ankle cuffs, the seaman finally took a short axe. With a few well-placed chops, he severed the chains and helped the castaway climb aboard. The first mate had suggested they lower a cargo net when the boat reached the side of the Sara Blue because it was evident the castaway was weak, stiff and would have much difficulty climbing the rope ladder to the deck. Shortly thereafter, the man was lifted from the small boat onto the deck.

"Stand back, men," the captain said. "Give him some water laced with rum. And Harry, run and get some bread for him to eat." The man was short, his skin so burned by the sun and wind it was difficult to tell its color. Probably a half-cast, by the look of him, thought the captain.

Mr. Johnson noticed the man's right ear had been notched at the lobe in the manner of some slave traders. "Did ye notice his ear, sir?" he said quietly to the captain. "He's probably a runaway slave."

Captain Shepard nodded. As the man gulped water and tore wolfishly at the bread Harry had given him, the captain sent the crew about their duties. Breed and Lita stayed beneath their awning but could hear quite well as the captain questioned the man, whose physique was one of great strength. A thick neck and shoulders, wide and muscular, gave him the appearance of a two-footed bull.

Indeed, when asked his name, the man answered, "El Toro!" and leered, smiling in the direction of the women. His language was as polyglot as his appearance, some pigeon English, a dash of African dialects, but mainly native Spanish.

Captain Shepard spoke to him sharply in Spanish. "Keep your eyes to yourself or over you go again, this time without your log. Now what were you set adrift for, and I want the truth!" Breed understood the captain, but the man spoke too rapidly for her to comprehend his answer. Lita touched Breed's arm. When Breed turned to her, Lita drew her right hand with the forefinger outstretched across her neck. Breed's eyes could hardly believe what they saw.

"He slit somebody's throat?" Breed asked. Lita nodded. Breed was shocked and full of questions, but it was time for her to go to the galley and start the evening meal. She saw the cook hovering behind a stack of canvas, waiting for her, so she rose to go and told Lita to send Harry as soon as possible to the galley.

Guayaquil lay before them. The captain sent the rescued man below in the care of two crewmen. "Put him in the brig and bring him some food, but for God's sake lock the door securely or he'll have the gold from your ears!" the captain said. Several of the crewmen wore gold rings in their ears, so the threat struck home and the castaway was led none too gently away.

When the Sara Blue was under sail, a breeze through the portholes kept the heat in the galley bearable. But with the ship anchored only miles from the Equator in mid-August, the heat was suffocating. Breed and Lita had already discarded as much clothing as was modestly allowed. Breed longed for a cool tub to bathe in, like the one at the convent. She cooked great chunks of ham from some of the last hanging in storage, serving it over rice in a spicy gravy full of onions and peppers, just the way the crew liked it. All the while, she longed for a cool, light dish, perhaps just fruit and cheese. She laughed aloud at the thought of the reception such a meal would receive from the ever-hungry crew.

The evening was well advanced before Lita and Breed were again sitting under the awning. The sun was down but the tropical twilight lingered. The captain and first mate had dined ashore, so Breed and Lita ate supper on deck and enjoyed the cooler air. "Crikey, I always thought Boston in summer was the world's hottest place...little did I know!" said Breed as she fanned herself with one of the woven palm fans they had picked up in their shopping. They could hear the crew jumping from the aft deck into the water. There was much splashing and ribald joking among the men, most of which went completely over Breed's head. Envying their swim, she considered asking the captain's permission to do the same. But she feared sharks and she knew Mrs. Potts would not have approved. However, she thought, I'd rather face a shark than Mrs. Potts in me shift, dripping wet!

Shortly, one of the provision boats arrived from shore and the irrepressible Harry with it. He went aft as soon as he was aboard to deliver the various purchases the crew had bid him make. Finally, after waiting what seemed hours, Breed had the boy sit down and tell them in detail about the castaway. Harry was sucking on a sticky sweet and taking so long to begin the story, Breed wanted to box his ears.

"Well, you see, we are down river from Guayaquil, Ecuador. It's one of the country's largest cities and a port." Harry paused for a prolonged suck, then continued, "But it's on this big river that flows so fast out to sea, we can't use the port 'cause we couldn't get up river against the seaward tide. Anyway, that's what Mr. Johnson says. Well, this castaway was a slave in Guayaquil, only he ran away. But he was caught, you see, and that's how they punish runaway slaves. They send them down river on a log, chained, so they can't swim ashore."

Harry paused again to finish the sweet, then continued. "The captain says he's a bad 'un. He admits to murder, self-defense he called it, but he must have done more than run away to get 'logged.' Seems the senors feel if the alligators along the river don't get him, the sharks that wait at the mouth of the river will!" He finished his story and drank some of the lemonade that Lita offered him. Breed was aghast at Harry's account of Ecuadoran justice, and his mention of sharks confirmed her decision not to ask to swim in the ocean.

"Captain told him he could work above deck during the day," Harry said, "but he has to sleep in the brig 'cause he's a fugitive and though us Americans don't hold with feeding bad 'uns to sharks, we don't trust 'em either. And when we reach San Pedro harbor, he's to go his way." He translated this last bit to Lita and then left to go about his chores.

By the time the girls were ready to sleep, their cabin had cooled somewhat. It was preferable to the deck, which was now alive with flying creatures of every description that had migrated from the shore to welcome them. As the women lay in their bunks, nearly asleep, Breed spoke to Lita, haltingly, in Spanish. "What will become of us, I wonder? We, too, are...." She tried to think of the word for castaway but finally said, "We, too, are... abandonado." In the dark, Lita kept her own counsel but vowed her friend would never be abandoned while she lived.

In the early morning, the Sara Blue set sail for her final port, San Pedro, the harbor town of El Pueblo de Nuestra Senora La Reina de Los Angeles, the City of Our Lady, Queen of the Angels. The castaway, El Toro, swabbed the decks and helped in the galley, so Breed often came in contact with him. That he was "a bad 'un," as Harry had said, she had no doubt. But he did have an ingratiating smile, with his polyglot chit-chat. The two young women decided to make him a shirt and a pair of seaman's trousers, so when they reached Los Angeles he would have more than his ragged pants. His clowning amused them during the voyage north, and Breed was shocked one day when she learned he was not to be allowed out of the brig for the remainder of the passage because he had been caught stealing in the crew's quarters. When she sent his dinner down to him, she tried to add any tasty leftover from the captain's table. A few days before they reached port, Breed and Lita went below with Mr. Johnson and presented the prisoner with his new linen shirt and trousers of dark worsted. El Toro was visibly moved at the thoughtfulness of the two young women, and possibly even meant some of his various vows of homage and appreciation.

After a few days, Captain Shepard announced they were off Baja California, or lower California, which still belonged to Mexico. Tomorrow, he said, they should see the Sara Blue docked at San Pedro. Breed, usually compliant and calm, looked stricken. She pretended to need something from their cabin and rushed below. She spent some time crying, then calmed herself and faced up to the morrow. All that John Loughlan could do was ship them back to Boston, and if he refused to have anything to do with them, they could find work. She washed her face, took a deep breath and went back on deck, determined to let the future take care of itself.

Both girls were up and dressed well before dawn when Harry was sent to tell them to come on deck. "Good morning, ladies," said the captain. "If you will look starboard, you will see the coast of California yonder!" The captain had changed from the usual white shirt he wore to a dark alpaca suit and a string tie. He looked quite handsome with his dark beard freshly trimmed and in clothes befitting the captain of a vessel such as the Sara Blue. "We should reach San Pedro this afternoon if the wind continues," he said.

Breed helped the cook prepare breakfast, more for something to do than because he needed help. Lita went below to finish their packing. When the crew was settled at breakfast, Breed took a tray on deck for the captain and Mr. Johnson and sent Harry to tell Lita to join them. After breakfast, both the captain and Mr. Johnson were in an expansive mood at the prospect of a successful voyage completed, so Breed plied them with more questions about California. She tried to slip in one or two regarding John Loughlan. Though full of information about Los Angeles, Captain Shepard was reticent on the subject of his cousin and the Rancho Dos Aliso.

Finally, she gave up and looked resignedly at Lita. Her friend, in return, rolled her eyes and gave a slight shrug. Mr. Johnson had excused himself, but the captain remained to have a morning cheroot. The three sat quietly for a few moments. The captain had left his leather cheroot case on the table with a box of matches. With only a questioning glance at Hugh Shepard, Lita removed one of the cheroots, put it between her lips and proceeded to light it. Breed nearly dropped her coffee cup. After the initial shock, the captain threw back his head and laughed aloud. "By God, senorita, you keep a man guessing," he said. Lita merely looked at him, appearing to thoroughly enjoy the cheroot, which clearly was not her first.

Breed was too embarrassed by Lita's smoking to say a word. In her mind, she could see what effect such an act would have had on her mentor, Mrs. Potts. "Sure, she would have fainted!" For the first time, Breed began to realize that the new world she had entered could either be for her good or to her detriment. If something was "different" or even shocking, it did not mean it was necessarily bad or wrong. She decided she must rely more on how she felt about something and less on how Mrs. Potts, thousands of miles away, would feel.

The rest of the morning was spent gathering their possessions. Shortly after noon, they heard one of the crewmen aloft in the rigging shout "Land Ho!" They returned to the deck after putting the finishing touches on their more formal traveling attire and could see the houses and buildings along the shore. Sandy beaches gave way to rocky, jagged inlets. In the distance, high palisades dropped into deep boiling surf. The two young women, so different in appearance, stood together at the rail, presenting a unified front to this new world.

Excitement raced through the crew. This would be their first

American port in months. San Francisco was the acknowledged leader as the best town in which to take shore leave, but San Pedro and Los Angeles were close behind.

Captain Shepard began issuing orders, first to one man then another, as they scrambled aloft to furl the sails that had taken them and their ladyship thousands of miles. Soon, the Sara Blue was waiting patiently at the harbor mouth for the harbor pilot to guide her to her berth. When all was in readiness, Mr. Johnson sent word for the crew to gather on the deck.

The captain stood in front of the crew, a cheroot in his mouth and his visored cap pushed back on his head. He waited until the men had arranged themselves into some semblance of formation. "All right, you blackards," he barked. "We have had a safe journey. This is Tuesday. We sail for San Francisco on the tide Sunday. Mr. Johnson has the harbor watches. Check with him, have a bit of fun, but don't forget where you have to be on Sunday next! If I have to go searching for my crew, you will spend time in the brig when I find you. Ye get only half your pay so you won't lose it gambling at the Pink Lady or to one of Madam Louise's girls, and to make sure you're here come Sunday!" The crew groused a bit, but on the whole accepted the captain's dictum, knowing he was one of the most trustworthy and fair men with whom they could ship out.

Hugh Shepard turned to Breed and Lita, who were standing at the rail observing, and continued, "Now ladies, I'll put no such strictures on you. You get your whole pay and my thanks. It's probably a first in the history of the sea, when sailors actually gained weight on a voyage!"

The men cheered and whistled in agreement. Old Davey Hornby, the ship's carpenter, stepped forward. Ducking his head in embarrassment, he held out to Breed a small bag made of sail cloth. "Ah, Missy," he said, "this here is from the crew for you and the senorita, with our thanks for all them good victuals and all and, yes, your music!" He quickly dropped it into her hand and scuttled back into the crew's ranks. Breed brushed away tears and smiled at the men. In a voice on the verge of cracking, she thanked them, and she and Lita promised to pray for them when they were once more at sea.

"Better to pray while they are on shore leave. They be in a lot more danger!" said Mr. Johnson, half-seriously.

Moments later, the harbor master's craft hailed them and the pilot, Mr. Durkins, came aboard. The captain greeted him as an old friend and they began exchanging news as the Sara Blue made her way into the harbor.

CHAPTER TWELVE

Wind had blown every cloud from the sky and it was brisk by the sea. Breed noticed, however, it was not so farther inland. Touching Lita's arm, she pointed to a great pillar of smoke rising for what seemed miles and asked Mr. Durkins where it came from.

"Well, Miss," he said, rearranging the quid of tobacco in his mouth, "it's the first of the fires. Everything out here gets so durned dry around about September that we always have at least one big fire. Used to just let 'em burn themselves out, but the land's getting so settled that folks are nervous if one starts too close to town or their spread." He spat expertly over the side and continued, "This time it's Francisco Navarro's Rancho, out where it meets the Mission San Gabriel." He paused a moment, then continued, "Say, Captain, there's a message for you concerning the ladies. John Loughlan has taken his men to help fight the fire and won't be able to welcome you himself." Here, he smiled his tobacco-stained grin and added, "little lady," this to Breed who was a good half-head taller than the pilot.

"Damnation!" barked the captain, "and what am I to do with your baggage?" Hugh Shepard did not relish having to stay with Breed and Lita. He too was looking forward to a visit to Madam Louise's. "That yellow-livered bastard, he's just afraid to meet his new bride!"

Breed jumped at his words. "Captain, surely you're going to explain. I mean...," she trailed off helplessly, as the captain bellowed irritably for the first mate to bring glasses and a bottle for him and Mr. Durkins.

Lita, who had remained in the background, watching Breed's worry and distress, came forward and stood beside her. Hugh Shepard, realizing they were closing ranks on him, spoke more softly so that only the girls could hear.

"John Loughlan wanted a wife, with three little girls. He needs a wife, so why not you? You could do worse." Captain Shepard had grown fond of Breed and spoke sincerely. He admired his cousin John and felt the two might do well together. Breed started to answer, but the captain was called to speak with the pilot.

"God help us, he's meaning it!" said Breed, more to herself than to Lita. There was no time to say anything more. The Sara Blue had slipped into her berth and the crew was swarming over her, securing sails and shore lines. The girls went below and with Harry's help brought their few belongings on deck. When they finally stood together with their carpet bags, Breed's guitar and the small humpbacked trunk surrounding them, they looked like two forlorn waifs. The captain was on the wharf talking to a swarthy little man in a large, straw hat. He pointed first to the ship and then to a horse-drawn wagon standing a short way down the wharf. After a moment's more conversation, Captain Shepard clasped his hand on the man's shoulder and cheerfully bellowed to Harry to unload the ladies' belongings and to store them in the wagon of Sr. Morales. He was absolutely purring, he was so pleased with himself. "Come ashore, Breed. Here is Pedro come with a message from John."

Exchanging worried looks, the two women disembarked from the ship that had been their home for months.

Breed could tell that whatever the message, it pleased the captain, and she wondered if they likewise would be as pleased. Captain Shepard turned and, giving them a satisfied smile, explained, "Mr. Loughlan has arranged that you will go and stay at the home of Sr. Morales till the fire is under control and he can come for you. Pedro will drive you there."

The meeting with John Loughlan postponed, Breed gave a sigh of relief. Even the usually unperturbed Lita looked less strained at the news that they had been provided for. But then Lita touched Captain Shepard's sleeve to gain his attention. She pointed at Breed, then brushed her fingers across her own face, looking at him questioningly. Breed was puzzled, the question of color had never entered her mind, but Hugh understood at once. He looked at her, thinking to himself what a handsome woman she was, then in Spanish answered her unspoken doubt. "Lita, you will both be welcome. This is California. Besides, if I'm not mistaken, Sra. Morales is a lady of some color herself. Someplace in her family, they were not all Spanish grandees! Come now, girls," he said, jubilantly herding them toward the waiting wagon.

So, amidst the calls of goodbye from the crew, the two young women were packed unceremoniously into the waiting buckboard. "It's that happy you are to be seeing the last of us, Hugh Shepard!" said Breed, with just the faintest break in her voice.

"Nonsense," he answered as he helped them settle amongst their belongings. "I'll be out to the place in a day or so. Must see my nieces and check on you two. Don't worry. Everything will be fine. I'll talk to John." With that, and hardly a backward glance, he left them. The driver of the wagon gave a cluck and a tug at the reins and they were off. The horses were evidently eager to return to their stable and feed bags because they went at such a fast pace that both girls were to hang on for dear life.

The rapid progress away from the harbor and all the new and different sights kept the two young women engrossed, so neither could dwell on the precarious position. As they drove along, they marveled at the thriving town. Occasionally, a hot blast of wind from inland reminded them of the forest fire to the north. After they had been riding more than an hour or so, the horses began to climb a high hill. Soon, they arrived at their destination.

The Morales' home was a huge Victorian edifice. Three stories high and decked with so much wooden gingerbread it reminded Breed of the cookie house Mrs. Goody had made one Christmas for the young ladies at the Weathermorn Home. There were deep porches on all sides of the house and cupolas crowned the roof wherever possible, and everything was painted bright yellow! The fields on either side of the road, leading to the house, were bleached nearly white by the summer sun. However, several large areas and the beds on either side of the brick walk were ablaze with flowers of every color and hue. The house was so placed on the crest of a hill that it had a fine view of the sea. Breed's first impressions were of spaciousness and comfort and a great deal of money liberally applied to make it so. She noticed a brick walk that led from the front of the house out over the hill to the cliffs and promised herself a good walk before dark, should her hostess agree.

As Pedro was helping them descend from the wagon, the front door flew open and one of the fattest women Breed had ever seen came sailing out. She came down the steps, her tiny feet booted in the latest Paris fashion, and gave each bewildered young woman a bone-crushing embrace. She was as tall as she was wide but so tightly corseted in a day gown of grey silk bombazine that her appearance was that of a huge Pouter pigeon. Her black hair, so lacquered that not a tendril was out of place, was piled on her head. On her cheeks, just in front of each ear, lay a flat curl, like an inverted question mark. The newcomers were now joined by several maids and two young girls, perhaps Eliza's age, who were dressed in the same expensive style as Sra. Morales. The two young girls introduced themselves. The younger was Serafina, the older Mira. Sra. Morales rattled off instructions to the driver and the maids, and then taking an arm of each of the arrivals she led them into the house, shooing the rest of her household ahead of them.

The hostess took them at once to their bedroom, explaining that she too had once been aboard a ship for a long time when she had come to San Pedro from Caracas to marry Sr. Morales. The first thing they must desire was a bath! Breed murmured her appreciation and tried to get a word in, but the good woman continued to effervesce half in English and half in Spanish. "Bathe and dress, then come down to the parlor. We will be waiting for you. My dear young ladies, we are so happy you have arrived safely!" She gave each a pat on the arm and sailed out of the room, saying in her rather confusing speech, "Aheeee, so romantic. Juan is very fortunate! Ah Madre de Dios, to be young again."

The girls closed the door and smiled ruefully at each other.

"There's no doubt about it, Lita. Sra. Morales is going to be very disappointed when she finds out I'm not Elizabeth."

The bedroom was a large square, light and airy. The heavy hand of Victorian décor had not yet reached above stairs as the room was simply but comfortably furnished. As the women unpacked, one of the little maids came to the door. She announced, in very careful English and accompanied by a wide grin, that the bathroom was just down the hall and the tub all ready.

Breed was tempted to soak and linger in the huge wood-and-tin tub, but not wanting to keep their hostess waiting she bathed in record time. By the time Lita had finished her bath, Breed was dressed.

Though her hair was still damp, she stood in the window combing it dry. During most of the voyage, she had worn it in a bun or a thick, single braid hanging down her back. But when she began to put it up again, Lita shook her head and indicated Breed leave it down. After a moment's hesitation, she did, thinking to herself, "For sure, when did you ever see a housemaid with her hair flowing to her shoulders!"

They went downstairs together and into the parlor that was Sra. Morales's pride and joy. It resembled something out of Godey's Ladies' Book and, in truth, Sra. Morales was the first to admit she had seen pictures of such rooms in the venerable periodical.

The walls were papered in a deep magenta, and seemingly every inch of space in the large room was filled with great carved pieces of furniture: chairs and settees, love seats, all upholstered in velvet of various shades of red. Even the piano bench was covered in red plush, with natty gold tassels at the corners. The floors, save for a few fine Turkish carpets, were of golden oak, so highly polished that Breed knew even Mrs. Potts would have approved. The only concession to location and temperature were the huge windows in the south and west walls. And though they were draped, curtained and shaded, as was the fashion, they were open and a cool offshore breeze made the room comfortable.

As they entered, Sra. Morales jumped to her feet and began her nonstop, rapid-fire conversation. She reintroduced her daughters, Mira and Serafina, and drew the two newcomers to a corner of the room. An ancient woman, so tiny one would mistake her for a child, sat there in rusty black clothes, with a black lace mantilla over her upswept, white hair. She sat so still, she seemed carved from dark stone. Only her black shoe-button eyes and gnarled brown fingers moved, the latter over her beads in silent prayer.

"And this is my husband's Tia, Sra. Montez y Ballesteros. She is nearly one hundred years old!" said Sra. Morales, proudly. Breed made a little curtsey, murmured the appropriate words and had time to marvel how easily the part of "the lady" was coming to her.

Just then, one of the maids announced dinner and Sra. Morales, with the ancient woman on her arm, shepherded them all into the dining room. Neither Breed nor Lita was prepared for the lavishness of the meal. Fresh shellfish was followed by a gazpacho-like soup and then tender young leg of lamb, surrounded by fresh vegetables, and several baskets of hot breads and hot rolled tortillas. If this was a usual meal in the Morales household, it was quite evident to Breed that both the daughters of Sra. Morales would soon resemble their mother in physical appearance!

The moment grace was said, followed by a suitable Thanksgiving to God for the safe arrival of the honored guests, Mira and Serafina piled their plates high and began to eat with a gusto unapproached by any of the Sara Blue's crew! The meal was delicious. The novelty of another person cooking, after the long weeks on shipboard as cook, gave Breed and Lita good appetites, which pleased Sra. Morales to no end.

After the first few minutes of serious eating, Breed felt she should speak with her hostess. In halting Spanish she said, "Senora Morales, your hospitality leaves both Lita and me feeling very unworthy. We can never repay your kindness." The rotund little woman smiled and nodded but continued to eat, so Breed went on, "My friend, Lita, as you maybe have noticed, does not speak. An old injury. She is not deaf, though, so should you wish to speak with her, please do so." Whereupon the eyes of the other women at the table turned toward Lita in sympathy. She looked at each in turn, smiling gravely and with a quick look at Breed bowed her head a little and returned to her plate. She was still careful of her food and cut everything in small pieces that needed little chewing.

As the meal progressed, Sra. Morales became more inclined to talk. Soon the women were chattering back and forth, asking questions about Breed and Lita's voyage. Breed, in return, asked about California. She would clearly have liked to bring up the subject of Loughlan but felt shy so did not.

The dessert, a huge plate of custard glistening in a pool of caramel sauce, had just been served when one of the maids hurried in, announcing that the senor and the young masters had just ridden into the stable yard.

Sra. Morales jumped to her feet. Once again, she was a veritable whirlwind, giving orders to the maids to prepare baths for the senor and sons, reset the dining table and have dinner ready for them shortly. All with asides to her daughters as to how they must help. She bustled away down the long hall and could be heard still marshaling her household, as a good general should.

Sr. Morales, his three sons and most of the men who worked for him had spent three days fighting the same great fire that had detained John Loughlan. In moments, Breed, Lita and the old one were the only ones left at the dinner table. After finishing their flan, Breed helped the old woman back to her comfortable chair in the parlor corner while Lita began to stack used china on a tray to clear the table. The kitchen was in an uproar and the maids welcomed the helping hands as they reset the table. Then, in an attempt to keep out of their hostess' way until she had her menfolk settled, the two young women withdrew to their bedroom.

Lita sat down by the west window to catch the early evening light and took out her sewing. Breed stood watching her friend, wondering at the delicate stitches and patterns she created with her needle and thread. As a parting gift for Hugh Shepard, she and Lita planned to give him two fine linen shirts. Lita was doing the finishing work and monogramming them now. Breed offered to help but both knew her sewing to be acceptable but uninspired. Lita would work faster alone, indeed preferred to do so.

Breed paced back and forth a few times, full of nervous energy. Finally, taking her old shawl from her carpet bag, she told Lita she was going for a walk along the cliffs. Lita nodded, engrossed in her sewing. Breed closed the door gently behind her and hurried toward the stairs. She could hear the voices of the Morales men and the senora behind the doors as she passed down the hall. On the stairs, she met a young man ascending, surely one of the Morales sons. He was tall, with dark brown hair and a mustache. His skin was olive, but not as dark as his mother's, and his eyes were as blue as Breed's own. They widened with surprise and interest when he caught sight of her.

As they met halfway on the staircase, he gave a slight bow and, never releasing his gaze from hers, introduced himself: "Senorita, your servant Diego Morales." He was so self-assured and imposing that Breed at once felt shy and clumsy. She acknowledged his greeting and, with a nod of her head, ducked by him down the staircase to the front hall. She was out the door so rapidly, she found herself breathless as she followed the path to the cliffs.

The long summer evening was drawing in, but the last rays of the sun painted the clouds over the ocean every shade of rose, pink and gold. Breed walked with long strides to the cliff's edge and wandered along the fenced walk, her shawl over her head and shoulders to ward off the chill. Her mind was a jumble of thoughts and emotions. What to do? Where to go? How would John Loughlan react when he found he had been jilted and saddled with two unknown women? Every once in a while, the face of Diego would intrude itself and the worries would begin anew.

Shortly after Breed began her solitary walk along the cliffs, a horseman rode into the Morales stable yard. He threw the reins to one of the stable boys and hurriedly dismounted, dusting his clothes and smoothing his hair as he walked unceremoniously through the back door and to the busy kitchen. Young Serafina was helping the maids prepare to feed her father and brothers. When she caught sight of the horseman, she dropped the soup ladle back into the kettle and went to him.

"Juan, we have been waiting for you, your betrothed is beautiful, and she is so nice, we...." The young girl rattled on as she took the man's arm and led him into the dining room, where her family was gathered.

John Loughlan was thirty-six and of slightly above average height. He was large-boned, with wide shoulders and narrow hips, and looked well in his denim trousers. He was clean-shaven, with auburn hair that tended to curl on his forehead and at the nape of his neck. His weather-beaten skin was tanned from long hours riding the range. His high cheekbones flanked a nose once broken and healed with a hawk-like hump. His eyes were grey and deep-set. Loughlan was sweating profusely, whether from nervousness or because he wore a beautifully tailored Norfolk jacket when the day was still warm. He was impatient to meet his new bride-to-be but allowed himself to be seated at the table with the family. The Loughlans and the Moraleses had been close friends since John Loughlan had first come to Alta, California, as a boy.

A troop of maids began serving the menfolk, but when Sra. Morales pressed John Loughlan to eat he declined. He patiently answered the ladies' questions regarding his daughters and his household, but with such a distracted air that it was evident his attention was elsewhere. He wondered where she could be, then realized Diego Morales had spoken to him. "I beg your pardon, Diego, what did you say?" he asked, but the whole family dissolved into laughter, the young men teasing him for being such an impatient bridegroom.

Finally, Sra. Morales took pity on the embarrassed man and spoke. "My sons, hush, do not make fun of Juan. Your time will come all too soon!" Turning to Loughlan, she informed him, "Your Golden One is out walking along the cliff. She too was undoubtedly impatient and nervous to meet you. Go out and find her." Her phrase Golden One puzzled Loughlan, but he let it go. He reddened under his tan and had the grace to look embarrassed when, as he rose from his chair, it fell over backward with a crash. Everyone laughed with him and called out various words of good luck, the young men choosing some less elegant suggestions for him to use upon meeting his new senorita.

Nervous and excited, he hurried out of the house and around to the brick walk that Breed had taken to the cliffs. He saw her ahead, facing the sea. The skirts of her gown were billowing behind her in the sea breeze, her head covered by a shawl. The sound of his arrival was muted by the crashing of the waves on the sandy cove below.

He stood a few feet behind her, trying to decide how to greet this young woman who had come so far and would soon be his wife. He ran his fingers through his hair and resolved to continue. He took the two short strides that brought him to her. Breed, hearing his footsteps, at last turned just as he put his arms out to embrace her.

The shawl slipped from her head, revealing hair the color of golden wheat, with streaks of near-white. Not the dark, brown ringlets of Elizabeth Staunton, but the straight, pale, golden locks that Breed's deep sea tan and blue eyes accentuated! Loughlan looked at her for a second, puzzled, but had already drawn her to him.

"Welcome to California, Miss Elizabeth," he said. Breed tried to tell him of the mistake, but he kissed her.

"I'm not Eliza Staunton."

John Loughlan pulled away. "You are not Elizabeth Staunton."

❧ CHAPTER THIRTEEN ❧

The sun had set and it was growing dark rapidly. The two stood looking at one another a moment longer, then Breed turned and began to return to the house now ablaze with light and activity.

John Loughlan walked beside her as she, in halting words, explained who she was and why Elizabeth Staunton had not come. He remained silent, so Breed went on. She explained about Lita and finally asked if the two of them might stay with him until a ship going back to Boston could be found. His silence continued and Breed began to babble from sheer fright. "We are both very good workers. I am a cook and Lita a seamstress of great ability...."

Loughlan's thoughts were in turmoil. He had set his mind on the woman in the small tintype the lawyer Hawksbury had sent him, a small, delicate Elizabeth Staunton. Instead, here was this tall woman he had only to bend his head a bit to kiss. He brushed the remembrance of their kiss away... this vibrant, irritating, young woman!

He felt cheated and his ego had been dealt a severe blow—that his intended bride should have jilted him in mid-ocean, and for an Englishman!

They reached the steps of the front porch and John Loughlan still had not spoken or even intimated that he had heard and understood all that Breed had told him. Breed, on the verge of nervous tears, continued to chatter inanely about their voyage and Captain Shepard. At the mention of Hugh's name, John Loughlan stopped short and growled, "By God, I'll strangle the bowlegged bastard!" He muttered something over his shoulder to Breed about "tomorrow" and headed for the back of the house and the stables. She stood waiting on the porch a few moments, gathering courage to enter and confront the Morales family. In a very short time she saw the angry man, mounted on the largest horse she had ever seen. He rode out of the drive in a fury. She lingered a moment longer, blaming herself for the poor beginning. Then, with a prayer, she entered the house.

Not wanting to intrude on the family gathering, she walked toward the stairs. She was captured, however, by the ebullient Sra. Morales, who drew her into the parlor where the whole family was gathered. Sra. Morales introduced her husband—"Mi esposo, my husband Roberto"—and their three sons, Diego, Antonio and Marco. Breed saw Lita sitting on the overstuffed sofa with Serafina and went to join them. As she crossed the room, she felt the eyes of Diego Morales on her. Her arrival had evidently interrupted a family entertainment. Mira, the older daughter, stood before the great marble and oak fireplace. When all were settled again in their places, she began to sing a lilting Spanish song. Breed gathered that the song was about a young girl who wanted to put her long hair up and have a suitor but was being told she was too young.

Mira's voice was clear, though not strong or particularly in tune, but she sang with such enjoyment that everyone smiled. They all clapped and praised her at the song's end and then it was Serafina and Marco's turn. The hearth rug was rolled and moved aside so that there was a clear space. Antonio began to strum his guitar slowly. Then, as the two dancers began to sway, he played faster and they danced a jota from the mountains of Spain. They danced well together, with natural grace and vigor, and the family gave shouts of encouragement.

Despite her worries, Breed was drawn into the gaiety of the group and thought the two young people the most beautiful sight she had seen. When the cheers and clapping ceased, the two dancers bowed with theatrical flourish and took their places, well pleased with their reception. "Now," said Sr. Morales, "one of our young ladies entertain." He looked at Breed. "Senorita," he said, "I understand you play the guitar. Will you play for us?"

Breed, flustered, shook her head. "I only wish I could play half as well as Senor Tonio," she said, "but I've only just learned and would be embarrassed." She halted, only to see Mira enter the parlor, carrying her guitar. As the young girl laid it in Breed's lap, Diego took his brother's instrument and came to stand before Breed.

"Senorita, let us play together. You lead and I will gladly follow." His brothers and father laughed.

Mira giggled and said, "The Golden One has made a conquest!"

"You forgot yourself, daughter," Sra. Morales snapped, noticing Breed's discomfort.

Feeling foolish but realizing it would be ill-mannered to refuse, Breed tuned her guitar, smiled and began strumming a piece she had learned from her sailor teacher. As she played, Diego effortlessly accompanied her, his stronger style only enhancing the tune. All the while, he stared at her, until Breed finished, confused. "Behave yourself, Don Diego," said Sra. Morales. "You must forgive my eldest son, senorita. He is only recently returned from Mexico City and the ladies there made much of him and turned his head." All laughed, even Diego, with a rueful look at Breed.

Sr. Morales, who had not uttered so much as one word the whole evening, spoke up and in Spanish asked, "Will not our other honored guest entertain us now?" Evidently his wife had not had time to tell him of Lita's inability to speak. Breed at once started to make apologies for her. But to Breed's astonishment, Lita went to the piano and seated herself. After a moment's thought, she began to play Chopin's "Raindrop Etude." She played as though lost in the heart of the music, with such mastery that her audience was awed. When Lita finished, all begged for an encore. With a smile toward Sr. and Sra. Morales, she played an old Spanish love song that they evidently knew, for the senora's eyes grew misty, and the man put his arm around his wife lovingly. When it was over, everyone exclaimed at the magic of Lita's playing and all began to talk at once. Sra. Morales bustled out and in a moment was back announcing coffee and dessert in the dining room.

Breed took Lita's arm as they walked. "You sly boots! Why did you not tell me you could play the piano? And so beautifully!" Lita squeezed Breed's fingers and gave a small shrug, thinking to herself there was much to tell and one day she would.

The visitors excused themselves soon after dessert, Breed explaining they were tired. Sra. Morales followed them into the hall and as they started to ascend to their bedroom she said, "Do not worry about Juan. He is impetuous, he will return. A lovers' quarrel, he has been alone too long."

Breed tried to explain, but Sra. Morales raised her hand and continued, "Your Juan is a shy man who hides it with bluster and temper. Be patient, he is a good man, loving and faithful. He will give you many strong sons." She looked over her shoulder, as though to be sure they would not be overheard, and said vehemently, "That other one, she gave him three daughters and heartache!" Then, looking guilty for having said so much, she kissed both girls and bid them to sleep well.

Breed lay awake long after the house had grown quiet. Her mind was in a whirl, so much had happened and so much was still unresolved. Finally, she said her prayers and fell into a deep, dreamless sleep.

John Loughlan rode as one chased by a thousand furies. When he reached town he went straight to Madam Louise's establishment. A young stable boy, standing by the front walk, was nearly bowled over when Loughlan reined the galloping horse to an abrupt stop. All in one motion, he threw himself from the heaving animal and curtly told the boy to cool down the horse and feed him. The angry man nearly kicked in the front door when it didn't open to his knock quickly enough. He gave his hat to the maid who answered his ring and demanded to know the whereabouts of Captain Shepard. The maid calmly led him to a small receiving room off the main entrance hall and ran to fetch Madam Louise.

John Loughlan paced to and fro in the small room like a caged animal and nearly pounced on Madam when she entered.

Madam Louise was forty-seven. Though her age was beginning to show, she still was an attractive woman. She knew John Loughlan as a friend of Hugh Shepard but had not met him as a patron. She looked at him speculatively, wondering if he would be interested in the new Chinese girl, but after moments of silence offered Loughlan a drink instead. "Where is Captain Shepard?" he asked, gruffly.

"Captain Shepard will be with us shortly," she answered. Loughlan threw himself onto the chair beside a desk and fiddled impatiently with the glass of brandy.

Madam Louise had plied her trade for nearly thirty years in and around the harbor. She had a canny ability with money and had made many shrewd investments over the years so that she could have, by rights, retired to a more genteel life. She frequently contributed to the orphanage in Los Angeles, and those of a sentimental bent said it must be in memory of some sad event in her past. The more cynical view, as expressed by the Mother Superior of the orphanage, was that Madam Louise's heart was a lump of coal and the donations were just and equitable for frequently the foundling babies in the town were born to young women in Madam's employ.

Since healthy, fairly attractive young women were still in short supply in the West, an unexpected pregnancy was not allowed to curtail one's earning power. And upon the rare occasion when one of Madam's alumni married, the blushing bride would make a visit to the orphanage and, with her new captive groom in tow, choose a supposedly random foundling to start her family.

Just when John Loughlan felt he must go find Hugh Shepard himself, the good captain knocked and entered, looking rested and refreshed after an afternoon spent with one of Madam's most knowledgeable young ladies. He advanced with his hand outstretched but Loughlan jumped up, brushed aside his cousin's greeting and looked as though he might take a swing at him instead. Madam Louise realized there might be trouble and hurried from the room in search of the house bouncer, stationing the man in the hall.

Shepard, still in a jovial mood, chose to ignore Loughlan's glowering expression. He put his arm around Loughlan's shoulders. "By George, John, you are looking fit," he said. "How are the girls? Tell them I have brought them each a new storybook." When Loughlan remained silent, he continued smoothly, "And what, pray tell, do you think of your new bride?" He knew full well what was bothering his cousin but decided to try bluffing his way out of the puzzlement.

Loughlan shook his cousin from his shoulder and roared, "Hugh, what in God's name have you done now?"

Shepard shushed him. "Mustn't disturb the ladies, old man," he said.

Loughlan began again, this time with lowered voice but no less irate. "What happened to Elizabeth Staunton? And what am I supposed to do with this... that servant girl?" Here, he remembered in a flash his welcoming kiss to Breed and her token struggle that gave way to warm acceptance. He cursed his thoughts and continued, "Am I to take these two women of questionable background into my home?" Wounded pride goaded him on.

Shepard was shocked at his words. The many weeks of close association with Breed aboard the Sara Blue had made him forget her previous station in life. In truth, she no longer looked the same young woman. Her hair, once dull and lank but now bleached by the tropical sun, was the color of ripe wheat. Her skin, spotty and drab, had given way to a glorious, creamy tan, glowing with health and causing her eyes to seem bluer than before.

"By Jove," the captain thought, "I've been looking at her all these weeks and just now really see her." He thoughtfully lit a cheroot, then turned to the angry Loughlan. "What could I do, John? Miss Eliza and her young man jumped ship, and my chasing them all over the Atlantic to fetch her back would have only caused scandal. And you're right, Breed's not the woman for you. She needs some taming, does that one." Loughlan had slumped into a chair. The last few days spent fighting the forest fire were beginning to tell. He was very tired. "Come now, John, let Madam send one of her girls to you and we will talk again in the morning." He gave the exhausted man a tug up and they walked out into the hall where Madam Louise, attended by the little maid and the hulking bouncer, hovered by the door.

Loughlan refused the offer of company but did accept a bed. As he trudged up the stairs, he turned and said to Shepard, "Why are women always so much trouble?"

Late the next morning, the two men ate breakfast together. Shepard proposed that Loughlan allow the two women to stay at his ranch until he returned from the Sara Blue's passage up the coast. Then he would take the two aboard for the return voyage to Boston. Grudgingly, Loughlan agreed and sent word to the Morales household that he would be there soon to take the young ladies to his ranch.

The message arrived just as the Morales' and their guests were sitting down to lunch. The girls had spent a quiet morning in their room, working on the shirts for Captain Shepard and doing Lita's English lesson.

Diego Morales had sent one of the maids up with his invitation to show Breed his mother's gardens and to take a walk along the cliffs. She declined, feeling things were complicated enough without the involvement of the very attractive eldest Morales son.

Loughlan arrived around two in the afternoon. He was subdued and asked to speak to Breed privately. When they were alone, they stood facing one another but neither looked directly at the other. "Miss...Miss. I'm sorry, I didn't catch your name yesterday," he said.

Breed flushed and answered, "Bridget Mary Seastrum. I'm called Breed for short," and she turned to the window.

Loughlan found it much easier to talk to her back. He began again, "Miss Seastrum," but she interrupted him.

"Breed."

"Yes, Breed. Captain Shepard explained everything to me, more or less, and I have agreed to take you and your friend out to my ranch till he returns from the voyage north with our shipment of wool." Breed nodded but said nothing, so he continued, "The whole time shouldn't be more than six weeks. Perhaps you could teach my daughters a little, while you are with us. Naturally, I would pay...."

Breed turned and said, in her best imitation of Lavinia Potts, "Mr. Loughlan, if you are kind enough to give me shelter till our return to Boston, the least we can do is help you and your family any way possible." She looked at him and noted that his collar was frayed and a button was missing from his coat. For a man who she knew was financially comfortable, he looked unkempt indeed. She almost added, "We will get you straightened out too me Bucko!" but the flush that mounted Loughlan's cheeks warned her that he was embarrassed by their conversation. So she smiled instead and lowered her eyes meekly.

Shortly, servants placed Breed's and Lita's few belongings into the wagon and the Morales family gathered on the front porch to bid them farewell. Sra. Morales embraced each and presented them with muslin scarves to keep the dust from their hair. She patted John Loughlan's arm maternally and told him to bring them and his daughters back for a visit when the hot weather abated.

As Breed settled herself on the high seat of the buckboard, Diego Morales stood close to the wagon. He took her hand and kissed it, saying, "Till we meet again, Senorita!" Poor Breed was so flustered she could only close her eyes and hope no one had seen.

Lita evidently realized the discomfort that any long trip in a wagon could create and had chosen to sit in the flat bed on a pile of hay. Sra. Morales had hastily sent for an old patchwork quilt to make it more comfortable.

At last, with a hitch of the reins from the wagon driver, the horses moved off. Loughlan rode alongside and for the most part was silent. As they traveled inland, the cool breeze dissipated and the air became increasingly hot and dry. The vegetation also was changing. There were fewer trees and everything looked parched.

After about an hour's drive, they stopped at a general store to water the horses and give the girls a chance to stretch their cramped legs. The proprietress, a Mrs. Munson, knew Loughlan and brought cool lemonade for all. Loughlan spoke with her about the forest fires. Then, standing before a glass case containing penny candies, he chose several bags of different kinds. When he caught the girls watching him, he collected the bags and stalked out to the wagon. "John is a good papa," Mrs. Munson volunteered. "He always takes his little girls a treat when he stops by. And them Horehound drops for his cook, Blanca, she do fancy them, don't you know?"

Once more on the road, Breed joined Lita in the wagon bed. The sparsely populated lands on either side of the road began to show signs that they were nearing a large town. There were more buildings, ugly wooden ones with tin roofs for the most part, and people could be seen working in the fields or passing them. The heat was stifling and so dry it hurt to take a deep breath. Both girls felt wilted and lifeless. "We are on the outskirts of Los Angeles now and should be in the town proper in half an hour," Loughlan said. "We can stop now, if you are too tired, and continue in the morning, or we can have dinner in town, then continue to the ranch. It will be at least twelve o'clock when we reach home, but traveling at night would be a good deal cooler."

The word "cool" caught Breed's attention. "And can you and the horses find your way home in the dark?" she asked. Loughlan assured them that traveling at night was safe, if somewhat slow, so it was decided they would have an early supper in Los Angeles before continuing to the ranch.

El Pueblo de Nuestra Senora La Reina de Los Angeles, the City of our Lady Queen of the Angels, was approaching the one-hundred year anniversary of its founding. It was much larger than Breed had anticipated but still a frontier town compared to Boston. When they reached the Pico Hotel, John instructed the wagon driver to see to the horses and himself and return for them in two hours.

The Pico was quite elegant and Loughlan appeared to be a frequent patron by the welcome the party received. He engaged a room for the ladies, so they might freshen up, and told Breed he would meet them in half an hour in the dining room. They hurriedly tidied themselves and Breed insisted Lita stretch out on the bed for a few moments' rest. Half an hour later, they joined Loughlan, who stood waiting at the entrance to the dining room. Breed thanked him for the extravagance of the hotel room for such a short time, but he brushed her thanks aside. "We keep rooms here always for just such occasions," he said. "Either Hugh or I are in town frequently. My mother used to spend several days doing her shopping, and it was convenient."

The meal was a silent one, each person wrapped in his or her own thoughts. As dinner progressed, several people stopped to speak to Loughlan and to glance curiously at Breed and Lita. The forest fire seemed the main topic of conversation, the various men comparing experiences with Loughlan. When an elderly couple stopped to chat, Loughlan made no move to introduce the young women. "Well, now, John, aren't you going to introduce us to your friends?" the old woman asked. Loughlan looked confused, then began haltingly.

"Sorry, Ma'am, this is Miss Bridget Seastrum and her friend Miss Lita...." He stopped and looked inquiringly at Breed, who in turn glanced at Lita and quickly offered, "Costa-Nunez, Senorita Costa-Nunez!" Loughlan was relieved and nodded.

Lita inclined her head at the introduction and smiled ironically.

Mrs. Childers, for that was her name, welcomed Breed and her friend to Los Angeles. Then, as she and her husband were leaving, she gave one final shot. "We shall be waiting for an invitation to your wedding soon, John!" This parting sally seemed to banish Loughlan's appetite. He told the girls to finish their dinner while he went to see about the wagon. Then he left the table.

When he had gone, Breed put her hand over Lita's and asked quietly, "Was it all right? Your last name, I mean? Does it remind you too much of the past?"

Lita looked at Breed fondly and shook her head. Taking her ever-present pad of paper and pencil, she wrote laboriously in English, "It is well." Breed sighed in relief and returned to her dinner with relish.

Half an hour later, the early summer twilight found them once more on a dusty road heading north out of Los Angeles. As it grew dark, their pace slowed and the young women in the wagon bed dozed.

🍂 CHAPTER FOURTEEN

The moon rose and Breed was awakened by the baying of a coyote. The lonely sound frightened her and she asked John Loughlan if it were a wolf. "No wolves hereabouts," he said. "It's just a coyote, and they're only as big as a medium-sized dog."

Since he seemed inclined to talk, Breed asked him a few questions. "Mr. Loughlan, what are your daughters' names, and how old are they?"

Loughlan took so long to answer, she thought he was going to ignore her, but finally he answered, "Annabelle, Marguerite and Nicole. Belle is almost eight, Daisy is five-and-a-half and Nicky, the baby, is almost three."

When he did not continue, Breed tried hard to find another subject that would keep him talking. "And were you born in California, Mr. Loughlan, sir?" she asked, knowing full well of his

Boston past. Again, Loughlan hesitated before answering. Finally, in a rush, he went on.

"No, my mother, sister and I came west in 1855. I was fifteen. My father had gone to the gold fields in '49 and chanced to save a man's life there. They were both mining the same stretch of river, and Ramirez stumbled into deep water and was washed down toward the rapids. My father, as strong a swimmer as Ramirez was not, was able to reach him and drag him ashore."

He stopped and Breed, afraid he would not continue, asked breathlessly, "And then what?"

So Loughlan picked up the tale, "Carlos Ramirez was from California. When it became evident that the river was played out, father and Ramirez had each made small strikes and came away with a respectable fortune. Ramirez invited my father to return with him to his rancho at Los Angeles. Carlos had left his wife and mother to care for things while he went prospecting, but when they reached the ranch they found the mother had died and the young wife had returned to Mexico and her family." Loughlan fell silent, then lighted a cheroot and continued, "Carlos was sick at the events and made plans to return at once to Mexico, so my father bought him out with his pickings from the gold fields and sent for us." Loughlan took a deep breath and spurred his horse so that it bounded ahead of the wagon, where it stayed the remainder of the journey.

Breed was satisfied and did not mind his abrupt departure. It's probably the longest speech he's made in his life, she thought to herself. Sure he's not one for words!

Slowly, the winding road had been rising and finally, in the distance, Breed saw lights. The moonlight was so bright, she could clearly see the house they were approaching. She nudged Lita to wake her and then gave her whole attention to the rancho.

The hacienda, such as it was, sat on the crest of the hill they were climbing. The two great sycamore trees that gave the rancho its name stood in the walled patio at the front entrance. These, and many other trees, gave the hilltop a sheltered look. The hacienda itself was a long building with an open gallery running the length of it. It was protected from the sun by cloistered-like arches similar to those Breed had seen in Havana. On the Spanish tile roof, Breed saw several chimneys. The adobe walls reflected the moonlight and the air was filled with the scent of night-blooming honeysuckle that climbed over the walls on one end of the gallery.

John Loughlan rode ahead of the wagon and called a greeting to those standing in the light of the front door.

By the time the wagon drew up to the entrance, he had dismounted and given his horse into the care of a ranch hand standing by the steps.

The two young women tried to brush off the dust of the journey and tidy themselves, but before they got far with their toilette Loughlan was at the wagon's side offering his hand for them to climb down.

He gave instructions to the driver to unload the luggage, and then with a curt nod toward the open doorway he signaled to the weary travelers to enter his home.

Breed and Lita walked up the flagstone path to the front

steps. They were a little stiff from the long ride, glad it was over but apprehensive about meeting the household of Rancho Dos Aliso.

The front door opened wide and standing just inside were three Mexican women smiling broadly. Peeking from behind the middle-aged senora's skirts was a girl of eight. Mentally, Breed recognized Belle from her father's description.

John Loughlan introduced the three women: Blanca, the cook/housekeeper; Susu, her non-too-bright niece; and Rosa, the children's nursemaid. Seeing Annabelle, he drew her to his side and with an arm around her shoulders introduced her to the travelers. Belle smiled shyly and announced that only she had been able to keep awake to meet them.

The kind Blanca, seeing how tired the travelers were, spoke in heavily accented English. "Come, senoritas, your rooms are ready. Rosa, go bring hot water so they may wash." Gratefully, they followed her while Belle took her father off to tuck her in.

Lita's room was small but freshly painted. The one window faced east and had a deeply recessed sill where several red clay pots of herbs and flowers sat. The floor was polished oak planks, with two small rugs, and on the bed was a beautiful patchwork quilt. Seeing that the hand had brought her small portmanteau and other belongings, Breed and Blanca left her and went farther down the hall. Blanca explained that the children's nursery was between Breed and Lita's rooms, and that the room at the west end of the hall was Sr. Loughlan's.

During dinner, Breed noticed that Lita had only toyed with her food and that she seemed withdrawn. So as Blanca was saying good night, she asked if it would be too much trouble to get a cup of warm milk for her friend. Breed explained that Lita had not been well.

Blanca was at once solicitous and hurried out to the kitchen for the drink.

Before Breed had finished undressing and washing, the cook was back with two large mugs of frothy hot chocolate on a tray. Breed thanked her for her kindness and wished her good night. Wrapping herself in her shawl, for the evening had become quite cool, she searched her portmanteau for the small bottle of drugs that would ease Lita's pain and assure her a good night's sleep. She added the drops carefully to the drink, stirring it thoroughly, and took it down the hall to Lita's room.

Lita was already in bed, her complexion an ashy hue that alarmed Breed. "Are you ill, Lita? Is it more than the pain?" she asked. Lita shook her head and reached for her pad and pencil. She laboriously wrote in English, "Head Hurt." Breed, relieved that it was nothing more, gave her the hot cocoa. She sat on the foot of the bed while Lita drank, explaining where her room was and describing it to her friend. The drug soon took effect and Lita dozed off. Breed turned down the oil lamp, added the comforter on the rocker to the covers on Lita's bed and gently closed the door as she left the room. In her own bed, she said her prayers and was asleep in moments.

The morning came cool, clear and bright. Breed lay half-awake, luxuriating in the quiet, snug in her warm bed. She realized that the click of the bedroom door, carefully opened, had wakened her. Opening her eyes, she saw three little girls. They were as much alike as peas in a pod, save for their size, and were standing just inside the door. Belle had the smallest by the hand and Daisy, the five-year old, stood close to her sisters, sucking her thumb. Moments passed before Belle finally spoke, "Good morning, Miss. We came to see you."

Breed pulled herself up in the big, double bed and patted the covers. "Come sit here, introduce your sisters, and we can visit."

"That would be nice," said Belle, "but Nicky is soaking wet and will wet your bed too!"

Before Breed could say anything, Daisy took her thumb from her mouth and said disapprovingly, "She smells too." The five-year-old went on, "Rosa says she's much too big to still be wetting herself, she's almost three, you know." Here, the miss of almost six sighed in disappointment at her baby sister's shortcomings. The unchastened Nicole smiled cheerfully, delighted to be the center of attention.

"Go, Belle, and get Nicky a fresh nappy and nightgown," Breed said. "You other two climb up here. You will take cold standing there barefoot." Belle was back in a moment with the dry garments, and Breed stripped Nicky of her wet nightclothes and redressed her. Then, rummaging in her portmanteau, she found some of the gifts that Eliza had purchased in Boston for the girls... a book for Belle, a jump rope with its own carrying case for Daisy and a small baby doll dressed in pink for Nicky.

While the girls admired their gifts, Breed went to the bathroom. What luxury to have indoor plumbing in one's own home! Opening the other bathroom door, she found a great tub almost as grand as the one at the convent in Havana. There was a large metal container at the foot of the tub and it was hot to the touch! A hot bath! She could hardly wait. Returning to her room, she again went into her portmanteau and produced the three small aprons that Eliza, Lita and Breed had made for the girls. She helped them put their aprons over their gowns and asked them to show her their nursery.

Belle was torn between her desire to look at the new book and her need to follow this tall blonde woman and be close to her. Belle could only just remember her own mother. Elaina Loughlan had not been a particularly motherly young woman. She considered her duty finished with the children's birth and had quickly relinquished them to the care of servants. Breed, sensing that the little girls wanted to stay with her, took Nicky in her arms and, shooing the other two girls before her, went into the large nursery.

Two wide windows faced north, offering a beautiful view of the foothills and mountains in the distance. There was a fireplace with a high, brass fender flanked by deep cupboards on one wall. Two small beds and a high baby's crib were arranged along the other wall. There were shelves and cupboards under the windows, and thick chintz-covered cushions laid along top to turn them into window seats. In the middle of the room was a round child's table, four little oak chairs and an adult-sized rocking chair. Breed made a note to see if the ranch had its own carpenter. The room had once been cheerful and gay, but the day-to-day wear and tear and the lack of any refurbishing had given it a distinctly dreary appearance.

Breed helped the children dress and was shocked by the condition of their wardrobe. Their clothes were in such a state of disrepair that even Aunt Kate's many offspring would be better dressed. Rosa, the nursemaid, evidently was not much of a seamstress. The clothes were clean but frayed or torn, and Belle had completely outgrown most of her things!

Breed realized how long this house had been at sixes and sevens since its mistress had died. She vowed to take things in hand for the time she and Lita were there.

When all were dressed and sporting the new aprons, Breed let the children lead her out to the kitchen. Blanca, the cook, was kneading bread at one end of the long kitchen table. A middle-aged man, dark and heavyset but with a pleasant expression, sat eating his breakfast. He stood up when she entered, and giving a slight bow introduced himself in heavily accented English. "Welcome, senorita, I am Huron Del Gado, Senor Loughlan's foreman." Breed smiled and said good morning to them and put the youngest child into the highchair drawn up to the table. She then asked Blanca if she had a fairly large bowl with a lip that she might use. When the cook produced one, Breed sent Daisy back to the nursery with instructions to bring out one of the little armchairs.

Susu, at the cook's instructions, set out a plate of hot tortillas and dished up bowls of refried beans for the girls and Breed. Breed took a china mug from one of the cupboards and poured herself a cup of what had to be the strongest coffee she had ever tasted. Only a large quantity of sugar and milk made it palatable.

Breed's mental list of things to be seen to was growing fast. Surely, she thought, good New England oatmeal porridge, or even eggs, would be better fare for the children.

Daisy returned, lugging the little chair, and Breed took it to Huron Del Gado, who had finished his meal but was lingering over coffee. She turned over the bowl that Blanca had given her, placed it onto the seat of the chair and used a kitchen knife to mark its size.

"Sure, now, Sr. Del Gado, could you please cut a hole just this size in the chair and fix it so the bowl slides in and out?"

The foreman looked puzzled for a moment, then laughed when he realized what she desired. "Si, si, senorita," he said. "I will do it at once!" Patting Nicky on the head, he gathered up the chair and bowl and left the kitchen.

Breed doubted that Lita would be up for the heavy, and from its appearance, highly seasoned meal the cook had provided. So she asked Blanca if she might make something light for the invalid. Blanca was only too happy to have Breed take care of Lita's breakfast. Susu showed Breed the larder and in a few minutes she had scrambled half a dozen eggs, made a less vigorous pot of coffee and toasted some of Blanca's bread. As she was arranging a tray for Lita, John Loughlan entered the kitchen and the little girls began chattering all at once. Breed poured him a cup of her fresh coffee and took Lita her tray.

It took only a few moments to make Lita comfortable. Breed insisted she remain in bed for a while longer, promising to return for the tray shortly. In the kitchen she found Belle and Daisy settled, their father between them and the girls vying for his full attention.

Breed divided the eggs, giving each of the older girls a small bowl and making plates for their father and herself. Loughlan and Breed faced one another across the table, ill at ease and unsure of how each should act. Sitting next to Nicky's highchair, Breed fed the three-year-old from her plate. The cook at the other end of the long table beamed at them and said something in Spanish. Loughlan flushed, Breed catching the words "happy family."

The Master of the House ate with evident enjoyment. When he

had finished his second cup of coffee, he thanked Breed. "I know you must have cooked it, because Blanca's menus are pretty predictable. In fact, she claims she only knows how to cook three meals: one breakfast, one lunch and one dinner!" The cook laughed and said, "Sra. Loughlan, your mother, she teach me to be housekeeper, not to cook!"

Breed gave Nicky the last of her toast and said, "And you really are a fine housekeeper. I noticed how spotless everything looked, even though there are three small children in the house!" John Loughlan nodded in agreement as Blanca glowed with pleasure.

Taking the bull by the horns, Breed said, "You know, Blanca, I'm a cook. Why don't you return to being housekeeper, which you do well, and I'll cook." Loughlan looked alarmed at the suggestion but relaxed when he observed how delighted Blanca was to get out of the kitchen.

Breed decided to strike while the iron was hot. Carefully avoiding Loughlan's eyes, she busied herself wiping the children's faces and plunged ahead. "And Mr. Loughlan, while we are at it, could not the girls have some new things? Lita is a gifted seamstress and if we could obtain some nice gingham and muslin she would be glad to sew for them."

The girls began to clamor for new dresses. Nicky, who usually only spoke in Spanish, smiled shyly and whispered to her father, "Papa, me too."

Looking all the world like a stallion surrounded by bothersome magflies, Loughlan stood up. He hurried to the back door, telling Breed to do whatever she saw fit. He slammed the door so hard, the dishes in the cupboards rattled. In seconds, the door opened again and the beleaguered man stuck his head in to say, "Tell me when you want to go to town and how much money you'll need." Again, he was gone, this time closing the door a little more gently.

Breed and Blanca grinned at one another. Breed set about clearing the table and spoke to the girls, "Come you now and get dressed. We have much to do!" Rosa took her charges off to the nursery and Breed went to Lita's room.

"Are you feeling any better now, dearie?" she asked her friend. Lita put her hand over Breed's and nodded gravely. Relieved, Breed launched a detailed account of the morning's happenings. "These poor children are practically wearing rags! Himself says we can go and shop and I'm to take over the kitchen." Breed stood up and walked to the window. "He's very gruff, is Mr. Loughlan, and not half as handsome as Captain Shepard or Don Diego." She continued almost to herself, "I'm sure he has a fearful temper...." She stopped and gazed out the window at the hillside and the mountains beyond.

Lita watched her intently, waiting for Breed to continue, but the moment was shattered as the little girls came running in. Breed told the girls about Lita's inability to speak but explained it was her only difficulty. "She's a fine seamstress and a talented piano player and my very good friend." The girls stood gazing at this paragon in awe and delight. Life on the ranch was not notably exciting. Rosa, their nurse, tended to keep them indoors where they were easier to watch. Any change in their routine was welcomed.

Telling Lita she would be in the nursery, Breed and the children left her to wash and dress. As they went through the children's wardrobe, Breed made a list of their needs. "Sure, you all need new knickers, and Belle, there's not a dress here that still fits you!" Quiet Daisy took her thumb out of her mouth long enough to request "pink knickers, please." Everyone laughed, and Breed promised if some suitable pink material could be found she would have them.

Lita and Blanca joined the busy group at the same time. Blanca, jumping at the promise of relief as cook, asked the senorita what she had planned for lunch and dinner. She prayed she had not changed her mind.

Breed left Lita busy with the children and went with Blanca to inspect the larder and see what provisions were available. Lavinia Potts in Boston would have been amused and edified at Breed's imitation of Lady of the House. She went through the storeroom items, asking all sorts of questions about what was available and what they should purchase on their shopping trip into town.

The ranch farm supplied eggs and chickens upon request, and milk was brought in every morning. There had been a kitchen garden in John Loughlan's mother's time but it had gone to seed from lack of care. Breed made a mental note to take the children for a walk later and look over the grounds. She arranged for three hens to be killed and plucked for dinner and had the older woman show her the intricacies of the coal stove. Before leaving the kitchen, she put on eggs to boil and admired the former cook's loaves of bread that were rising on the long trestle table.

Back in the nursery, Lita had already begun to refurbish the children's clothes. With her needle flashing, she was lengthening one of Belle's dresses.

"I want to go for a walk, will you come?" Breed asked. Lita raised her hands in mock horror. She could not understand this desire of Breed's to be constantly on the move. Even on shipboard, when her duties as cook allowed it, Breed had spent hours walking around the decks. Seeing Lita was content with the sewing, Breed took the little girls off to explore.

❧ CHAPTER FIFTEEN ❧

Breed was amazed at the stark beauty of the land. The hot summer sun was beginning to heat up the cool morning and all around on the hillside the grasses and wild oats were burnt a golden yellow.

The valley below was heavily forested in cottonwoods and sycamores. Everything looked dusty and scorched. Around the back of the sprawling rancho, Breed found signs of a once-flourishing kitchen garden. A few cabbages and hardy herbs still grew among the weeds and grapes flourished along the fence post. Breed and the children tasted the grapes and agreed they were small but good. Belle ran back to the house for a large basket and Breed filled it with the fruit they picked. There was a small irrigation ditch in none too good repair running from the wall of what must be the bathroom down the hill to a small orchard. There were several trees, healthy and either bearing ripening fruit like the plum tree or still ripening like the green apple and orange trees. Breed was delighted. The plums looked ready to pick. In fact, the ground beneath the tree was littered with fallen fruit. Daisy was sent back to demand another basket, and they spent some time gathering the windfalls from the ground and other reachable ripe fruit from the tree.

The little girls were in their element as guides and grew excited when Breed promised they could help her replant the garden in the spring. It was becoming very warm, so Breed decided to postpone the rest of the tour. She took the children and their booty back to the kitchen and announced they were going to make plum jam.

Breed set the girls to washing the fruit, while Susu showed her the cellar storeroom where old Mrs. Loughlan had kept the produce she had put up. Sure enough, the empty crocks and mason jars were neatly stored on a shelf alongside two great blue enamel pans used for making preserves. Breed and Susu filled pans with jars or crocks and returned to the kitchen. Blanca and Lita had joined the girls and were busy sorting and preparing the fruit. Blanca suggested they do the actual cooking outside in the summer kitchen, which would keep the big kitchen cool.

In warmer climates, many homes were supplied with an outdoor kitchen. Breed was interested to see the large adobe oven. It was shaped like a beehive and stood nearly four feet high with a door that opened to shelves and the fire pan. Blanca's morning bread was in the oven at that moment and she checked it to see if it was done. On the other side of the "kitchen" was a small windowless adobe house the size of a large chicken coop. When the housekeeper opened the door, Breed was surprised by the chilly, damp air that met them. Blanca pointed to the thick walls and explained that this was the rancho's cold room. Breed noticed a tub of butter and several tin jugs of milk sitting on shelves. A large smoked ham hung from the rafters.

Tito, a ranch hand, rode in around noon and told the women that Sr. Loughlan would not be in for lunch. Blanca filled a goat-hide water bag with fresh water, wrapped one of the just-baked loaves and a chunk of cheese in a napkin and gave it to the man to take out to Loughlan.

The women worked through the hot afternoon, stopping only to put the two younger children down for a nap and to occasionally nibble at one of the ripe juicy plums. Everyone was so engrossed with jam-making they were almost able to ignore the heat. Breed saved some of the nicest plums and made two large tarts for dessert.

As the afternoon wore on, a cool breeze sprang up, so they opened the long shutters at the parlor windows. Blanca bemoaned the loss of her usual afternoon siesta and even the little girls were beginning to run down. Shortly after five, Breed sent the young maid, Rosa, into the house with the little girls. She gave her instructions to bathe and help them dress for dinner, as even the fastidious Belle was sticky and stained from the jam-making.

Satisfied that the light supper she had planned was nearly ready, Breed went to her room to freshen up, as did Lita. Breed wanted her first meal as cook at Rancho Dos Aliso to be one of her best, so that John Loughlan would not feel cheated in their bargain. She stood before the mirror and brushed her hair, rewinding and pinning it into a secure bun at the back of her head. As she stood a moment in front of the mirror, her thoughts wandered to Loughlan, how his dark hair curled on his neck just the way little Daisy's did. Catching herself, she blushed and tied a fresh apron around her waist before returning to the kitchen.

Later, Loughlan entered the kitchen, his hair still damp from a dousing under the backyard pump. He stood on the threshold and sniffed appreciatively. The fragrance of hot jam, fresh baked bread and chickens simmering in a pot was almost too much for a hungry man to bear. "When do we eat?" he half-shouted.

His wife, Elaine, had not been much of a hand in the kitchen, but he remembered that during his mother's lifetime the kitchen had this particularly enticing smell.

The little girls greeted him joyously and showed him precious plum tarts made with their own hands. He complimented them and promised to taste each one. Breed shooed them out of the kitchen to the now shady veranda where Lita brought a large pitcher of cool lemonade. It had been made from lemons, according to Blanca, from a tree down by the corral.

When supper was almost ready, Huron Del Gado came in carrying the little chair with the pot attached. There was much interest shown by the older girls and they wondered aloud if Nicky would, indeed, use the marvelous contraption. Breed laughed and assured them she would when she was ready, and sent the three of them to put the little chair in the nursery.

Blanca insisted that Lita and Breed sit with "El Senor" and the children in the dining room. She and Susu would serve them their dinner. Huron Del Gado declined to join them and ate in the kitchen because, Loughlan said, "he's making wolf's eyes at Rosa!"

Dinner was a success. The chickens, in their thick creamy gravy with rice and a dish of plum sauce, were delicious. The still warm plum tart with a mound of whipped cream put the final touch to Breed's reputation as "good cook." John ate so much he was nearly comatose.

"Senorita, I congratulate you," he said, pushing back his chair. "That was the best meal I've eaten in this house since my mother died!"

Breed looked pleased. "If it would be all right with you, Mr. Loughlan, we will go to town tomorrow as the larder is truly bare. Sure, I used the last of the flour to make the tarts and gravy!"

Loughlan, in the expansive mood of a well-fed man, agreed, telling them to leave early before it got too hot. He would have a wagon and driver ready at four in the morning The older girls begged to go, and Breed agreed if they went to bed at once. Torn between missing the evening's unknown excitement and their desire to go into town, they finally followed Rosa, who carried the half-asleep Nicky.

Breed and Lita cleared the dining table and prepared to help in the kitchen with the cleaning up, but Blanca would have none of it. "The cook, she is not the dishwasher. You go out on the veranda with El Senor, and Susu will bring coffee." Breed thanked the older woman and admitted she was tired.

Loughlan was lounging on a wooden chair, smoking a cheroot. He rose when he saw them and set two more chairs beside his.

The view from the veranda looked south over the foothills to the town of Los Angeles and past, to the distant sea. As the summer evening drew in, it was one of peace and tranquility. Breed sighed, as much from her enjoyment of the quiet as from tiredness. It had truly been a busy day. Lita had brought her ever-present basket of sewing and was mending a little girl's frock. She occasionally cast covetous glances at Loughlan's cheroot but controlled her desire to smoke for fear of shocking the staid senor. After a few minutes of mutual silence, Loughlan spoke. "I received word from Hugh, from Captain Shepard today," he said. "He has picked up a cargo for Oregon, wool I think, for a new mill up there and is going to be gone awhile, so you might as well settle in."

The fragrance of night-blooming jasmine and honeysuckle filled the air as a breeze came from the sea to cool the evening. The companionable silence was interrupted by the hustling Blanca, bearing a tray of coffee and another piece of the plum tart for Loughlan. She bade them good night and, with Susu in tow, could be heard going down the path behind the rancho to their small adobe casa.

Loughlan consumed the tart and coffee with lightning speed and sat back, the picture of contentment. Breed decided to chance a few remarks. "Your home is so different from the other houses we have seen since we arrived. It's not wooden like the Morales' home."

John answered, "We had only been here a few years when the earthquake in '56 happened. It struck with such force that the ranch house was almost demolished. When we went to rebuild, my mother insisted some changes in the general design be made. My father used to say she had tried to have an adobe Cape Cod cottage and it just got away from her. She wanted the red barrel tiles on the roof and loved her gardens and the veranda but wanted large rooms with lots of windows to see the mountains." He finished and gave his attention to his cheroot.

"Sure, it is a lovely, comfortable house," said Breed. She would have liked to sit longer in the cool darkness with this man, but all were tired and would be up early to leave for the trip into town.

Breed stood and told John Loughlan good night. He rose clumsily to his feet and, after a slight hesitation, thanked them for the excellent dinner.

"You should wait till after supper for the trip home to avoid the heat." He paused, then continued, "The mercantile on Spring Street is where we shop, so just charge what you need. And the Chinaman Hung Mi Sing has a dry goods store on Flower and you can charge what you need there too." Breed thanked him and went indoors with the coffee tray. "Use the rooms at the Pico Hotel to rest before you return," he called to her receding back.

Instead of parting at Breed's bedroom door, Lita came in. Indicating the small chair by the window, she gave Breed a little push toward it. Breed sat down. Lita, taking the brush from the dresser, removed the hairpins from her friend's hair and brushed it with long, even strokes. Bleached by the sun to the color of ripe wheat, her hair rippled like a golden wave. As Lita brushed, the exhausted Breed, slumped in the chair, all but purred.

Unconsciously, Lita had chosen this way to show her appreciation and love for Breed's many kindnesses to her. The young Irishwoman had never been waited on in her life. To the contrary. Since the age of thirteen, she had been a maid of all work and companion to young ladies under the care of the Reverend and Mrs. Potts. The novelty of being attended by Lita was the height of luxury. After a few moments, she began to talk about the coming shopping trip into Los Angeles. Lita braided Breed's hair into a long plait. Then she poured water into a large china basin on the nightstand and helped Breed out of her dress. While Breed washed, Lita fetched a fresh nightgown from the dresser. When Breed was in bed, Lita extinguished the oil lamp and quietly went to her room. Breed turned on her side and for a few moments before sleep came thought of John Loughlan, his little girls and the new adventure before her.

At dawn the next morning, the excited party of shoppers was on the road to town. The buckboard wagon's bed had been padded with straw and the old quilt thrown over it to provide a bit more comfort to the shoppers. It was quite cool and stayed so until well after sunrise. The young women and the two little girls were deposited at the Pico House Hotel, on John Loughlan's instructions, to have breakfast before starting their shopping. Manuel Carozone, a ranch hand, was the driver and told the girls he would be at his sister's shop next to the plaza should they need him before evening.

As the small party moved hesitantly through the hotel lobby in search of the dining room, they were pleasantly surprised to encounter Serafina Morales and her oldest brother, Don Diego. After explanations on both sides of their presence in Los Angeles, Don Diego escorted the group of chattering, excited females into breakfast.

After they had ordered their meal, Diego questioned Breed about her new home and how she liked it. When she continued to give him short answers containing little or no real information about herself, he switched his attention to the little girls. He delighted them with his description of plans for the great fandango his father and mother were planning when his sister was married. The pretty bride-to-be simpered and acknowledged congratulations. "That is why we are in Los Angeles. Diego has brought me to choose material for my wedding dress!"

Breed was so relieved at no longer being the center of Diego Morales' attention that she volunteered, "We, too, are shopping for material. The girls all need new winter things and God knows Lita and I are threadbare. We are to go to a shop owned by a Mr. Sing."

Serafina beamed and noted, "But how remarkable. We too are on our way to Hung Mi Sing's. We will all go together."

Breed looked in confusion at Don Diego, who in turn smiled smugly, bowed and murmured, "We will have our little visit yet, senorita."

When breakfast was finished, Serafina insisted the ladies go up to her room. It was agreed they would meet her brother half an hour later in the lobby.

The young women and their charges were more than willing to freshen up after the long wagon ride. The half hour passed quickly. Serafina was full of her forthcoming marriage and several times she teased that Breed, whom she still called Elizabeth, would be the next to the altar.

It took them a few minutes to reach Sing's emporium, a rather unimposing storefront on Flower Street. The one plate-glass window had a hodgepodge of ladies' frufru, a black mourning bonnet, lovely lifelike silk flowers, reams of French lace, ribbons and bolts of work-a-day gingham cloths.

As they entered, the shop was busy. But when the young Chinese man in charge saw the Morales sister and brother he came quickly to the party. Bowing ceremoniously, Sing's number-one son welcomed them. Don Diego introduced Breed and Lita and the little girls, mentioning that Breed was to be the new Mrs. Loughlan.

If the young man had been pleased to see the Morales siblings, the mention of John Loughlan's name acted like a bolt of lightning. He bowed repeatedly, accompanied by giggles from the little girls, and his nice face was split by an enormous smile. "Please come this way. You are honored guests and my father will want to attend to your requirements himself," he said as he rushed them to a more private showroom. After seating the ladies, he bowed again and hurried away to find the elder Sing.

"Sure all that bowing and bobbing is enough to make you seasick," Breed whispered behind her hand to Lita. Lita, used to the attention of shopkeepers, merely smiled and looked aloof.

The room was a rainbow. Great bolts of silk from Japan were stacked high on red lacquered tables that had dragons for legs. There were beautiful sheer gauzes from India, rich velvets from Belgium and France. The wall shelves were full of shimmering satins and wools from Scotland.

In moments, the Sings, father and son, returned. The bowing and welcoming commenced once more. When the two men finally showed signs of slowing down, Don Diego explained his sister's need, with his mother's instruction that Serafina's final choice be approved by Sing the Elder. Breed asked the younger Sing to help her and Lita choose wool for winter dresses and "about twenty-five yards of pretty gingham, for the little girls need pinafores and I need aprons. Then let's see...." Here, Lita touched her elbow and drew her aside. On her little pad, she had printed in English, "a gift for her" and pointed to Serafina, engrossed in choosing the material for her wedding dress. Lita had found a bolt of fine white French lawn and showed it to Breed. Breed was delighted by the idea and asked how much material they required. When Lita counted out twenty yards, Breed asked, "So much?" Lita pointed to the little girls, and Breed realized they were much in need of new underclothes too.

The little girls had been wandering through the shop, almost in a daze with the excitement of the trip into town and the shopping. Sing Jr. brought them each a sweetmeat to nibble on because they were so well-behaved. They finally came to Breed, lugging a bolt of yellow satin with small slant-eyed rabbits hopping over it. "Miss, oh Miss, could we please have some of this for Nicky? She would love the little bunnies!"

Breed was touched to see they remembered their absent baby sister and agreed. Turning to Lita, she murmured, "We can make some knickers for Nicky and maybe that will encourage her to stay dry." Lita nodded in agreement but was preoccupied looking at Serafina, mentally taking her measurements for her gift.

During the lull that occurred while Sing Jr. and a sales lady wrapped the purchases, the elder Sing invited the party to step back to the family's quarters for a cup of tea.

Passing through a heavy oak door painted bright red, they found themselves in another world. The bare floors in the room were highly polished. A few beautifully carved low chairs and a long chest lacquered in black and touched with gold were the only furnishings. A wide ceiling-to-floor window provided a magnificent view of a garden, cool and quiet and hidden from the street by a high wall.

The elder Sing was very pleased with everyone's reaction and asked the ladies and Don Diego to be seated. The little girls were already out in the small garden examining the carp pond and cage of chirping finches.

Sing rang a small brass gong with a little hammer. A moment later, a handsome Chinese woman in a black silk gown entered, carrying a ladened tray. On it were small, handleless teacups and a teapot. Behind her came a small boy of three or so, carefully carrying a basket filled with tiny cakes and sweetmeats.

The woman knelt beside the lacquered table. She set out the cakes on a plate, poured tea into each of the little cups and gave them one at a time to the little boy to offer their guests. Breed thought she must be Sing Jr.'s wife, or perhaps even the daughter of the house. Not more than thirty-five, she had clear ivory skin that almost glowed against her black hair. Her serene expression made it obvious that a sitting room full of strangers did not disturb her in the least.

Breed was more than a little shocked when Sing proudly introduced her to the assembled group. "This is my wife and my number-two son. She does not speak English, but nonetheless, you are welcome to our humble home."

While the party drank the fragrant tea and nibbled on the little cakes, Sing explained that she was his second wife. After his first wife died, he had been very lonely. John Loughlan had commissioned Captain Shepard to bring the unworthy Sing a picture bride when he returned from one of his China voyages. "Life was again full and happy," continued the older man. "Indeed, John Loughlan has arranged that Captain Shepard bring number-one son a bride when he soon returns to China."

Everyone beamed at everyone else. Even Lita seemed lifted from her usual melancholia.

After the package-laden party left Sing's emporium, Diego

convinced Breed they should have dinner with him and Serafina before leaving for the Loughlan ranch. Not knowing how to decline gracefully, and half-wanting to do it, Breed consented. Serafina suggested the little girls return to the hotel for a rest and Breed gratefully agreed. So, with only token resistance, Belle and Daisy climbed out of the carriage with Serafina and Diego when they reached the hotel. Breed and Lita would continue to the general store.

❧ CHAPTER SIXTEEN ❧

The long, hot afternoon was almost over when the two young women, arms full of their purchases, arrived back at the Pico House. Manuel had met them at the general store to load the wagon and received instructions to meet them at eight at the hotel.

Tired and hot, Breed and Lita were met by Serafina, who told them the little girls had napped and were now refreshed and tidied. Breed thanked her, and then she and Lita spent time freshening up and visiting with Serafina, hearing the exciting plans for the girl's wedding in the spring. The little girls sat on the carpet, playing with jacks that Diego had bought them.

Lita helped Breed pin her hair into a French roll. It was just like a picture in the Ladies' Day magazine they had purchased at the dry goods store. Serafina was entranced and begged Lita to help do hers the same way. As they talked, Annabelle asked Breed, "Will you and Papa be married before Serafina? I do hope so."

Embarrassed and at a loss for an answer, Breed laughed ruefully. "We will talk about it later, Dolly," she said. And before Serafina could say anything on the subject, Breed herded the little girls out of the room with a promise to meet in the lobby.

Descending the grand staircase to the lobby, Breed felt herself quite the figure of elegance. Her hair, brushed first against her head and then wound in the French roll and secured with a pretty tortoise shell comb, did make her look, if not quite beautiful, at least very smart. Though her plain, grey surge skirt and simple white blouse were not the latest fashion, her newborn self-confidence and happiness made those who saw her smile admiringly.

At the foot of the staircase, handsome and cool, stood Don Diego Morales. His look was so intense, Breed felt her old awkward self. But she refused to let him see how he affected her. Diego took her arm and murmured, "You wear a crown of gold, my heart," though his voice was so low, Breed was not sure she had heard him correctly. With his next breath, he told the little girls to go into the patio where a waiter would bring them lemonade. He and Breed would stroll in the small hotel garden.

They walked in silence, her hand still tucked into the crook of his arm, his other hand possessively over it. Finally, with mixed emotions, Breed decided she must explain her situation.

"Senor Morales," she faltered. The pressure of his hand on hers gave encouragement and she continued, "Diego, I must tell you about myself. I am not Elizabeth Staunton. I was her maid, her companion, if you will. She met someone on shipboard and they eloped when our ship made port in Buenos Aires. Lita and I are only stopping with Mr. Loughlan till we can take a return passage to Boston. He had kindly allowed us to exchange my being his housekeeper for our room and board...." She paused, on the verge of tears, waiting for Diego Morales to speak.

When he did, his words made her wonder if he had even been

listening. "You are the most beautiful, most vibrant woman I have ever known. I think I love you! John has been my friend since we were boys and I would not speak when I thought you were his 'esposa,' but now!..." He took the startled girl into his arms and kissed her so passionately she felt her knees weaken. Only when he heard the little girls calling to them did he release his embrace. Breed looked around wildly for somewhere to run. He evidently had not understood a word she had said! Realizing his abrupt declaration had alarmed Breed, he smiled at her, drew her hand through his arm and turned toward the patio. As they came out of the screening shrubbery to join his sister, Lita and the little girls, he whispered, "We will talk again, mi amor."

Somehow, Breed muddled through her dinner, carefully avoiding Diego's gaze. Serafina was so thrilled about her wedding plans that she and the little girls, so full of chatter about their day, kept the table from silence.

Later, when Manuel arrived with the wagon, they took leave of one another. As Diego helped Breed into the wagon, he whispered, "Te amo, until we meet again."

The young women were quiet as the wagon left the bustle of the town. Indeed, Breed was sunk in a deep study. The little girls, exhausted from the excitement of the day, had finally run down and were asleep on the blankets among the parcels and boxes of groceries.

Finally, after a prolonged silence, Lita put her hand on Breed's and touched her fingers to her lips. Breed blurted out the whole episode with Diego. Lita listened, realizing that Breed was speaking more to herself than to her friend.

The evening wore on, the cool night settled in, and again all was silent save for the clop, clop of the horses' hooves on the dirt road. Lita was half-asleep and Breed had sunk into a deep reverie, her thoughts disconnected and unclear, when she heard the wagon's horses neighing.

Quickly, Manuel had reached down to the boot of the wagon. He had a rifle in his hands, ready to fire. Breed gasped in fright, for herself and the rest of the party. She had heard Blanca speak in lurid terms about the outlaw Vasquez, who roamed as far north as Sacramento and south into Sonora, Mexico. Rumor had it that he and his gang of cutthroats were in the area, having raped a rancher's wife and stolen fresh mounts from the corral. Breed sat tense and hardly breathing as the horses neighing was answered by that of another horse in the darkness. Her ears strained to hear ahead but she heard only Manuel cock the rifle.

Then, out of the shadow of overhanging trees rode John Loughlan. He announced himself to Manuel, who laughed nervously and put the rifle down. "Hey, boss, you almost have a few holes in you. I think you are Vasquez!" said the relieved driver.

"Saints be praised," Breed whispered to herself. "Sure, you gave us a fright, Mr. Loughlan," she said, as he rode alongside the wagon.

He begged her pardon for frightening them. "It was so quiet at home, thought I'd just come meet you," he said, sheepishly. "Did you get everything you went after?"

Breed felt such a sensation of relief and happiness that her tiredness evaporated and the exciting happenings of the day poured out. When she reached their visit with the Sings, she paused for breath and asked, "What is a picture bride?"

Their conversation woke the sleeping children. The girls began to chatter at once, telling Loughlan of the day's adventures. Later, sitting on Breed's lap, thumb in mouth, Daisy asked sleepily, "Why did Don Diego kiss you, Miss?" Loughlan had Annabelle up before him on his horse and Breed hoped he had missed the child's sleepy question. There was no way to tell because he immediately kicked the horse and it shot ahead of the slow-moving wagon. When the horse and riders failed to return, Breed realized they had continued on to the ranch.

In the confusion and excitement of their arrival home, Breed did not have time to speak again to her employer. Just before she fell asleep, she thought of the long day just passed and marveled at how her life had changed. She smiled in the darkness at the picture of John Loughlan riding alongside the wagon and how pleased she had been to see him. Then, the memory of Diego Morales and his kiss flashed into her thoughts. She felt disturbed and uncomfortable. Why, she wondered, did one man make you feel safe, the other that you were walking on dangerous ground? Unresolved, she fell asleep.

Late the next morning, Breed was awakened by the arrival of the three little girls. Belle carried a cup of Blanca's strong coffee, Daisy a spoon and small pitcher of cream, and Nicky proudly presented a basket containing one of the cook's hot breakfast rolls.

She sat up in bed and made room for her visitors. "What will we do today, Miss?" asked Belle.

"Why sure, today we must put all our purchases away," Breed said, "and get Lita started on the sewing too." Daisy volunteered that Lita had been up a very long time and had material strewn all over her room. Nicky announced she was going to use her potty chair so she could wear the yellow bunny bloomers Lita was making for her! Everyone was properly impressed and Breed gave her a big hug.

When Breed and the little girls went to the kitchen, she asked Blanca if they were to expect El Senor home for lunch. She was informed that he would be gone for several days. A ranch hand had arrived from the Santa Barbara property early in the morning with word that a wildcat had been stealing sheep. "So, all the men who can be spared have gone with Senor to hunt the cat," Blanca said.

When asked how long a wildcat hunt lasted, Blanca replied, "Maybe a day, or maybe a week. Then, if they get el gato, they will all get drunk. And if they don't get him they will get drunk anyway!"

The next few days were spent happily working in the summer kitchen, finishing the jams and some preserving Breed wanted to complete. They also sewed the various pieces that Lita felt Breed or Rosa could do properly. And then in the long twilight Breed would insist Lita join her and the girls for a walk around the property.

One afternoon, as Breed, Lita and the girls sat on the veranda conducting a reading lesson for Belle and an English lesson for Lita, they noticed a single rider. His horse kicked yellow dust about as he came up the road from Los Angeles. At first, all thought it was John Loughlan. But as he passed the two sycamores at the bottom of the hill they realized it was Don Diego Morales.

"Don Diego, how nice to see you," said Breed, just barely suppressing a blush.

"Uncle Diego," said one of the girls, "Papa is on a wildcat hunt at Santa Barbara!"

"I know," he said.

Feeling happy if not a little giddy, Breed asked Diego if he had eaten dinner. Not yet, he said. She went indoors and called Blanca. "Senor Morales is here and has not had his dinner. Will you put something... No, I'll do it." She hurriedly heated some soup, cut slices of bread and a piece of pie and set it all out on a large tray. She added one of the good linen napkins from the dining room and a mug of coffee.

When she reappeared on the veranda with the food, she found Diego settled comfortably in the chair where John Loughlan usually sat. Nicky was on his lap and Belle stood before them reading competently from her McGuffy. Daisy, thumb in mouth, was pressed close to Lita, with Lita's arm protectively around her. Belle brought out Breed's guitar and, while the young man ate, Breed sang their favorite songs, first in Spanish, then English. The little girls were enthralled, so they did not go willingly when Rosa came to take them to bed.

Breed had been sitting next to Lita. But shortly after the little girls went in, Breed realized that Lita was about to leave her and Don Diego alone on the veranda. It was almost dark, so Breed hoped Diego did not see her grab Lita's skirt and tug on it when Lita started to rise. Lita looked at Breed questioningly. Breed, however, kept her face toward Diego and continued talking to him, so Lita settled back and took one of her cherished cheroots from its tin box in her skirt pocket and lit it. After another hour of agreeable conversation, Don Diego realized he was not going to have time alone with Breed. He rose, kissed each woman's hand and thanked Breed for his supper. As he was going down the path to where his horse was tied, he called back, "Mi corazon, I go to Mexico on business, but when I return, we will speak!"

In the kitchen, while they put the dishes to soak and had a last cup of coffee, Lita wrote on her little pad, "And WHAT was that all about?"

Breed was embarrassed and a little flustered. "Sure, I don't know, dearie, but Don Diego goes too fast and it was just better you be close by."

The heat of early September eventually gave way to cooling near the end of the month. In the evenings, Breed and Lita wore their shawls and the patio was used after dinner less frequently. Loughlan was away from the rancho several days a week. He had property in Santa Barbara to the north, and south toward San Diego.

Breed's life was busy and full. She cooked, taught the little girls and when Lita allowed helped with the sewing and mending. When John Loughlan was able to join them for a meal or an hour's time, she felt almost giddy with happiness. She refused to dwell on why she was happier when her employer was present but knew one day she would have to deal with the questions.

Lita seemed content and enjoyed the company of the little girls. Breed knew she was still far from robust and insisted Lita rest every day, joking to the little girls after lunch, "Now we must put our two babies to bed for a little rest." When Loughlan was home, Lita watched how he and Breed behaved in each other's presence— occasionally smiling to herself as she bent over some fine handiwork or one of the children's books she was learning to read.

The first week in October started out as though it were mid-August. A strong Santa Ana wind blew over the mountains from the desert, heating the valleys and flood plains. Loughlan had been invited to a formal dinner party in Los Angeles. He would be in town Friday, attend the party on Saturday and return Sunday. Breed carefully pressed and packed his dinner clothes and fresh things for Sunday. "Sure, himself doesn't seem all that excited about going to the party," she said to Lita as they watched him ride between the gates early Friday.

The hot wind continued to blow through Friday and Saturday. Breed and the little girls went tramping over the hills behind the rancho, leaving Lita to sit on the veranda and smoke a cheroot in peace. By evening, the heat had taken its toll on all. After an early supper of cold chicken and pudding, everyone agreed bed would be welcomed.

Breed first took a leisurely bath. At seventeen minutes to ten she was just drifting off to sleep in her bed. Then, the earth shook. She was nearly frightened out of her wits as her bed and the glass windows rattled and all she could think was to get to the children as quickly as possible. The noise of the ground shifting and roaring ceased as suddenly as it had begun. Breed grabbed her shawl and carefully sidestepped a broken flower vase that had fallen from the dresser. Lita met her in the hall and together they went to the girls.

The nursery night-light had fallen over, breaking its chimney, and books had fallen from the case. Otherwise, the room was intact and only Belle had wakened. She sat in the middle of her small bed, hugging her favorite rag doll, Lucinda. The younger girls still slept soundly as only exhausted children can.

Breed went back to their bedrooms and got their boots in case there was more broken glass in the house. Then the young women and the little girl made a tour of the rancho. The kitchen was the hardest hit. Several jars of preserves had fallen from their shelves and dishes were smashed on the tile floor of the pantry. Breed made a note to have Huron Del Gado put wooden slats along the shelves and doors on the dish cabinets, similar to the Sara Blue's galley. Soon, they were joined by the cook and two housemaids who had come up the hill from their little casa. Breed made hot cocoa for everyone and they spent the next hour or so tidying the house and calming each other's nerves.

Every little while, the house would rock again as a small aftershock rolled through the area. When this happened, the young Susu, Blanca's none-too-bright niece, jumped and started screeching prayers in rapid, unintelligible Spanish. Finally, Breed sent the two young maids back to their beds. When Belle began to cry at the thought of returning alone to her own bed, Lita indicated she might come in with her. Breed made a game of it, saying as she tucked the two in, "Sure, I have the biggest babies in all the Californias. Now, Belle, when the bed rocks just pretend you are at sea with your Uncle Hugh on the Sara Blue."

In the kitchen, Blanca had just finished mopping the pantry floor, so Breed told the older woman to sit down while she put the pail and mop outside. Then the two women sat quietly, each drinking another cup of hot cocoa. But the house and grounds kept moving. Just when they were lulled into thinking all was calm, a jolt that seemed strong as the first would rock the house to its foundations. Blanca began to tell Breed of the earthquake in '57. It had done such damage to the whole area, and to the Rancho Dos Aliso, in particular. "Senor Juan was just a young boy, his mama and he only just came to live here," Blanca said. "La Senora, the good God rest her, helped many who were injured or had nowhere to live after their houses were destroyed. She did nothing here, even though the rancho had much damage. Walls cracked and adobe fell everywhere."

Breed realized for the first time that the town might have sustained damage and that John Loughlan might be hurt. "Blanca," she said, "do you think El Senor and the men who went into town will be all right?"

Blanca stood up, put the two mugs in the tin sink and said, "Si, senorita, he is like a cat, always lands on his feet. Be sure all will be well." Wrapping her shawl about her snugly, she bid the younger woman good night and went down the hill to her bed.

Breed sat a few minutes longer and finally decided she could do nothing about the trembling earth. She would still have to be up and about in only a few hours, so she also went to bed. She dozed fitfully until close to three in the morning, when the sound of approaching horses brought her wide awake.

The party John Loughlan had attended was in full swing when the quake struck. The home hosting the party sustained quite a bit of damage, and the women guests insisted their menfolk take them to their own comfortable homes at once. Several people were injured, so Loughlan helped make them comfortable until a doctor was located. Then, after thanking his hosts, he claimed his horse at the stable and took off for the rancho in great haste.

About an hour out of town he caught up with several of his

ranch hands who had been to town with their pay. The evening's amusements having been so rudely interrupted, they had decided to cut short their stay. After purchasing several bottles of tequila they were on the way home. "Hola, Senor," said Huron Del Gado, the foreman offering a half-empty bottle to John Loughlan as El Senor rode up to the group. All were excited and talkative after the quake and liberal doses of tequila. So the long ride went quickly, as did the bottles.

On the ride home they had seen little damage in the countryside save for a small landslide along a canyon wall. But Loughlan was still worried about those at Rancho Dos Aliso. When they reached home, he left his horse with his foreman and climbed rapidly up the hill. He arrived at the kitchen door just as Breed came in. Her hair was loose from its braids and shined in the light of the oil lamp she carried. The much-washed flannel nightgown she wore beneath a shawl did nothing to accent her appearance, but Loughlan still caught his breath at the sight of her. He remembered Elaine, his beautiful wife, her dark hair all soft curls, her night garments the finest silk and ribbons.

He shook his head as if to chase an unwanted thought from his mind. "Is all well here?" he asked. "There's quite a bit of damage in town, but everything looks safe hereabouts." Embarrassed at being caught in her nightclothes, Breed told him quickly what had happened, then turned to go back to her room. She heard Loughlan come through the kitchen and follow her. She reached her room the same time he did. He was so close behind she could smell the combination of his shaving soap, the horse he had ridden and the spirits he had very evidently had his share of. As she put the lamp on her dresser, Loughlan tugged at her shawl and it fell from her shoulders.

Breed stepped away from him and felt the side of the bed against her knees as John reached for her and engulfed her in his arms. He bent to kiss her, but in one swift movement she pulled away, raised her leg and kneed him in the groin.

"Oh, my Christ!" the man gasped as he bent over in agony.

Breed stood to one side, looking with mixed emotions at her employer. "Sure, Mr. Loughlan, you've had too much to drink."

"That, I have," he said through clenched teeth, "and I'm going to lose it now!" Breed took her washbasin from the little stand and held it for the violently retching man. Afterward, he sat slumped on her bed, weak as a kitten and embarrassed beyond belief. Breed wrung out a towel in the pitcher on her stand, wiped his face and gave him a drink of water to rinse his mouth. "Breed, I'm sorry," he said. "Just give me a minute and I'll be on my way. Guess champagne, wine and a large amount of tequila don't mix." While he spoke, Breed tugged off his heavy jacket and then, one arm at a time, his formal coat. "No, I'm all right, really," he muttered.

"Mr. Loughlan, I've seen me uncle and cousins much worse for wear than you this minute. I also know how to take care of a great drunken sot." With that she pushed the unresisting man back into her bed. Lifting his legs, she arranged him tidily for sleep, first removing his shoes and stiff shirtfront. He was asleep before she could hang up his clothes. She turned the lamp down, went around to the unoccupied side of the bed, pulled back two quilts and climbed in beside the sleeping man.

Just as she was falling asleep there was another aftershock. She leaned close to the warm, strong body beside her, feeling entirely safe, and slept.

Morning came all too soon. As usual, the younger girls were up with the birds and wondering why Belle wasn't in her cot. They took themselves to the kitchen, thinking the rest of the family was there. The kitchen was empty! No one had even started their porridge or Papa's coffee! Daisy took Nicky's hand and said, "Come baby, let's go find Miss."

Daisy carefully opened Breed's bedroom door and saw her father, asleep with his arm thrown across the still sleeping Breed. The two little girls were delighted, and they went around to Breed's side of the bed, intending to join the two people they loved most. Breed awoke, from a pleasant dream of being wrapped in a beautiful fur coat, to find the two little faces close to her, their little hands gently tapping on her forehead. She moved John's arm and then, putting her finger to her lips, threw on her shawl and led the littles from her room.

"Your Papa was very ill in the night so I let him stay with me," she said. "Belle is in with Lita. It's been a very long night so we must let them sleep." She took the girls into their room, lit the Franklin stove to warm the nursery and set about helping the girls dress. Shortly, the aroma of brewing coffee filled the house. Breed realized that the cook had come up the hill and started breakfast.

Hooking the last of Nicky's pinafore, Breed gave each of the children a quick pat and told them to tell Blanca to give them their porridge.

Quietly, she opened her bedroom door. John Loughlan had removed himself and his clothes, so she hurried and washed, dressed and tidied her room. Lita came to her door on her way to the kitchen and the two young women went to breakfast.

An unknown man sat at the end of the long table nursing a cup of coffee and finishing a piece of pie. He stood as the two entered and Blanca announced offhandedly, "He is Ed Dunn from the sheep farm, El Norte. There has been some damage from the earthquake and they need senor Juan to come at once." John Loughlan joined them and Blanca produced a great platter of ham, eggs and toast for him. Breed poured him a cup of coffee without meeting his glance. The little girls chattered, and Belle had to tell her father in great detail about the night's excitements. Lita sat toying with her food and watched Breed and Loughlan speculatively. When she caught Breed's eye with a questioning look, Breed had the grace to blush and give a tiny shake of her head.

Promising to take the children on a walk shortly, Breed spoke to her employer, "Mr. Loughlan, will you be gone long? Could we pack an overnight bag for you?"

"Thank you, yes," he said without looking at her, busying himself with the youngest of the girls. "I may be gone several days. Blanca will get my saddlebags for you." Quickly, Breed followed the cook into the hall. Blanca opened the long carved chest outside the nursery and pulled out the large leather saddlebags.

"Just working clothes and a warm jacket," Blanca said. "It gets cold at night there." So saying, she hurried back to the kitchen.

It took Breed only a few minutes to find and pack several changes of clothes and gather Loughlan's razor, soap and strop. As she was buckling the bags closed, John Loughlan came into his room, dressed to go, spurs and hat already in place. Dismayed, Breed noticed he also was armed with a large six-shooter in a tooled leather holster. He saw her look and said, "Ed Dunn brought word that Vasquez and his gang were seen near Trancas, so I best be prepared." They stood awkwardly, looking at each other and not knowing what to say. "Breed, I'm sorry about last night," he said, hurriedly. "I behaved badly. It won't happen again." With that, he turned and left the room, calling for the little girls to "come say goodbye to your Papa."

Breed returned to the kitchen and found Huron Del Gado and one of the ranch hands on ladders checking the stove chimney for damage. "Senorita," Huron Del Gado said, "it is necessary we go over our house to be sure all is well. Did you notice any cracks or displacements?"

"Oh, Glory," Breed said, "I never even thought about house damage. Lita, did you notice anything?" Lita shook her head and, herding the children before her, went out the back door. "She's right, of course," Breed said, following Lita and the littles. "You get on with your work, senor. We'll keep the children out of your way."

The day was much cooler, a hint of fall in the air. Lita had walked the children around behind the house and down into the little orchard. She took a seat on the wooden bench in the shade. "Miss, please push me," begged Belle, sitting on the rope swing Breed had put up.

"No, me first," said Daisy, hopefully.

"Sure, the seat's wide enough for the two of you," Breed said. "Get aboard." And then she sent the swing flying. Later the two young women spoke about the frightening happenings of the night before, and Lita brought up John Loughlan's presence in Breed's bed. When she had read Lita's questions, Breed blushed. In a low voice, so the frolicking children could not hear, she explained. Then Lita wrote carefully, "If he touches you again, I will kill him."

Lita then stood up, dusted her skirt and returned up the hill to the house. Breed sat quietly, trying to come to terms with her own feelings and all that had happened. Soon, however, the girls came flying at her and she was engulfed in arms and legs.

"Miss, tell us a story, please," echoed Belle and Daisy as Nicky climbed into Breed's lap, "about Momma Rabbit."

"You mean 'Mrs. Rabbit, the Fox and Strict Obedience?'" Breed asked. "But you know that story by heart!" The girls nodded their heads and squirmed in anticipation. "Very well, but after this we must find another favorite story."

As the afternoon drew to a close, Breed gathered her charges and went into the house. She had shaken her feelings of sadness and embarrassment over the encounter with John Loughlan and resolved not to let her emotions rule her so.

"Here are three dirty little rabbits for you to wash," she said, handing the little girls over to the nursery maid. "What shall we have for dinner, Blanca?" she asked the cook.

"Senorita, something light. It is just for ourselves, since all the men have gone. They won't be back for quite four days." Breed tried not to show her disappointment. She hadn't realized Trancas was so far away. Everything was such a long way away here in the West.

"Well, let us just make a large pot of soup then," she said, putting on her apron and taking out carrots and onions to scrub and chop.

For the next week, there continued to be aftershocks, usually small, but just enough to keep the household on edge. John Loughlan remained away and the house of women ran smoothly.

Autumn in California came to the rancho. Breed marveled at the beauty of the mountains, gold from the long drought but clear and sharp in the cooler weather. Lita and Breed spent one day in town, shopping at Mr. Sing's for lengths of wool to make winter dresses for the fast-growing girls and other fabrics to use in their Christmas gift sewing. Breed also stopped at the stationers for school supplies, including new slates and a more advanced reader for Belle.

Loughlan's long absence was explained. The bandit Vasquez and his men were back. They had raided a homestead and killed a ranch hand north of Trancas. Loughlan, as a landowner, had joined the posse but so far they had little luck locating the elusive outlaw.

It was November 1, All Saints Day, and John Loughlan was still away. Everyone was tired and cranky from the Halloween party Breed had given. First the huge pumpkin had to be carved to a proper Jack-o'-lantern. With three helpful little girls, this took longer than anyone would have imagined. Then they all had to bob for apples. Finally they sat with Blanca, Rosa and Susu around the fire munching on apples and popped corn. Breed told one or two mild ghost stories. Later, after the girls had gone to bed the women sat long in front of the fire, frightening one another with tales guaranteed to give nightmares.

The next day just after noon, a rider arrived with a packet of mail and newspapers from Texas and announced, "Vasquez and his gang escaped again. The reward for capture had been upped to ten-thousand dollars, dead or alive." Breed offered him a meal. "No thank you ma'am. I still have deliveries to make, so I'll eat later." Breed heard him speaking to Huron Del Gado about the Vasquez gang and their latest crimes. She thanked God the criminals were far away.

During the night there was a sharp aftershock. Breed awoke, nervous and worried. Lighting her chamber candle, she went first to the nursery to be sure the children were all right and then looked in on Lita. Evidently Breed was the only one who had felt the quake. Her nerves were still frazzled, so she went to the kitchen to heat a cup of milk. The huge iron stove that dominated the kitchen was still hot and she set a small pan of milk to heat. By the lamp light on the table she noticed Loughlan's saddlebags dumped by the back door—and Loughlan himself slumped asleep in the old kitchen rocking chair.

They both became aware of one another at the same moment. "Is everything all right?" she asked the tired, saddle-weary man.

He nodded and started to tell her about the dead rancher and his wife, who had been assaulted. Then he thought better of it and to change the subject said, "Do you often entertain gentlemen in your night clothes?"

Breed, mortified, turned to leave, but he rose from the chair and reached for her arm before she could. "Come sit here awhile," he said. "It was a cold ride but I wanted to get home to...." He paused, pulling her to him and burying his face in her hair. "To see you." He held her tightly to his body, one hand tangled in her hair, the other at the small of her back. Breed could smell the horse he'd been riding for hours, the smell of a man. She knew she should free herself from this compromising situation. Knew it was unsafe to stand there in a nearly dark deserted kitchen with this man. And she knew there was no other place on earth she wanted to be. Loughlan gently tugged her head back, seeking her lips. "Breed, please come to me," he said. I...."

She didn't know what he was going to say but she put her fingers to his lips, quieting him. "Turn down the lamp," she said, "and we will go to bed." He did and they went arm in arm to his room.

Late in the night it began to rain and Breed woke to the sound of the wind beating the branches against the window. She was wrapped in John Loughlan's embrace, her head on one arm, his other arm around her, his hand cupping her breast. "John," she whispered to herself, "I love you, God help me!" Then she settled herself again and with a contented sigh slept.

Breed woke early before the house began to stir and untangled herself from the sleeping man's arms. She pulled on her nightgown and, after gathering fresh clothes and her sponge and bath towel, went and drew herself a long, hot bath.

As she lay soaking, the water easing her aching muscles, thoughts chased one another through her mind. What will he think of me? Will he marry me? Could he love me? She shook her head to clear it and said aloud, "I must get the bed linen and put them to soak at once or the Venturas will be scandalized." The Venturas were the three sturdy dark women of undetermined age who arrived every two weeks to spend the day doing the laundry.

Just as Breed opened the hall door, John Loughlan left his bedroom. Each saw the other and both saw Lita coming to call Breed. Lita stopped and looked appraisingly at the two. Breed blushed to the roots of her hair and Loughlan wore an uncomfortable, guilty look. Lita, with not so much as a nod to either, turned swiftly and headed to the kitchen.

Breed stood there holding her nightgown and bath towel, unsure of how to react. Loughlan came to her, cleared his throat and said quietly, "As God is my witness, Breed, I didn't know it was your first time. I wouldn't have laid a hand on you...." He looked away. Breed was stunned. Not love, not even like, he had thought she was a whore!

"Think nothing of it, Mr. Loughlan, I didn't," she said. And with all the fury she could muster she slapped his face and, swallowing hard, ran to her room.

She wanted to throw herself on her bed and cry for hours. But the little girls would be looking for her, the cook would want to plan the day. There was a tap on her door, and it was briskly opened. Lita held her small slate in her hands and wrote, "Is it to be marriage?"

Breed shook her head. She stood up, wiped her tears and said as steadily as she could manage, "It was a mistake, not all his fault and you are not to even think of... any revenge."

Lita's look was as sharp as daggers. It was evident she held her feelings back only with great effort. She cleaned the little slate and wrote, "For now." Then she put her arm around Breed and, giving her a comforting hug, went with her to join the family.

The kitchen was in its usual morning uproar, the little girls vying for their father's attention. He was deep in ranch business with Huron Del Gado. No one seemed to notice Breed's red eyes or that she was quieter than usual. And shortly the men left to spend the day counting stock on the range.

The next week for Breed was the most difficult she would remember since her father's death. Guilt-ridden and heartsick, she kept herself busy with the children, house cleaning and thoughts of how she and Lita could leave Rancho Dos Aliso before Captain Shepard returned from the Pacific Northwest. At night, she said her prayers and allowed the tears she denied herself during the day.

John Loughlan, on the other hand, spent so much time away from the house the children complained. So, for three evenings in a row he read to the little girls, each allowed to choose their favorite for that night. Lita and Breed stayed late.

At the end of the week, Breed had calmed herself and could even speak to Loughlan about household matters and the children in a cool, detached voice. He had not yet looked her in the eye.

At dawn on the 8th of November the household was awakened

by pounding on the back door. A man had been sent to outlying ranches to gather a posse. The bandit Vasquez had struck again, leaving death and destruction behind. The Sheriff of Los Angeles and the townspeople had decided to chase the bandit and his crew and catch them once and for all. The plan might take them as far as Mexico, but they were determined to hang the lot of them this time. Loughlan hurriedly told Breed to fix breakfast for him and the three men he would take with him. He went back to his room to pack his bags and a bedroll. Huron Del Gado had come in dressed and armed by the time Loughlan returned to the kitchen. He and three of the ranch hands, along with the townsmen, were eating pancakes and slabs of ham as fast as Breed and Lita could make them. "Huron, you must stay here," Loughlan said between gulps of coffee. "We can't leave the women undefended. Who knows where the blasted devils are."

"Si, Boss," the older man said. He was disappointed but knew Loughlan was right.

In less time than Breed could imagine, they were ready to go. She had wrapped food in a flour sack along with the water bag. As Loughlan hurried out the door behind the men, she gave it to him saying, "Go with God and safe home."

Loughlan was halfway down the path to the stable when he turned and saw Breed still in the doorway. Her skirt had been hastily pulled on over her nightclothes and her shawl was tied across her front. Loughlan came back. His arms were loaded with his saddlebags, bedroll, rifle and the food sack, but he learned toward her and said quietly, "Breed, we will talk when I come back." And then he was gone.

Minutes later, as the cook and girls bustled in, they could hear the mounted men leaving Rancho Dos Aliso at a gallop on the road south.

And now a time of waiting began. News was hard to come by and usually only fourth or fifth hand. At first, it was rumored that the gang had fled north. Then that there was an attack on a rancho along the San Gabriel River and the gang was trying to get back across the border. Huron Del Gado made a pallet in the kitchen and slept there at night with guns close at hand.

The first two weeks the weather held and Breed kept the children busy with walks and games outdoors. Lita, never one to walk save when shopping, worked on the Christmas dresses and winter clothes for the girls. Winter arrived and, save for an occasional break, it rained and blew cold winds down from the mountains. Breed prayed nightly for the safety and comfort of the huge posse still on the trail of bandits.

The first week in December the weather again became mild, even balmy by Boston standards. Manuel, a ranch hand, brought word one morning from John Loughlan. In a terse note to Breed he wrote, "Vasquez and half the gang have been captured. A sort of trial will be held tomorrow. Then we will hand them over to the hangman. I should be home within the week. Tell the girls I miss them—everyone." He signed the note at the bottom with his initials, J.L.

Two days later, Breed was amazed to receive a long, happy letter from Eliza. It had been written in August and had been sent via the diplomatic pouch and a British frigate bound for San Francisco. She loved her new home, Edward's mother and two elder sisters were kindness itself and the doctor had confirmed her pregnancy. Her life was complete! She had written dear Mr. and Mrs. Potts in Boston and enclosed it in the envelope with her and Edward's wedding announcements. She had done the same for Breed. Eliza rattled on in her letter, happy and contented with her new life. She closed with warm regards to Lita and Breed and looked forward to hearing about their lives in California.

Breed couldn't help herself. The tears fell as she reread the letter, partly in relief and partly in self-pity. How differently things had turned out for her. Her lapse into such a state lasted only a short while, however. Quickly wiping her eyes, she carefully arranged a smile and went in search of Lita, who was hearing Belle's reading in Spanish. Settling the little girls before the nursery fire with milk and cookies, she and Lita read the letter again.

Lita, always sensitive to others, knew what Breed was feeling. She took her friend's hand and held it, as much in comfort as in reassurance that things would work out for Breed.

Had the house been less full of children and the day-to-day demands of running it, Breed might have given way to her deep feelings. As it was, she taught the little girls, spent long hours on the Christmas sewing with Lita and worked with the cook, teaching her how to make old-fashioned Christmas cakes. Several times she started to answer Eliza's happy letter. But she felt that because she and Lita were in limbo and could not say what their futures held, she put off writing again.

The second week in December, John Loughlan arrived home

badly sunburned, wearing a beard and with a heavy cold. He looked exhausted, and Breed insisted he go right to bed after a hot bath. That evening, everyone sat around him as he ate a huge meal that Blanca had prepared and brought to him at Breed's instruction. He was still worn out but gave them a mild version of the hunt for the bandits and their capture. When the children were sent to bed, he told the assembled adults everything, including the mass hanging of Vasquez and members of the gang captured with him. It was thought that a few others might have escaped across the border.

As Loughlan finished, Breed went and got a bottle of brandy and two glasses so Huron Del Gado and John could have a nightcap. Then she turned everyone out. Before she had put another log on the small fire and an extra quilt on the bed, Loughlan was asleep.

❧ CHAPTER EIGHTEEN ☙

Breed awoke feeling ill. She could hear the little girls chattering to their father in his room. She was thankful they had not come first to her. Getting out of bed gingerly, she washed and dressed and went to the kitchen to set the breakfast table. Usually the first cup of coffee was as welcome as the sun. But as she poured it she smelled the two small fresh trout and hash browns that Blanca was preparing for Loughlan and made a mad dash for the water closet. As the day wore on she felt better, but she could not keep anything down. She caught Lita looking at her several times and knew they both had the same thought.

Her periods had never been regular, so she really hadn't been worried the past month. Now, however, there was little doubt that she was pregnant with John Loughlan's child. She would give John a few days and then, if he hadn't said anything, she would tell him that she and Lita would be moving into town to wait for the arrival of the Sara Blue.

Early in the afternoon, the girls dragged their father down to the barn to see a newborn colt. Lita and Breed had a quiet time to talk. Breed was still nauseous and had seen and heard enough at her Aunt Kate's to realize she was pregnant. She spoke calmly to Lita and begged her not to say anything to John. Lita agreed, grudgingly. As they sat drinking coffee in the warm kitchen, Lita held up her hand and listened. Soon, Breed heard it too: a lone horseman coming at full gallop. He would soon be at the front gates. The women ran to the front window and saw the rider coming up the road from Los Angeles.

John and the little girls also had heard the rider as he came up the path toward the house. Breed and Lita realized the visitor was Captain Hugh Shepard, returned early from his voyage north.

"Hello," he shouted as he swung down from his mount. "This is a fine welcome!" he said, and then announced, "I've come to spend Christmas!" Everyone was delighted to see him, and he was taken in at once to the kitchen for a quick meal. The girls kept asking what was in his bulging saddlebags, and John Loughlan questioned his cousin about the trip north.

The next few days were hectic, getting the house decorated for Christmas, baking cookies and breads and finishing the Christmas sewing. Breed hardly spent two minutes alone with John.

Breed had told the girls about the Christmas trees that were put up in houses in Boston, and they begged for one too. So, early Christmas Eve morning, Hugh and the warmly dressed little girls started out to look for a small pine tree to chop down and bring home. Loughlan stayed and, when all was quiet, called Breed in from the kitchen.

She came into the small room he used for an office, wiping her hands on her apron, trying to look calmer than she felt.

He took her hands in his and, looking at her, said, "Breed, will you marry me? I know I'm not going about this right, but we need you—the girls need you..." And then, in a rush he added, "...and love you."

Breed was stunned, weak in the knees and nearly in tears. She asked, "Are you sure? For me to stay just for the little ones?"

Loughlan took her in his arms and whispered, "Won't you stay because I love you?"

She nodded into his chest. "Had best tell you," she said, "it's pregnant I am and this time next year there will be four children at your table!"

He laughed and swung her around, "My dear girl!"

Breed was so happy she could only smile.

The children burst into the room. "Uncle Hugh needs help with the tree we found. Come now, Papa." So John withdrew his arms from around Breed, and she from him, and each went to their appointed tasks.

After dinner that night John Loughlan gathered them all together, even Blanca and Susu, and announced that he and Breed were to be married as soon as possible. The little girls were delighted and Lita looked as pleased as a cat who had just finished off the last of the cream. Only Hugh Shepard seemed surprised but wished the happy couple his best. Later, Lita and Breed took the little girls off to bed and excused themselves, leaving the men to their cheroots and brandy in front of the fire. Breed was exhausted. As she fell asleep she heard John Loughlan loudly exclaim, "God damn you say!"

John stood at the fireplace. Hugh slumped disconsolately in a chair. "Are you sure?" John asked him.

"Yes," Hugh answered, and both lapsed into a discouraged silence.

Everyone was awake early Christmas morning. The little girls ran from bedroom to bedroom demanding the adults get up so they could open their gifts. John seemed distracted but was pleased with the two plaid flannel shirts and the large work handkerchiefs. Hugh Shepard also received two shirts of navy blue flannel. The girls were wild over the new dresses and pinafores and matching rag dolls from Breed and Lita. Hugh had given Belle a paint box, Daisy a set of paper dolls and Nicky two books of nursery rhymes. He had brought Breed a beautiful woolen shawl from up north, and for Lita a gold chatelaines belt with a small pencil and pad of paper enclosed in a book not three inches long. There were also scissors and a chain for household keys. He also gave John and Lita boxes of Havana cheroots. John surprised the children by having Huron Del Gado bring in his gift—a large three-story nine-room dollhouse with lots of furniture. There was also a family of dolls to live in the house. For Lita, he had an elegant bottle of the finest French perfume.

Wrapping Breed up in her new shawl, he took her outside to the front patio where they could be alone. It was a beautiful, clean and crisp morning and the air was scented with the burning logs in the fireplace. They sat on the bench beneath one of the bare sycamores that gave the ranch its name. He held her hand and from his watch pocket took a beautiful gold ring with a large pearl set in a pronged manner. Slipping it on her finger, he said, "Dear girl, this was my grandmother's and was to go to Belle one day. But will you wear it until I can get you your very own?"

Breed was so happy the tears were spilling from her eyes even as she laughed. "Oh, my John, thank you!"

Holding her hand tightly, he said, "We must talk. I had planned to have us married within the month, but Hugh has brought us disturbing news. He says that while he was in San Francisco he saw my wife, and she did not divorce me!"

Breed felt as though she could not breathe. "Your wife!" she said. "What wife? I, we thought you a widower!"

"God that I were," snarled Loughlan. He stood up and began to pace back and forth in front of Breed. "I met Elaine de Val when we were both living in San Francisco. I was a student and she lived with her father at the French consulate. She was, is, beautiful: tiny, dark hair and eyes that you could drown in. She is also spoiled, self-centered and determined to have her way. We were married only three months after we first met. We took a short wedding trip to Mexico City, then returned here to the rancho. We spent a lot of time in Los Angeles, rather than here, and though she didn't particularly want children breezed through all three pregnancies. As long as my mother was alive and here, Elaine seemed satisfied. She had jewels, clothes, even her own French maid. And we, rather she, went out socially all the time. That's why we have two rooms at the hotel, her pied-a-terre she called it. When my mother died suddenly, Elaine was in her seventh month with Nicole. She seemed so lost, as soon as she was able to travel after Nicky was born, she told me she was going to live in Los Angeles. I thought it was just she needed a rest from the children and me, but she planned otherwise."

John stopped for a moment, looking at Breed and taking a

deep breath. "Elaine never had much to do with the care of the girls after two or three visits with them. In town it was evidently clear she didn't miss them and she was just a pretty lady to our daughters. So I stopped carting them to town to visit her. After six months I suggested she come home. She smiled bewitchingly and announced she wanted a divorce. She would live in San Francisco and must be properly provided for financially! I was stunned and hurt. I tried to talk to her, but she laughed and gave me her lawyer's name. I stormed out of the room, went to see the lawyer, signed a stack of papers and settled money on her. Then I went home to our children. In a few weeks, I heard she had sailed for San Francisco and was installed at the Royal Louis Hotel. Her lawyer sent more papers that I signed and I presumed that by then we were divorced.

"My daughters needed a mother, I needed a wife, so I wrote to Mr. Potts and you came into my life."

Breed had been sitting still as a statue, listening to him and not wanting to distract him from his thoughts. She stood up now and went to him. "My dear, do not worry. It will all work out now. Tell me how Hugh found out that Elaine had not divorced you."

"He met her at a party at one of her society friends' home. Hugh is always in demand at such doings. He's a real ladies' man, knows how to talk and drink, too, and all of that. By now there she was, dressed fit to kill with three young men dancing attendance. She asked after me and Hugh said I was planning to remarry. She laughed and said if I did I'd be a bigamist. She hadn't gone through with the divorce as being Mrs. John Loughlan gave her more social prominence than being a gay divorcee. So, dear girl, there you have it."

Breed did not know what to say. John Loughlan took her in his arms and kissed her fiercely. "By God, I leave tomorrow for San Francisco to settle this once and for all. She deserted us so there are grounds enough. Breed, I do love you, so please be patient. We will be married before the little one arrives, I promise!"

Breed was silent but she knew she could not marry a divorced man, ever.

Later in the day John and Hugh took the girls out for a walk. As they tidied the parlor and set the table for dinner, Breed told Lita all that John had said. Lita was shocked and threw up her hands in disgust. "Hombres!" she wrote on her ever-present pad of paper.

Breed smiled wanly. She knew full well how Lita would have settled things. Lita was writing again. Hugh had asked her to sail with him to China on the Sara Blue. Panicked, Breed asked if she wanted to. Lita shook her head and folded the linen napkins.

The thought of Lita's leaving, and of her own situation—pregnant, alone in a distant land from all she knew—almost brought her to tears. When the table was set, Lita drew Breed to the little bench in the hall, sat down and again wrote on her pad. "Where you go, I go. I stay till little one comes; when you marry I go to Los Angeles to sew."

Breed read the note. "To sew?" she said. "What do you mean?"

"I have shop?" wrote Lita. "Sew for money."

"Of course!" Breed was excited. "You will be like the ladies who make the clothes in the magazines!" The idea was thrilling. Breed forgot her own problems and began planning Lita's shop! She knew money would not be a problem, as Lita still had some of her diamonds and her pay from John.

"Much to plan," wrote Lita, "but first marriage and baby."

"Dear friend," Breed said. The two young women sat in companionable silence, and there the men and children found them.

The children were full of chatter and questions all through dinner. After the serving of the flaming plum pudding, John told the girls he must leave the next morning "on business" but would return soon. Hugh Shepard said he too would be leaving as the Sara Blue was ready for the trip to China. The rest of the meal was spent in deciding what treasure Hugh would find and what he would bring back.

Blanca, her nieces and Huron Del Gado had gone to a family Christmas at Blanca's brother's home over near Pasadena. They would not be back for another day, so Breed cleaned up the kitchen while Lita got the girls settled in bed.

Breed helped John pack a carpetbag with a change of clothes and his shaving things. "Would, will you come to bed with me, John?" she shyly asked.

"No, dearest, you're exhausted, I can tell," he said. "Once I get into your bed you won't be able to drag me out, and Hugh and I must be away early." They sat on John's bed, kissed and acted like any loving engaged couple.

In the parlor, Lita and Hugh sat one on either side of the fire, happily smoking the Christmas cheroots.

The men left very early in the morning. Breed had fixed a good breakfast to hold them until they reached Los Angeles. As they were leaving, she wished Hugh "Godspeed and safe home" and whispered to John, "Vaya con dios, mi amore." He kissed her and they were gone just as the day was breaking.

✣ CHAPTER NINETEEN ✣

In San Francisco, the holiday weather had not been pleasant. Elaine Loughlan was in the midst of a temper tantrum. She drank far too much champagne at the Christmas dinner party the night before and allowed Captain Broderick, her current favorite, far too much liberty in his attentions to her. Usually, she was very careful to guard against any behavior—at least publicly—that would compromise her, or give John Loughlan ammunition should he decide to follow through with their divorce. She would have to speak to Captain Broderick.

"Nette," she said, "bring me a headache powder now... then my writing case." Her lady's maid of several years, Annette Corley, could tell from Madam's voice it was going to be a long morning. Fortunately, there was a knock at the door of the suite. "Ah, flowers and a note for Madam," she thought as she took the bouquet from the bellboy. "This will sweeten her temper." Hurrying, because she could hear Elaine calling again, she put the note, a rose from the bouquet and the headache powder on the breakfast tray and took it to her Mistress.

The maid marveled that such a spoiled and pampered woman should look so well, so beautiful after the late hours she had kept and the amount of drink she must have consumed. Her dark, curling hair was in disarray and the blue smudges beneath her eyes accented her pale but perfect complexion. Unfortunately, all was spoiled when the beauty opened her rosebud mouth and snarled, "Where is my headache powder, fool?"

Arranging the tray on the bed, Nette handed her a glass containing the powder mixed with mineral water. As her Mistress drank, the maid produced the note and gave a short weather report. "It rains still, Madam, but there is hope of clearing tomorrow."

Elaine Loughlan ate her breakfast while Nette tidied the bedroom. After a few moments, Elaine announced, "My note is from Sir Francis Madfield. We met last night at the party. He's very wealthy, quite nice looking, older, of course. He will take tea here at the hotel this afternoon. What shall I wear?"

Nette knew better than to offer a suggestion. Madam cared for no opinion save her own where clothes were concerned. Shortly thereafter, Elaine told the maid to ready her wine wool with the lace collars and cuffs. She would wear the matching hat, too, the one with the small face veil. By now she was standing before the French doors that led onto a small balcony. "This wretched rain," the little woman said, petulantly. "If it had stopped, I could have eaten out there."

In another suite on the same floor, Sra. Costa-Nunez, widow of the late Dr. Costa-Nunez of Havana, Cuba, and her traveling companion, Sr. Alfredo Miguel Ramos, also were having breakfast and planning their day.

"Alfredo!"

"Si, my dear?"

"As it will be too wet to go for a drive this afternoon, we shall attend the photographic display the hotel is having," the woman said. "A Senor Mornay is the artist."

"Si, my dear," was his answer, and so the die was cast.

Sra. Costa-Nunez was well into her middle years. She kept the ravages of age at bay, though it took longer and longer. Her rather full figure was corseted into a small waist, her graying hair dyed and her face powdered and creamed and rouged into a pleasant-enough mask. It was her eyes that gave her away—black, with no light or life. Her smile never reached beyond her mouth.

Alfredo Ramos had been Carolina Costa-Nunez's lover for ten years. He had squandered his inheritance at the gaming tables almost as soon as he received it and, being of a naturally lazy disposition, he had seen his alliance with Carolina as a godsend. She was eleven years older than him and as mean as a snake when crossed. But one must do what one must. Besides, Alfredo was frightened of Carolina. One did not incur her wrath needlessly. He was still an attractive man. True, his dark hair was thinning, but the grey at the temples was distinguished. Of medium height and build, with only the smallest paunch, he was quite satisfied with himself. She fed, dressed and housed him exceedingly well. Life was comfortable.

The photographic display was held in the small parlor off the hotel's main lobby. M. Mornay, the artist, had arranged many of his photos in groups on small easels set on tables, each group representing a different subject. One of his most interesting settings was titled, "Aboard the Sara Blue." He had pictures of the men in the rigging. Of Captain Shepard at the helm. And one of three young women sitting under their awning, Eliza reading, Lita sewing and Breed playing her guitar. He had placed a note beside it: "Three Graces." There also was a picture of Lita alone, looking regal and aloof at the ship's railing.

Carolina Costa-Nunez, with the ever-present Alfredo, entered the room like a man-of-war under full steam. When she came to the display of the photos from the Sara Blue, she stopped, transfixed, and gasped, "Dios! Alfredo, attend... do you see, in the photo! The bitch Lita!" Alfredo did see and held his breath, fearing Carolina would make a scene. At that moment, M. Mornay joined them and began his chatter. Sra. Costa-Nunez turned slowly and looked at the little man. Her black eyes held him tightly, as a hungry snake would a mouse, and then she smiled and said with great effort, "Who... who are the three young women in this picture?"

"Ah, Madam, one of my best I feel," Mornay said. "They were shipmates with me on part of my voyage." Here, he made a grave error, not having really understood who and why the three women were aboard. He told Carolina, "The small girl is Mrs. John Loughlan of California, the other two ladies her companions."

Just then, Elaine Loughlan entered and stood to the rear of Carolina and Alfredo. She was dressed in her wine and lavender gown and wore a small hat of wine and lavender feathers, a face veil over her eyes. If one did not look too closely, she could be mistaken for a much younger woman. At that moment, a bellboy called to her from the doorway. "Mrs. Loughlan, Mrs. John Loughlan?"

Elaine turned. "Yes?"

"A telegraph for you, ma'am," the boy said, handing it to her and tipping his cap.

Carolina Costa-Nunez turned and looked closely at Elaine. Too vain to wear spectacles, she was shortsighted and saw only a small, dark-haired woman. Taking Alfredo's arm, she said, "We must leave." They walked rapidly into the lobby.

Elaine excused herself and opened the telegram. It was from John, telling her he would be in San Francisco shortly. Smiling at Sr. Francis, she tucked the paper into her small purse and said, "Nothing important. Shall we continue examining this display?"

"Righto and then a spot of tea," the gentleman answered.

Life was not easy the next few days for Alfredo Ramos. Carolina was sunk in gloom and drinking heavily. "The bitch Lita should be dead—or a slave on a plantation!" she cried. "What is she doing here in San Francisco? What is she? A lady's maid?"

"Carolina, perhaps she is not here, just because you see her picture with the woman Loughlan does not...."

"Silence!" she snapped. "She is here. I feel it, and she will somehow tell about my husband's death. You must remove her at once!"

Remembering how vengeful Carolina was, he had no doubt what she meant. Poisoning an ill old man was one thing, but trying to kill a young woman, especially one who seemed to have made important connections, was something frightfully different.

"Carolina, this is not possible," he said. "We should just leave San Francisco as quickly as we can. You said you wanted to return to Mexico City. What better time?" When the woman did not answer, he paced the room nervously, fiddling first with his watch fob, then his cravat.

"We must plan carefully," Carolina whispered. "Sit down and listen to me."

❧ CHAPTER TWENTY ❧

John Loughlan arrived in the city on the 28th of December and went immediately to the hotel. He identified himself at the front desk, reserved a room for the night and sought out his wife.

Elaine Loughlan was in the midst of a holiday tea she was hosting for friends and gentlemen admirers. Most of the older ladies had left and the "tea" had given way to a table of wine and liquors. There was much laughter and high spirits, to the point that Nette the maid bent down to Elaine as she was passing a tray of cheeses and hissed, "The gentlemen become too loud. They have had too much to drink. Remember your reputation, Madam."

Elaine gave the maid an irritated look but knew she was right. She beckoned Sr. Francis and Captain Slater and asked if they could start the boisterous men on their way.

As the party was clearing, John Loughlan arrived. He took one look at the condition of the room and several of the guests and he lost his temper. "Madam, we must talk now!"

Elaine had also taken a little too much in the way of liquid refreshment for so early in the day. She flared at Loughlan. "How dare you speak to me like that!" she said. "Do you not see I have guests?"

The four or five men and women who remained were very interested in the scene. They hoarded every look and word, for it would surely be the main topic of conversation at many dinner tables that night.

Sir Francis, not knowing John, began to intervene. "See here, sir, this lady does not wish to talk...."

Whereas, John said icily, "This lady is my wife and we have urgent business. I suggest... no demand everyone leave so we may conduct it. Thank you." The remaining guests paraded out. They were agog. Everyone had thought Elaine Loughlan a wealthy young widow—and here was a husband very much alive. And a very presentable husband at that, thought the ladies.

When the room was cleared, John turned to Nette. "Please leave us," he said. "See that we are not disturbed."

At first, Elaine was going to quarrel with John. But seeing the fury in his face, she shrank back onto the sofa. John Loughlan stood over the beautiful woman he had once loved. "I want us to be divorced at once," he said. "Either you seek it tomorrow or I will, and I have more than enough proof of your shortcomings, desertion only one of them!"

Elaine realized he was determined to divorce her. Allowing two tears to run down her cheeks would play havoc with her makeup. "You can have your divorce," she said, "but I will take the girls!"

John knew her so well. "Fine, I will have another family," he replied. "Boys this time. Let everyone in polite society see what a fine mother you are. People will be so surprised that you have such grown children. Take them gladly."

Biting her lip in anger, she looked at the man standing over her. People would call her an old woman with growing girls tagging always behind. When she saw neither tears nor threats would change his mind, and wondering who this new love was that could make John stand against her, she stood up.

"Very well," she said, pushing him aside. "You can have your divorce and your children. I plan to return to France shortly. Anyway, life here grows dull and provincial. Tonight, I dine at the Trumbels and my lawyer, Edgar Gates, will surely be there. I will tell him you will be in to see him in the morning. Are you satisfied?"

"Thank you, yes," he said. "You will, of course, be well provided for. Mr. Williams, our family lawyer, will see to our side of things." Picking up his hat from a table, he wished Elaine Loughlan "good evening" and walked out of her life.

In Carolina Costa-Nunez's suite down the hall, the two Cubans sat at a small table drinking. Alfredo was frightened. He knew Carolina's ability for vengeance. He also knew she would make him her agent. He hadn't actually killed anyone yet, but he sensed that only Lita's death would calm Carolina, who was acting like a person possessed.

"Tomorrow night, no wait, we must establish that we are, that we have no connection to these people," she began. "In the morning I will tell the hotel we are leaving. Find out what ships are sailing on, say, New Year's Day. Then we will put it about that you have become ill. You will take your meals in bed so that even that wretched hotel maid who helps me dress will see how ill you are. Then, New Year's Eve, when this Mrs. Loughlan will surely be out, you will slip into her room by way of our balcony, kill her and come at once back here and retire again to your sick bed."

"Madre de Dios," gasped the man, "have you lost your reason, Carolina? Why can we not just leave the country?"

"Coward," she said. "Because if Lita conveys the circumstances of my husband's death, we will both be in danger, and welcomed nowhere! No, we must make arrangements. Don't forget to complain of a headache while the maid is here tonight." She rose, patted the man's hand and said pleasantly, "All will be well."

John Loughlan was at Elaine's lawyer's office the moment it opened. When lawyer Gates tried to talk him out of the divorce, John repeated his threat to seek one on his own terms. Gates drew up the necessary papers to start the proceedings and had John sign them. They parted with the lawyer's assurances that everything would be expedited and he would contact Loughlan's Los Angeles lawyer soon. John thanked him and, carpet bag in hand, headed for the harbor and boarded a ship for home, leaving that very day on the evening tide.

The night that John Loughlan had left for San Francisco, a winter storm blew into Southern California and heavy rain drenched Los Angeles and outlying areas. The rain continued all the next day. The children played all morning with their new toys while Breed and Lita straightened the house. In the afternoon, Blanca and her nieces returned from their Christmas visiting. While the women dried out in the kitchen, the little girls brought in their toys and took the two young maids to see the dollhouse in the nursery. Breed asked Blanca, "Did not Huron Del Gado return with you?"

"Si, Senorita," Blanca answered, "but we met a posse from Los Angeles on the road. They said the hombres from Vasquez's gang who got away had been seen in San Fernando. Indeed, they had robbed a stagecoach. The posse was on the way to look for them and Huron went with them. He said our ranch hands will be back tonight, so we are all safe."

Blanca then began to tell all about the wonderful "Natividad" celebrations with her family. Breed was happy they had enjoyed themselves but was a little uneasy because there were no men on the ranch and bandits were about. The rain continued through the night and into the early morning. But then, without warning, the clouds piled over the mountains, the sun came out and a warm wind blew from the desert.

The children were wild to be outside and pestered Breed to take them for a walk. "We must wait till the grass dries," she said. "You go and play on the patio. Your swing should be dry." She sent one of the young maids out to keep an eye on the children and went to see why Lita hadn't come out yet.

When she opened Lita's door, she saw her friend still in bed. Lita's dark skin was ashy and she was clearly in pain. "Lita, why didn't you come and tell me you were ill?" Breed asked. "Is it a toothache again?"

Lita nodded and turned her face so Breed could see the swelling in her jaw. "Oh, you poor dear, I'll be right back."

Breed hurried to her room and took the small bottle of laudanum from the box on the shelf in her closet. She was very careful with it, as the nun in Havana and the good doctor in Los Angeles had warned her. She went to the kitchen, fixed a cup of hot coffee and added sugar, cream and several drops of the painkiller. She took it into Lita, absently tucking the small bottle into her deep apron pocket.

"Here you are, dear," she said, offering the cup to Lita. "Drink this while I plump up your pillows. It will still the pain and make you sleep." Lita drank the coffee and lay back on her pillows. The drug was fast-acting and in minutes Breed saw Lita's eyes close and the lines of pain in her face ease. She took the empty cup to the kitchen. "Lita has another toothache, Blanca," Breed said. "She's asleep now so we must keep the girls quiet. Will you pack a little picnic lunch? I'll take them off on a long walk."

"Si, Chica, but it is still so wet from the rain..."

"Perhaps it's drier now," Breed said. "I'll go out back and look at the path that leads down the hill. They love walking along that little stream." Putting on her wool shawl and the old boots she used to wear in snowy Boston, Breed went out to see if the wind had done its job. As she wandered down the hill, she found it hard to comprehend that it was a few days after Christmas and here she was walking in the warm sunshine, not really needing a shawl.

As she reached the bottom of the hill, she decided it was still damp. The girls, however, would be fine. Then she heard the soft jangle of a horse's bridle, and from behind a large stand of bushes two mounted horsemen approached.

😸 CHAPTER TWENTY-ONE 😸

"Good morning, gentlemen, may I help you?" She spoke pleasantly but became afraid when she noticed the men were dressed as Mexican cowboys: large sombreros and a great deal of silver on the horses' tack. The two men spoke quietly to one another, so softly she could understand only a word or two. Then the smaller and more disheveled of the two dismounted and produced a large six-shooter, pointing it directly at Breed. She could feel her heart beating so fast she felt faint. Should she stay or run, taking the chance he might shoot her? What if the little girls came around the house and saw them?

"What do you want?" she inquired, remembering there were no men at the ranch yet. It was up to her to keep them from the house.

"Senora, how many men in casa?" the small man asked.

Breed said, "Only seven, but the rest are in the east pasture and will be in for lunch soon." She prayed they believed her.

The mounted man said something to the other and told Breed, "Get on the horse quickly." When she stood her ground, he too drew his pistol and in a nasty tone told her, "We will hostage you. Mount now or you will be dead hostage!" The small man came closer, grabbed her arm and pulled her to his horse. Now she was truly frightened, not only of the banditos but also of the idea of mounting the great brown animal.

"Sir," she stammered." I...I do not know how to ride a horse." Breed thought it best they not know she understood Spanish. The mounted man was becoming angry. "Hoist the blonde cow," he yelled. "We must be on our way!" The small man holstered his gun, cupped his hands and ordered Breed to climb up. Breed had thought the morning sickness had passed, but it took all her concentration to keep from vomiting.

The mounted man snarled, "Get up, senora, now!"

She grabbed the saddle horn and with a boost from the small man hiked her long skirts up and threw herself onto the saddle. "God save us!" she gasped as the horse sidestepped and neighed.

"Move back, senora," the small man said. "I will be in front or my dear Paloma will not be happy." It took them a moment to arrange themselves. Breed did not want to hold onto the small man. He was not only scruffy but smelled quite rank. She again felt nausea. The horse trotted off after the other man. As they turned to the east and the valley, Breed looked back up the hill and saw Belle standing at the corner of the house watching them. Pretending to resettle her shawl, she turned and put her finger to her lips and prayed the child would not call and put the whole rancho in danger.

Belle watched as Breed rode off with the strange-looking men. Then she went into the kitchen. "Blanca, where has Breed gone?"

"Ah, Chica, she goes to see where you and your sisters may have a picnic."

"No, she's on a horse with two horsemen, wearing those big hats people wear at Fandangos," Belle said. "And they're riding toward the mountains."

"Madre de Dios, what do you say?" the startled cook asked the child. Belle repeated her story.

Poor Blanca did not know what to do. The strangers were surely banditos stealing away the senorita! Lita was deep in a drugged sleep, the ranch hands would not return until afternoon and the only man around was old Tomas, who was half-blind and could hardly mount a horse! She did not want to frighten the children, so she fed them and sent them to play in the nursery. And all the while she prayed for Breed's safety.

The two men and Breed rode east for an hour or so before climbing into the foothills. Carefully, Breed tried to keep track of the route they had taken. Hours of jolting atop the big horse had given her a splitting headache. And the difficult position of riding astride the horse was giving her discomfort elsewhere. "Thank God I wore me long johns today and my heavy boots," she thought. Occasionally, the men spoke between themselves, but they ignored their hostage.

CHAPTER TWENTY-ONE

"Please, senor, when do we stop?" she asked the small man.

"When him say we stop," he answered, pointing toward the lead horseman.

The winter afternoon was fast waning and she realized it would be dark all too soon. Would they tie her up? Could she try to escape? They were now well into the foothills, the vegetation mostly bushes and grass and very few trees. The landscape was littered with great stone boulders that must have been there forever.

Shortly, the men stopped in a small clearing. Many boulders formed a half circle. In the middle, she noticed what looked like an old fire pit. The men had used this spot for a camp previously.

The men dismounted. The small one led Paloma to one of the flat rocks and helped Breed climb off the horse. Breed could hardly stand. Now what, she wondered. The small man gathered a few twigs and dry grass and started a fire. The other unsaddled the horses, leaving only their bridles. He brought his saddlebags to Breed and, roughly, told her to fix them supper.

Sliding off the rock, Breed took the saddlebags and looked through them. A battered coffee pot, a sack of coffee with no water, some sausage and tortillas. The small man brought her his full canteen and gave a toothless smile. "We eat, si?" he said. "Then we rest, si?"

Breed looked down on him, rolled her eyes and thought, "Not we. Me, little man," and she put cut-up sausage in a small pan that had also been in the saddlebag. The sausage was so greasy she reached into her apron pocket for a handkerchief to wipe her hands. She felt the small bottle of laudanum. Again, she went into the saddlebag and found two tin cups. The men were busy settling and feeding the horses for the night. They were behind her and could not see as she nearly emptied the little bottle into the cups. When the coffee and sausage were ready, she poured coffee into the cups, filled the plates and took them across the clearing to the men. She returned to the fire, took a couple of the flour tortillas and a little sausage and sat down on a flat rock. Trying not to look too worried or guilty, she wondered if perhaps so much of the drug might kill the men? And once they were asleep, what did she think she could do?

It was night now. Across the fire ring the men were still eating, though Breed thought the big man seemed sluggish. He put down his empty cup and called for more, then toppled over. The small man had finished his meal. Leering, he patted the ground beside him and told Breed to come keep warm. She didn't move from the rock, so he rose and started toward her. He took ten steps and fell into the fire pit. Breed jumped up, ran and pulled him to one side and brushed off a bit of ash. She sat back on her heels. "Now what?" she mused.

All afternoon, she had tried to keep a sense of direction. The nearly full moon had just risen above the crest of the hill. She looked into the night sky and located the North Star, then took the gun belts the men had removed. She picked up two more tortillas, folded them into her pocket and approached one of the horses. "Come now, you great beast," she said. "We must take both you and your friend away." She untied the horses and, pulling them along, turned her back on the unconscious men and started out due west.

The path was hardly visible. After slipping and sliding, she realized the horses would do better leading her. She let Paloma take the lead. The two gun belts Breed carried were heavy, so within an hour she took one of the six shooters, stuck it in her apron waist and dropped the rest behind a rock. She traveled on in the chilly night, her skirt and petticoats tucked up to keep them dry as well to make it easier to walk. All sorts of sad thoughts raced through her worried mind. Would she find her way home? Or would she wander, lost in the mountains until she died? She missed the little girls, Lita, the rancho and most of all John Loughlan.

Breed and the horses walked for four hours. The moon was well on its way west, but she kept it always on her left. Calculating how long Lita slept when she drank just a small dose of laudanum, she decided the men would be unconscious for at least six or seven hours—if they weren't dead!

She must rest. She could tell the horses were tired too by the way they kept stopping. The night was full of noises. The hoot of an owl, the rustle of the bushes as small animals scurried for cover. Twice, she heard coyotes calling over the hills. Thankfully, they didn't sound close. "Blast," she said as she banged her leg on an outcrop of rock. "No farther, boys, we rest here." She tethered the horses beside the trail and lay down on a slab of granite, tucking her skirts around her legs and her shawl over her head and shoulders. Looking at the moon, she said a prayer for all she loved and asked the Virgin to lead her to safety. Then she slept.

Just before dawn, something woke her. She lay there, cold, stiff and trying to remember what had brought her out of sleep. Then it happened. It wasn't a sound but a movement within herself! Like a strong butterfly hitting her stomach! It was John's child. It had quickened. It was alive and she would do anything to protect it. It was so thrilling, her baby was letting her know she must be up and on her way.

"Saints, what I wouldn't do for a cup of tea or coffee and a nice bowl of mush," she thought as she relieved herself behind a bush. She rearranged her skirts and long johns, untying the horses and giving them a push along the trail.

Chewing on a tortilla, Breed realized that morning was upon them. She knew she must make haste and find help before the men woke up and followed her. She walked for three hours and recognized two things: the trail was gently descending and a buzzing could be heard. As she looked around she saw eight wooden bee hives just below her to the east of the curving trail. She also noticed a faint track leading from the hives to the valley floor. "Bees! That means there must be a farm not far away," she thought. Tugging the horses, she hurried as fast as she could to the track leading from the hive, down the path and over a small rise. In the distance, she saw a rather ramshackle farm, smoke rising from the chimney and cattle grazing behind the small barn. No more than a mile, surely, she gladly thought. Breed started for the farm, but stumbled while hurrying across a wash between the bottom of the hill and the fences of the property. She shot out her hands to stop her fall and skinned them badly. She stood up, brushing her skirts with one hand and wiping her tear-blurred eyes with the back of the other.

Despite her condition, Breed saw a wondrous sight: A large woman working a row in a kitchen garden!

Breed cried out, "Hello, please, can you help me, please?" The woman did not hear her until she had called out several more times.

The woman stood stock-still as the bedraggled young woman with a pistol stuck in her apron waistband led two horses to the small wooden gate at the end of the trail.

"Mrs., I'm Breed Seastrum, housekeeper at Rancho Dos Aliso over that way," Breed said, pointing westward.

The older woman, tall and sturdy, dark hair streaked with grey and pinned in a no-nonsense bun, noticed Breed's injured hands and her tears. She put down her hoe. "I'm Mrs. Muller," she said, opening the gate. "Come in."

As Breed entered, the woman called out, "Hans, Bette, Frida get up, we have company!" She pointed to a chair at the kitchen table and told Breed to sit. Breed gratefully did so as three youngsters came in to the small room. There was a boy of sixteen or so, large boned like his mother, a pretty girl of fourteen or so and another girl about ten. "Get you out back and stable the two horses," the woman said. "Bette, go make my bed, take a brick from the fireplace and get the bed warmed. This girl is frozen through."

Breed looked around as she sipped strong, hot wonderful coffee. The kitchen was hardly more than a lean-to but it did have a flagstone floor and oiled paper in the window.

Breed asked Mrs. Muller if she worked the farm alone. "Mr. Muller is with the railroad and don't get home often, so you could say I work it alone," she said. Both of the older children had returned and stood staring curiously at Breed as she ate bread and small pieces of cheese. "Mrs. Muller," Breed said, "we must get the sheriff." Then, to the astonishment of the whole family, she recounted all that had happened to her the day before.

They talked at length about what was best to do. It was decided that Hans would ride at once to Los Angeles to alert the sheriff. "Hans, you best take both horses in case the banditos come looking for Miss Breed," his mother said.

Excitedly, the boy asked, "Should I take Miss Breed's pistol, Mutti?"

Breed looked at him, smiled and said, "Not in this life, Bucko. After you talk to the lawmen, tell them I said you must stay at the hotel where John... where Mr. Loughlan has rooms. Eat, then come home in the morning." Disappointed but still excited about his errand, the boy left to saddle one of the horses. His mother wrapped bread and cheese in a napkin and filled a canteen with apple cider.

Everyone stood on the small porch and watched the boy mount up, the other horse on a lead.

"Hans, ask them to send word to Rancho Dos Aliso that I'm safe," Breed said.

"Goodbye," he said, "and girls take care of Mutti and Miss Breed." And then he rode off.

Mrs. Muller could see Breed was on her last legs. Leading her into the house, she pointed to a curtained-off area of the small room. "You get into bed before you fall down," she said, directing the exhausted younger woman. Bette and Frida stood at the foot of the iron bedstead and watched as their mother helped Breed out of her dress and boots, pulled the covers down and tucked her in as though she were nine years old. Breed turned her head on the linen pillowcase and saw that it had been beautifully embroidered with colored floss. Bette saw her looking at the words and blushed. Mrs. Muller told Breed that Bette made the pillowcase for her as a birthday gift.

"How beautiful," Breed said quietly. "It's like laying your head on a bed of wild flowers." Soon, she was sound asleep.

Mrs. Muller gave Bette the dress, Frida the boots. Brush them well, she told the girls, and put them behind the curtain. "Remember mine kinder," she said, "should strange men, one tall, one small, come walking out of the hills looking for her, we know nothing." And then she went back to her garden and hoeing.

Breed slept most of the day. When she awoke, it was late afternoon. She felt sore and hungry but otherwise in good health. Out back, the girls were shooing the few chickens into their coop, a sturdy one with river rocks as a base and a heavy door to latch.

Mrs. Muller came around the side of the house carrying a wooden bucket of millet. She saw Breed watching the antics of the girls as they tried to corral the chickens. "We must lock them up tight at night," she said. "The coyotes like nothing more for dinner than one of my plump hens."

In the small kitchen, they sat at the table and ate wonderful cabbage soup and chunks of cornbread with cups of still warm milk.

"Oh sure, Mrs. Muller, you're a grand cook!" Breed said. "I haven't had soup this fine since I left my aunt's house in Boston."

"Boston? You come all that way to be stolen by bandits?" Bette asked. The Mullers had migrated some years earlier from Pennsylvania by wagon train. With only the smallest sigh of disappointment, Mrs.

Muller said, "We were not always so poor, but my husband longed to go west, so here we are."

They were sitting around the fireplace now, with only the flames for light. Breed told them of the Sara Blue, Lita and Eliza and their final arrival in California. She was yawning, so Mrs. Muller banked the fire and sent everyone to bed. She would sleep with Bette, Frida in Hans' bed in the loft. Wishing all good night, Breed again climbed into bed, but this time she made sure the loaded pistol was on the floor underneath.

❧ CHAPTER TWENTY-TWO ❧

Hans reached Los Angeles well after dark and searched for the sheriff's office. Finding it, he tied the horses to a hitching post and went inside. He asked for the sheriff and said, "I have a message from Breed Seastrum of Rancho Dos Aliso."

The men in the room hushed and looked at Hans. A middle-aged man wearing a bandage told him to speak quickly. It seemed that the ranch hands at Rancho Dos Aliso had arrived home two nights earlier and heard from the cook about Breed's abduction.

After making a plan, Huron Del Gado sent a man into town to have the sheriff gather a posse and meet him and the ranch hands as soon as possible. They would leave at sun-up so they would be able, God willing, to find the trail of the men who had kidnapped Breed. The posse should follow the Dos Aliso men's trail. The men from Los Angeles had been gone twenty-four hours with no news and the sheriff had been planning to send more men out. The two men who took Breed were without doubt dangerous stragglers of the Vasquez gang and must be caught.

As everyone was asking questions at once, no one noticed when Don Diego arrived. He was dressed in evening clothes and looked very impressive. "Sheriff, I have just come from a dinner party at the

227

Mayor's and everyone is saying Breed Seastrum has been abducted," he said. "Is this true?" Most of the men knew Don Diego. His family was among the wealthiest in Southern California. They stepped aside and pushed Hans Muller forward. He told his tale again. Everyone was amazed at Breed's bravery and daring. "So she is safe, you say?" the Don asked Hans.

"Yes, sir. She told me to go to the hotel and sleep and come back tomorrow morning to take her home. Only she forgot to tell me which hotel."

"No matter, Chico, I stay at the same hotel," Don Diego said. "I'll help you get settled. Then in the morning, I will drive my chaise out to your homestead and return Breed myself."

The sheriff thought that sounded like a good plan. He and other men would go along and let "Miss Breed tell us where she left those dogs."

So the gathering broke up with a promise to meet at dawn. Don Diego took Hans to the hotel and saw that he had a meal and was settled for the night. Exhausted and sore from spending long hours in the saddle, Hans tried to remember everything that had happened so he could tell his mother and sisters. But he was sound asleep in minutes.

At dawn, the posse and others left for the Muller homestead, Don Diego in his one-horse chaise and Hans with the outlaws' horses.

In Santa Barbara, John Loughlan paced impatiently on board the ship from San Francisco, waiting for the cargo to be unloaded. He longed to be home with his children and his love.

In San Francisco, Elaine Loughlan was considering what she would wear to the elegant party at the British Consul's home. And in another suite just down the hall, a murder was being planned with great care.

The posse reached the Muller's about noon. They were excited at the prospect of the hunt and listened carefully to Breed's directions. After an hour's rest and a bowl of Mrs. Muller's soup, they set off.

Shortly afterward, Don Diego and Hans arrived. The two young girls came running down the path, calling to their brother and telling him of the excitement caused by the posse. Breed and Mrs. Muller came out onto the porch just as Don Diego climbed down from his chaise. Tossing the reins to Hans, he said, "Will you take care of the horse? Feed him, and not too much water." With that, he tossed the boy a gold eagle coin and went up the path to greet Breed.

"Santa Maria, what poverty" he thought. He greeted Mrs. Muller with a small bow and put his arms around Breed. "Mi amor, you are safe, God be thanked."

Breed laughed and wriggled out of his embrace. "Don Diego, what a surprise. Have you come to fetch me home?"

"Si, and the sooner the better. Everyone is very worried."

Mrs. Muller looked at the handsome Don, not quite sure she liked him. But hospitality won out and she said, "Come in, sir. You have had a long ride. I can only offer you a small lunch, as the posse ate us out of house and home."

"Gracias, Senora, anything is welcome," he said, "but we must start back to town quickly, as it grows dark soon."

Shortly, he had eaten and was ushering Breed out the door in the waiting chaise. "Mrs. Muller, how can I thank you for your kindness?" Breed asked as they parted. "You saved my life. I will repay you somehow." She hugged the girls and touched her cheek to the older woman's.

"Come Breed," Don Diego said impatiently.

"We will meet again soon, dear friend," she called out to Mrs. Muller as Don Diego helped her up into the chaise.

"The horses are yours, Hans," she added as they started down the road.

They had gone a few minutes in silence when Don Diego spoke, "So, you are a heroine, mi corazon. Start at the beginning and tell me all that has happened."

And so she did.

When she had finished, he shook his head. "You are wonderful!"

"I am tired, dirty and dying to get home," she answered.

"We will not reach town until very late, but you can stay at the hotel."

"No, I want to go home, not to town. Oh please, Don Diego, I must go home."

Diego looked at Breed a moment. "I leave for Mexico City in three days. Breed, come with me. We will be so happy, and you will love Mexico. Mi amor, come with me."

Breed listened to the handsome man asking her to go away with him, calling her his love. "Diego, you must know how much I value your friendship, so I must be true with you. I... I'm carrying John Loughlan's child."

"Yes, si, I know. The nursemaid is sister to Mama's upstairs girl and she told Mama. What does it matter? You can have the child in Mexico and we will have a good wet nurse for it. I know the perfect house for you."

Breed stopped him with a raised hand. "Diego, would you marry a woman already with child from another man?"

Twilight was fading but Breed was still able to see Don Diego's head snap toward her, noting the look of shock on his face as he said, "Marriage? Marriage? How could I marry you? Am I not affianced to Maria Esperanta de Gratisis? Why else would we go to Mexico City? She and I are to be married the Saturday after Easter!"

Breed was embarrassed and shocked. "You meant I should go to Mexico as your mistress?"

"Now, mi amor, think on it. Marriage would not be allowed, between one of my family and a... a gringa!" he said in a pompous tone.

Breed could only shake her head. Men, she thought, and began to laugh. It really was so ridiculous. The man was not even wed yet and already he was planning on installing a mistress. Well, it would not be her, thank God. Please Lord, she thought, let John come home soon.

"What is so amusing, Breed?" asked Don Diego in a huff.

"Nothing. Nothing," she said. "I'm sorry. It's getting cold and I'm tired."

Wordlessly, Don Diego reached behind the seat and pulled out a large wool Tartan lap robe. He almost threw it at Breed. She wrapped herself in it and shortly fell deeply asleep.

She awoke to the sound of voices as Don Diego drove the chaise into the back entrance at Rancho Dos Aliso. Breed sat up. "Sure it's good to be home safe and sound!" she said. The kitchen had oil lamps lit and at the sound of the chaise the door flung open and Lita and Blanca rushed out. They were followed by two of the ranch hands who had stayed behind to guard the family. Lita was first to the chaise and helped Breed down.

"Don Diego, you must stay the night," Breed said over her shoulder as she hurried into the kitchen flanked by Lita and Blanca. "You have been traveling all day. Please come in." One of the ranch hands took the horse and led it toward the barn for a good rubdown and feed. Don Diego entered after the women, his usual impeccable attire dusty and wrinkled and much the worse for wear after a long day on the trail. Seeing his expression, Breed spent several minutes thanking him and instructing Blanca to prepare a meal for them. He was still grumpy but she did not care.

Later, when they had eaten and Don Diego had retired with a glass and bottle of brandy, Breed told the two women her story. Blanca threw her large apron over her face every time Breed told some particularly frightening bit. After awhile, Lita wrote on her pad that Breed must be tired and in need of a bath, so Blanca wished them good night and Breed went to bathe. Lita had seen that there was plenty of hot water and brought a bottle of scented bath oil to add to the tub.

Breed hadn't realized just how stiff and achy she was until she felt her muscles relaxing. She closed her eyes and said a small prayer of thanksgiving for her safe return and her unborn baby's safety too. In her room, Lita had put a warming pan in the bed and it was as snug as could be. Before Breed climbed into bed, she took the small bottle from her apron pocket and again hid it high in her closet. Lita came back in, removed the warming pan and, pulling the covers up to Breed's neck, patted her head and kissed her forehead. Breed reached for Lita's hand, squeezed and was asleep.

The coastal schooner John Loughlan had taken passage on arrived at the port of San Pedro early in the morning on the last day of December. He was the first passenger off the ship and went at once to the livery stable where he had left his horse. The ride into Los Angeles took most of the morning and the lawyer's office was still closed for lunch. John Loughlan knew that most of the lawyers went to Cooley's Restaurant, close to the courthouse, so he did too. As he suspected, his lawyer, Mr. Williams sat at a round table with five other lawyers and businessmen. When they saw John approaching, several rose to speak.

"Well, sir, you have one sure hellcat for a housekeeper!"

"Quite a gal, your Miss Seastrum, John."

"What do you mean, sir?" John asked.

"You do not know about her abduction and escape?" asked Williams.

"What are you saying? Tell me, is Breed...."

"Breed is the talk of the town, John. Come, let's sit at that empty table," Williams said. "You will excuse us, gentlemen."

When they were seated, and a waiter had taken John's order for lunch, the lawyer told him all that transpired since he left the day after Christmas.

John stood up and said, "I must go home at once. I must see she is all right!"

"Calm yourself, John, she is well," Williams said. "She is a brave young gal. Don Diego took her home and assured us all she was tired but in excellent spirits."

"I still must go," John said. "What if those men come looking for her?"

"Wait, son," said the lawyer. "Eat. There's more. The posse found the campsite. One of the men had been killed by a mountain lion, pretty badly mauled, I hear. The other had left him and started east. They followed his trail and found him dead in a gully. Evidently he had slipped and fallen, breaking his neck. They found jewelry and money stolen from the last raid the Vasquez gang made out in the valley. Eat, then you can go."

John wolfed down a huge bowl of soup and bread, drank his beer and rose to return home. Suddenly, he remembered why he had been looking for Williams. "Sir, Elaine and I wish to be divorced as soon as possible. Her lawyer, Mr. Edward Gates, will be contacting you. As soon as it's final, Breed and I will be married."

With that, he threw a few bills on the table, jammed his hat on his head and strode from the restaurant. At the stable, he traded his horse for a fresh one and left for Rancho Dos Aliso.

❧ CHAPTER TWENTY-THREE ❧

New Year's Eve in San Francisco promised to be cold and clear. At four in the afternoon, Elaine Loughlan had already started her lengthy toilette in preparation for a gala at the home of the Van Houtons. Nette was busy pressing the elegant rose brocade ball gown that Elaine would wear as her mistress soaked in her bath.

"After my bath, you must do my nails in that rose-colored nail paint I had sent from New York," Elaine said. "Then, I will rest till half-past six. Be sure you don't let me oversleep, and order champagne and have it ready when Sir Francis and Captain Slater arrive." Nette bobbed her head in assent, thinking, Mon Dieu, one would think I was stupid. Tell me once... hmmm tonight Jean Paul will surely try and make love to me, and perhaps I will let him. She shivered in anticipation.

Said Elaine, planning her own evening's diversion, "As I won't be in till very late, Nette, you needn't wait up for me. I'll get myself ready for bed."

You and who else, Nette thought. The brave captain or the very rich Sr. Francis?

Just down the hall in the rooms of Sra. Costa-Nunez, a hotel maid had just brought in a tray of soup and hot mulled wine for the sickly Sr. Alfredo. He, in turn, was languishing in the bed, his throat wrapped in strings of linen reeking of liniment. If truth be told, he really did feel poorly. He did not know if he could cold-bloodedly kill someone. Carolina usually took care of the messy things they had done.

"Madame, I do think Sr. Alfredo has a fever," the maid said. "He looks right glassy-eyed to me."

"Si, he will remain in bed one more day and if he is still ill, we will send for a physician." Carolina wanted the woman to leave, but the maid kept puttering around.

"Will Madame need me tonight?" she asked.

"No, I will remain here with Sr. Alfredo, perhaps read to him."

Finally she left and Carolina sat beside the bed. "Let us go over your evening's work."

Alfredo groaned and asked, "Dearest Angel, must we... I ... do this? I will be truly sick. Let us wait."

She interrupted him roughly. "Idiot, do you not understand our danger? If Lita should tell anyone I, we, killed my husband, even if they refuse to believe her, a doubt will be cast on us and sometime, somewhere, someone will take her word. She must be removed permanently.

"Now, a little after ten, you will dress and climb over the balcony to the Loughlan suite. Use the knife I gave you to force the door should it be locked. Enter and find the viper and kill her. How I care not. Strangle, stab, just be sure she is dead."

Alfredo groaned again and turned away from his Angel of Death. Carolina rose, patted her hair and poured herself a glass of brandy.

At eight o'clock, Elaine was dressed in her new gown and looking beautiful. She added the diamond pendant John had given her as a wedding gift. Her satin slippers were the same color rose as her gown and, though a little loose, quite comfortable. Nette had piled high her thick, black hair and then curled it, weaving rose velvet ribbon and velvet roses in and out of the tasseled curls. Even Elaine was pleased, holding up a hand mirror to look at the finished product.

"You have outdone yourself, Nette. As soon as the gentlemen arrive, you may go. Enjoy yourself and happy New Year."

"Merci, Madame, and to you also," said the maid as she went to answer a knock at the door and let the men in. She served a tray of crackers, cheese and caviar. Then, as the gentlemen poured champagne and Elaine basked in their profuse compliments, Nette hurried to her small room on the other side of Madame's dressing room. She changed her black bombazine and apron for an attractive green wool gown with matching velvet wrap. A touch of powder to her nose, blush on her lips and a good spray of Madame's second favorite perfume and Nette was ready to take San Francisco by storm, or at least thoroughly enjoy herself for the evening. She let herself out the door in her room.

As she was leaving, she heard Elaine calling to Sir Francis to "come in off the balcony and close the door. The draft is appalling."

"One puff more, my dear, and I am at your service," he said. Coming in, he neglected to lock the door, and neither Elaine nor Captain Slater took note of the fact.

Close to nine o'clock, Elaine pulled on white kid opera gloves, allowed Captain Slater to help with her wraps and, with the men happily in tow, left the suite. The hotel lobby was filled with revelers and guests. Elaine, in her new gown and flanked by two handsome men in black tie and tails, knew what an elegant picture she made at the top of the grand staircase. Taking an arm of each man, she started down. Somehow, one of her new slippers slid on the carpet stairs and she nearly tripped. In fact, she would have if not for her escorts' support. Still, she somehow turned the heel of the dainty satin slipper so that the heel came off!

"Merde!" she said, realizing that she must go back and find another pair of shoes or spend the evening hobbling about. Controlling her fury, she told her escorts she must return to her suite for a fresh pair of shoes. They begged to accompany her.

"No, I will be but a moment," she said. "You call our carriage and I will change shoes and return at once." With that, she removed both slippers, lifting the skirt of her ball gown high enough to give anyone watching a sight of her trim ankles. She hurried back to her suite.

When she entered, she was met with a blast of cold air. Stupid man, she thought, he left the balcony door open. It is freezing!

"Nette, are you still here?" she called, hearing a noise coming from the maid's room. She went toward her dressing room and encountered a man dressed in dark clothes coming out of Nette's room.

"Who are you?" she demanded. "What are you doing here? Surely, you are the Spanish man from the next suite?"

Alfredo panicked when she recognized him. What should I do? he thought. She knows who I am!

"If you are looking for my jewels, I keep them in the hotel safe," Elaine said. "Now leave before I call for the police."

Trying to save the situation, he came close to her. "Where is your maid, the African?"

"Who do you mean, stupid man? My maid is French," she said over her shoulder, searching the closet for another pair of dancing slippers. He came up behind her just as she turned. She realized for the first time in her life there might be danger from a man and began to scream. But the rattled coward grabbed her around the neck to silence her while pondering what to do next.

She struggled, lashing out at Alfredo and badly scratching his face. Frightened and angry, he squeezed her throat as hard as he could. The bitch had injured him, how dare she! Where could Lita be, he thought, looking around wildly. What would Carolina say when he announced he had botched the job?

Elaine gave a shudder and went limp, her face discolored, her eyes bulging.

Alfredo looked at his hands around the throat of the lifeless woman and tossed her aside as though she were a child's doll. Panic-stricken, he tried to think what to do. He bent over the dead woman and tore the diamond pendant from her neck, put it in his pocket and, in absolute terror, let himself out the French doors to the balcony and hurried back to Carolina.

In the lobby, Sir Francis and Captain Slater were becoming

irritated. "Typical of the best of women. Never can decide on one article of clothing in a hurry," said Sir Francis.

"I'm going up to get her," said Captain Slater. "We will be late for the party. You go tell the carriage to wait." He climbed hurriedly up the staircase and went to Elaine Loughlan's suite.

He found the entry door not quite closed and entered, calling, "Elaine, my dear, we must hurry." He looked around the living room and, again calling her, went into the bedroom. Seeing it also was empty, he thought to look in the dressing room to see if the broken-heeled slippers were there. Perhaps she had changed shoes and gone down a different staircase while he was coming up the main. Opening wide the half-closed door, he found her lying on the floor, her beautiful face an ugly mask. "Oh, my God, Elaine!" He bent down but already knew she was dead. He had seen many men die and recognized it at once.

Almost running, he left the suite and went down the grand staircase to the hotel manager's office. At the door, he turned and saw Sir Francis at the entrance watching him. Captain Slater beckoned to the Englishman to come with him. When he was sure Sir Francis was on his way, he entered the office. The night manager, Horace Ridley, jumped up from his late dinner.

"Captain Slater, sir, what can I do for you?" he said. "Are you ill? Shall I call for a doctor?"

Sir Francis came in just as Captain Slater said in a horrified voice, "Call the police. I think Elaine Loughlan has been murdered!"

In Sra. Costa-Nunez's bedroom, Alfredo cowered under the

bedclothes as Carolina ranted and berated him. "Fool. Cretin. Imbecile! In the morning I will go down to breakfast to hear what is said and we will leave the following day for Los Angeles as I arranged. Get up and wash the blood off your face and put some salve on your scratches!"

Outside Los Angeles, it was well after sunset and a cold north wind whipped down from the mountains as John rode the last way home to Rancho Dos Aliso. He could see lamps shining in the front of the house, a truly welcoming sight. He rode on up to the stable yard where one of the hands was caring for the horses. He dismounted and went on up the hill to the house. He crossed the flagstone area leading to the kitchen and the back door and in seconds was surrounded by his daughters, all laughing and chatting at once. He picked each one up, hugged them and said, "Come, let's go in. It's getting very cold." As they headed to the back door, he saw the woman his eyes and heart had been searching for.

"Well, girl, can I not leave you alone a few days or you'll get up to mischief?" he asked Breed, grinning. He came up to her, stood for a moment, and took her in his arms. "My dear girl, thank God you are safe!"

Tears running down her cheeks, Breed returned his embrace. "Oh, John, I was so worried about you. We have sorely missed you!"

Lita entered the kitchen and shooed them out to the front room, where a fire was blazing. She signaled to Breed that she would get John's supper and bring it out. The little girls were full of news that Breed had been "kitsnapped." Breed and John sat side by side on the settee, holding hands, listening to the children and occasionally answering their questions. They agreed to wait until they were alone to share their other news. Lita came in with John's meal, as well cookies and cocoa for the rest. At half-past nine, she took the children off to bed, smiling at John and Breed.

The couple continued to sit before the fire, speaking in low voices, sometimes about what had happened while they had been apart, sometimes just lovers' words. "Hopefully, we will be able to marry well before Easter, Breed," he told her.

"Come to bed now, you must be worn out," Breed said, filling a warming pan to heat his bed.

"I'll not need that if you will come keep me warm," he said.

Breed, her free hand on her belly as she felt the baby do a somersault, cast virtue and propriety to the wind. "I will do that, John Loughlan," she said, smiling. "For it's a cold night and I too will be warm!"

❧❧ CHAPTER TWENTY-FOUR ❧❧

In San Francisco, the new year dawned clear and crisp. Polite society was aghast at the wanton murder of Elaine Loughlan. Sir Francis took to his bed with what was thought to be a mild heart attack. Captain Slater, still in shock, told the police about John Loughlan's visit and the apparent ill feelings between him and his wife. The chief of police mentioned this to the mayor at a meeting and that night at a dinner party the mayor mentioned it to the state attorney, Mr. McGonical. McGonical said, "Nonsense. I've known John Loughlan since he was a youngster, knew his father, and John took passage to Los Angeles on the same ship I came down on from Sacramento. We chatted a few moments before he boarded. Good man."

This, the mayor hastened to pass on to the police chief. It was decided that the crime had been one of chance, a burglar caught in her room when she returned to change shoes. The distraught maid announced that Madame's diamond pendant was missing—along with several other pieces of jewelry that she had carefully removed from the jewel case and hidden in a sewing box amongst her things.

The sheriff in Los Angeles was sent a telegraph. "We're telling of the death of Mrs. Loughlan and asking that a message be sent to John Loughlan asking him to come to San Francisco and oversee Mrs. Loughlan's last rites."

A day later, Sra. Costa-Nunez and her lover, Alfredo, left the hotel as she had previously announced and took passage to Los Angeles. Alfredo supposedly was still feeling unwell. He was swathed in a heavy cloak, a muffler that covered much of his lower face and a fashionably dashing felt hat that helped hide his upper face and eyes. Carolina had spoken to the police. "We heard nothing," she said. "So frightening it might have been us! But I was reading to my nephew and we really noticed nothing. Awful!" Here, she was able to squeeze out a tear or two and was hurriedly excused.

A lone rider arrived at Rancho Dos Aliso in the afternoon with the news of Elaine's death. John was in the corral breaking a horse when Breed sent word to him that there was a messenger from town. John knew the man. He rode with him on the hunt for Vasquez. "Well, Jim, what brings you out this way?"

"Hey, John, guess it's some bad news. Here's the letter from the sheriff." Breed, hearing this, took the man out to the kitchen for a meal. She and Lita had just set him a plate of cold ham, cheese and new bread when they heard John say, "Oh, my God. My God!"

She rushed into the front room and asked, "John, what is it? Is it Hugh? Tell me, dearest."

John looked pale but collected himself and gave Breed the letter. Reading it hurriedly, she gasped. "God rest her soul," she said. "Oh, what will you tell the children?"

"Nothing," he said. "They have all but forgotten her, and these last few months you have been more of a mother to them than she ever was."

He took her hand, "Breed, I must return to San Francisco and have a funeral up there. I'll be back as soon as possible."

"I'll go and pack your black suit," she said, hurrying to get his things together. "You tell the children you're going away again."

An hour later, John and the deputy were on the road to Los Angeles. Late that night, John was able to get passage north on a whaler.

Elaine's funeral was well attended. Her many socially prominent friends were there, more from a desire to see the handsome widower in person than out of respect to the dead. In their shallow little group, Elaine's murder was as a ten-day wonder before polite society forgot her. John spent an hour going through Elaine's effects with the maid, Nette. Finally, disgusted and impatient to be gone, he told her, "I don't know what, if anything, all this frippery and geegaws are worth, but you may take whatever you want. Then, bundle the rest and send it to the mission for the poor."

The woman was stunned. Thousands of dollars worth of clothes were all hers. She could open a shop. Then, feeling guilty about the jewelry she had taken, she said hesitantly, "Mr. Loughlan, there a few of Madame's jewels hidden in her dressing room. Let me get them."

But he waved the offer away. "Keep them. I'll tell the lawyer you are to have complete control of all this. The rent for the suite is paid for the remainder of the month. Thank you for your faithful service to Mrs. Loughlan, and goodbye." With that, he strode from the room. After a short visit to the lawyer, he went down to the harbor to find a ship bound for Los Angeles.

True to his words, he was back in Los Angeles in two weeks. He went first to the city clerk's office, then to the mission to see his old friend and schoolmate, Padre Miguel Gaurrio. The two had been at school in San Francisco and Padre Miguel had baptized all three of John's girls. John knocked on the door of the Padre's office. "Here's that bad penny, Miguel."

The priest rose from his writing table and came around to his visitor. Taking his hand in his own, he offered his deepest sympathies to his friend. "Thanks, Padre, but you know things between Elaine and me have been over for almost three years and now, well, it's really over. But that's not what I'm here about."

The priest took his arm and said, "Let's walk in the garden and tell me what I can do to help you."

The mission was old and had suffered damage in the various earthquakes but was a beautifully designed compound: the church to one side, attached by long, open galleries in the Spanish manner, creating a square. The garden, a tiled fountain and several shrines were tucked here and there amongst the flowers and vines that grew rampant. The many other offices, rooms, kitchens and workshops opened off the other side of the gallery.

The two men walked slowly and silently for a few moments before John blurted out, "How soon can I remarry? I had planned to marry the girl I sent for from the East as soon as a divorce became final, but now Breed and I can be properly wed."

"Remarry?" the Padre said. "John, your wife is hardly cold in her grave! Think of the scandal. Can you not wait a year? Even six months?"

John stopped walking. "I must marry her now. I want to marry now. She is pregnant with my child and I will not have it born a bastard."

They resumed their walk. After a moment or so, Padre Miguel spoke. "Easter is early this year. Then Lent starts early also. What about being wed on St. Valentine's Day? That way you will remember your anniversary."

John shook his friend's hand. "Miguel, thank you."

"Wait now," the Padre said. "Before you go off hell for leather, you and your lady must come to the mission to arrange everything." John agreed and was off at once for the ride home.

Meanwhile, at the Pico Hotel, Carolina Costa-Nunez and her paramour had settled comfortably into their new residence. More than two weeks had passed since their arrival and they had heard little of the murder in San Francisco. "The weather here is much nicer than in the north, I think," she noted as she and Alfredo had early tea in the small hotel garden. Alfredo only nodded in agreement, his mouth full of cream cake.

"Next week, I shall seek out a dressmaker and plan my summer wardrobe," she said. One had only to look attentive around Carolina, who preferred to do most of the talking.

Later that evening, as Breed and Lita sat by a lamp sewing baby clothes, Breed watched John reading to his children. "I never knew a man who spent so much time coming and going," she told Lita.

John heard her and said, "You would too if you received such a welcome as I do every time I return."

CHAPTER TWENTY-FOUR

They smiled across at each other.

John had told her of the wedding date and the need to go into town. He also told her he wanted to have the doctor look her over.

"John, sure I'm as healthy as a cow," she said. "My good aunt had seven confinements and a doctor never crossed the threshold."

"You are not your aunt or a cow, dear girl, and you will see the doctor," he said in a firm voice that Breed had come to know meant no argument allowed. It was planned that Lita would go with them to look around for a possible spot for her shop.

The two women agreed that they would first go to the dry goods store to find out if Hung Mi Sing and his wife might have suggestions. "Besides," Lita wrote, "we need more diaper material and some to make gowns for you as you enlarge!" It was decided that they would take the little girls as a treat and take turns watching them. While John and Breed went to see Padre Miguel, Lita would watch them. When Breed and Lita went to shop, John would take over. They spent the next day packing for the two-day trip and John went around the Rancho with Huron Del Gado to check on what needed to be done.

The wagon was used for the trip into Los Angeles so that there was plenty of room for grips and carpetbags. John had the wagon bed piled in fresh, sweet-smelling hay and Breed covered it with blankets.

It was hardly daylight when the travelers left Rancho Dos Aliso, but it promised to be a beautiful day, clear and cold. As before, John rode alongside the wagon. Sometimes he would take one of the girls up in the saddle with him and ride ahead and back.

Watching how delighted the girls were to ride, Breed said to Lita, "I will never understand how they can be so brave around such huge beasts!"

And Lita wrote, "They also smell." Both women smiled. After three hours, they opened the picnic basket that Blanca had provided. As the wagon plowed along the bumpy road, John tied his mount to the wagon's gate and sat with them for lunch. There were small little meat pies called empanadas, thick sandwiches of ham and cheese, a sack of oranges, a jug of coffee kept hot in wrappings and hot bricks, and the last of the Christmas cake. When he had eaten, John took over the driving of the wagon so that Jorge, the ranch hand, could eat. As they came to a small grove of trees and bush, Breed suggested they stop so the girls could go to the toilet. When they returned to the wagon, all the children lay down, their heads in either Lita or Breed's laps, and were asleep in moments.

Shortly after noon, the wagon pulled up to the rear entrance of the Pico Hotel. Everyone climbed down. "I'll go with Jorge to the livery stable to bed the horses and freshen up," John said. "Breed, I'll be back for you around four to go see Padre Miguel." John gave the bellboys instructions to take care of his party and then left.

Just off the main hall, in a rather dark and dank area, Alfredo Ramos was enjoying a dalliance with one of the hotel maids. Carolina would be busy with the hairdresser for hours. The maid, a pretty young thing, plump and willing, was inclined to tease before she allowed the handsome Cuban his desire.

As he fondled her breasts, she whispered, "Careful, there are hotel guests arriving. Look, they might see us!"

Alfredo glanced around. He realized they were well in the shadows, but then he saw her: Lita—alive and surrounded by a tall, blonde woman and little girls!

How could this be, he thought, nearly ill as he remembered how Elaine had looked. His hands dropped from the young maid. He reached into his pocket, gave her a few coins and said, "I must go. We will meet again." Then he went out the rear entrance and walked the busy streets.

He was frightened. Carolina would find out Lita was here. She was determined to finally silence the black woman, but he could not kill again. He still had nightmares about killing Elaine. Carolina must not ask him to commit murder again!

Unknowingly, he had wandered into the less desirable area of town. There were few sidewalks and every storefront was a low saloon or boarding house. He went into one, got a glass and a bottle of liquor at the bar and sat at a small table toward the back. It was only mid-afternoon but already there were quite a few disreputable-looking characters at the bar. Alfredo realized he was drinking too much, had been drinking too much since San Francisco, but he could not help himself. He felt someone's eyes on him and carefully looked around. At another table, just to one side but in the shadows sat a seedy looking person, a seaman, by his dress. More than a little drunk by now, Alfredo lifted his glass toward the stranger and with his foot shoved the other chair out in invitation.

After a moment's hesitation, the seaman picked up his glass and joined the Cuban. When the men realized they both spoke Spanish, they conversed idly.

"What port do you sail from? What are you doing here?"

Then, in Alfredo's drunken brain, an idea was spawned. "Senor, are you interested in making some extra money, say twenty dollars?" he asked.

The seaman nodded. He poured himself another drink and said, "Si, who do you want me to kill? Your wife? Her lover?"

Frightened, Alfredo looked around to be sure no one had heard. "Yes, I do want you to kill someone," he said. "It must be soon. Tonight. Tomorrow by the latest."

The seaman grinned an ugly smile. "Just tell me who and where, senor, but it will cost you thirty dollars!"

The men continued to drink and Alfredo arranged for the seaman to meet in the alley behind the hotel's rear entrance at ten o'clock that evening.

Jim Stein, the young deputy who had brought John Loughlan word of Elaine's death, by chance entered the saloon for a drink before going home to Mrs. Calhoun's boarding house. Standing at the bar, he saw in the mirror the reflection of Alfredo and the seaman, sitting together and talking.

That's a real odd combination, he thought, a well-dressed dandy and a dirty, disheveled seaman. Wonder what they are up to? Just then, the two men walked past and out the door. Shortly thereafter, Jim left thinking now of his dinner and perhaps a game of cards with Essie, Mrs. Calhoun's daughter.

John Loughlan returned to the hotel for Breed and off they

went to meet the priest. Breed liked the Padre, who was soft spoken and friendly. He invited them to stay for supper but John explained that they had the girls at the hotel with Lita, Breed's friend. On their way back to the Pico, the couple laughed and were as silly as school children. In a little more than two weeks, they would be man and wife. Each felt so fortunate in having the other, they were giddy.

At the hotel, Lita and the girls were dressed in their best, waiting to go to dinner. The evening had become overcast and the air smelled definitely of rain, so it was decided they would dine at the hotel rather than a restaurant.

When Alfredo returned to the hotel, he found Carolina dressed and ready to go down to dinner. She had spent the day with the hairdresser. She wore a new gown and was ready to socialize.

Alfredo knew they dare not go to the dining room, in case they encounter Lita. He poured them both a stiff brandy and told Carolina about the arrival of Lita and the others. She went pale. Then rage took over and she threw her half-empty glass at the wall. "She is a witch! She is trying to frighten us. It is voodoo! This time she will die!"

Alfredo nodded, pouring another brandy. He was used to her rages, but this one frightened him. Her careful makeup became a mask and her eyes resembled nothing so much as those of a snake seeking its prey.

"Silencio," Alfred said sharply, and Carolina stopped her pacing and violent language in surprise. "I have found a man, a seaman whom we may employ. He will come to the alley tonight for instructions." Alfredo knew she must be convinced to use the seaman to kill Lita.

He could not go through that again. Having gained her attention, he spoke quietly of his plan, then rang for a waiter to order dinner sent to their room.

Later, as the waiter served them, Alfredo idly asked, "Who is the family with the three little girls? They do not look a bit like their mama."

"Ah, sir, so romantic," the waiter said. "The tall, blonde lady is to be married shortly to Mr. John Loughlan. The lady of color is their companion. and the little girls his by his earlier marriage."

Alfredo looked at Carolina, gave a small smile and asked, "Do they reside here in the hotel all the time?"

The waiter was enjoying the chance to talk. "Ah, no sir. They have come to shop and make arrangements for the wedding and reception here at the hotel afterward."

Carolina could keep still no longer. "Shop? Where?" The waiter puffed himself up and announced, "I did hear they plan an early start in the morning and will go to the Chinaman's for material first!"

Alfredo gave his mistress a slight shake of the head. Then, giving the waiter a generous tip, he sent him on his way.

Late that night, Alfredo and Carolina, both heavily cloaked, met the seaman in the dark alley. They gave him his instructions, and a third of his money. As they parted, Carolina hissed, "She must be dead before dusk. Return here and receive your reward!"

At dinner, John, Breed and Lita discussed wedding plans. John said he had ordered invitations to be sent to the ranch. Breed and

Lita could address them. He then proceeded to tell them of the plans for a reception afterward. Breed looked from him to Lita in panic. "Reception?" Breed said. "What do you mean? John, no one will come! You... you are marrying your housekeeper!" Her voice quivered, and Loughlan rose and went to her.

"Dearest, you don't understand," he said. "California is a new country, not staid and stuffy like Boston. To be sure, there will be talk, but only by those who mean nothing to us. You will be Mrs. John Loughlan. That is all that anyone need know."

Lita wrote, "We are all tired, let us go upstairs." He nodded his head and, taking Breed's hand and tucking it in the crook of his arm, set sail out of the crowded dining room. The little girls and Lita moved ahead like leaves before the wind.

Later that night, as the women prepared for bed, Breed thought, I can send an invitation to Aunt Kate and Eliza and the Potts and, oh, to Cook. They will be so surprised and pleased for me.

Early in the morning, Dr. Husselman, the Loughlan's family physician, arrived to give Breed a check-up and to see how Lita and the little girls were getting along.

Breed was embarrassed, having never been examined by a physician, and insisted that Lita stay with her. When Dr. Husselman had finished his exam, he took a peculiar-looking instrument from his black bag. He put two parts into his ears and placed a small cup hanging by rubber tubes onto Breed's stomach. He looked pleased with himself and kept saying, "Hmmmm." The women were intrigued. Asked Breed, overcoming her nervousness, "What is that thing in your ears?"

As proud as a peacock, Dr. Husselman told them it was a stethoscope recently arrived from New York. It allowed a doctor to listen to his patients' hearts and lungs and helped in diagnosis. Both Breed and Lita were properly impressed.

The good doctor washed his hands and put on his coat, excusing himself to join John Loughlan.

"And how is she?" John asked.

"As healthy as a brood mare," the doctor said. "You know she is pregnant?"

John nodded. "Yes, we are looking to the arrival of our child," he said.

"Well, you better be ready because if I'm not mistaken your bride-to-be is carrying twins!"

The doctor took out his pipe, stuffed and lit it. "Come, girls, let me look at you," he said, giving John a grin.

When they were alone for a few minutes, before Breed and Lita went shopping, John told Breed what the doctor had said. She was shaken.

"Twins?"

Giving her a quick kiss, he laughed and said, "I'll be the envy of all the Californians. My own harem! Six women at my beck and call!"

Breed, in a daze, again said, "Twins." Then the little girls and Lita joined them.

It was arranged that the children would go with their father, allowing Breed and Lita the morning to shop at Sings. Breed also gave John a grocery list. They parted company, agreeing to meet for a late lunch back at the hotel.

Late January and the sky was blue and clear, just chilly enough to appreciate a shawl. Breed mused aloud, "To think, back in Boston there will be snow and ice and oh, the wind. So cold. I love California!"

Lita, having never seen snow or frost, merely nodded in agreement. She was busy observing the different businesses as they passed, her mind excited with thoughts of her own planned shop. As they passed a small alley, only a few doors from Sings, a man accosted them. He was evidently a seaman, by his dress, but wore new cowboy boots.

At first, Breed thought him a beggar. She reached into her pocket for her change purse but then her eyes opened wide in surprise. He bowed low and said in Spanish, "Senoritas Day and Night."

Breed gasped. "El Toro! What are you doing here?" Lita too was surprised, but not as trusting as her friend. She glanced around to make sure there were other people close by.

"What am I doing here, Miss?" the man said. "Well, not what I thought I would be doing. I will not keep you, only long enough to say again my thanks for your kindness to one abandoned soul. For the clothes you made me while aboard the Sara Blue, the food that gave me strength and the coins you pressed into my hands before you parted from the ship, I thank you. Take your lives as my thanks. You will not see me again!"

With that, he backed into the alley, turned and ran.

Puzzled but glad he had gone, the women continued on to Sings. "What an odd man," Breed said, and Lita nodded.

The Sings were delighted to see them. Though Saturdays were usually very busy, it was early enough that they were the only customers. They spent a small fortune on material for the wedding. A soft and beautiful blue velvet that matched her eyes would be used for Breed's wedding gown. Sing produced bolts of elegant wool prints from Liberty's of London, dear in price but perfect for the little girls' dresses. Lita decided that she, as maid of honor, would wear a matching shirt waist with a dark blue skirt she had recently made for herself. Writing the word "twins," Lita gave it to Breed, who blushed and told Sing the younger they would need material for nappies and planned for "other things." Mrs. Sing came and, in her careful English, invited them to have a cup of tea. Breed was more than willing, as she found the choosing and planning exhausting. Lita, though, was in her element.

They retired to the lovely garden room and soon the elder Sing joined them. As they sipped their tea, Mrs. Sing hesitatingly inquired about Breed's adventure with the kidnappers. Breed obliged by telling them all. Then, after a note from Lita, she relayed Lita's plan to open a dressmaking shop in town. She asked if Mr. Sing had suggestions as to where the best location would be, and would he be willing to supply the materials she would require.

Sing the elder stood and bowed, pouring out a stream of pleasantries. He realizes we will be useful to one another, Lita thought, but he does not know I will be in charge. It was agreed that over the next few months, the Sings would keep their eyes open for a suitable site for Lita's shop. Lita, using her own money, bought several bolts of material that she would make up as samples to display to her future customers.

The women thanked their hosts and returned to the hotel. As they walked, Breed told Lita they would never be able to finish all the sewing by the thirteenth day of February. She thought they should send a letter to Mrs. Muller and ask if her daughter Bette could come and help them. She knew the family could use the money.

They arrived at the Pico, Breed giving instructions to the Dos Aliso ranch hand about picking up the purchases at Sings as Lita wandered into the small morning room off the main lobby. As Lita stood looking idly out the French doors to the garden, she felt the hairs prick at the nape of her neck. Someone was watching her. She turned slowly and looked at the people who were scattered around, reading and writing. There, across the room looking at her in shock, and yes, fury, sat Carolina Costa-Nunez. The sheer hatred that emanated from the woman was almost a slap, and Lita was glad other people were in the room. She nodded toward the woman who had tried to kill her, who tried to have her sold into slavery. Then she quickly left the room. She looked for Breed in the lobby but there was no sign of her or John. A bellboy came up to her and said the Loughlan party waited for her in the dining room. She fled to the safety of their family circle.

Carolina, in the hotel morning room, was on the verge of hysterics. Only the tightest hold on her emotions kept her from screaming, from going after Lita and strangling her or committing whatever crime it took to silence her. Fortunately, Alfredo entered moments after Lita left. Seeing Carolina in what he knew was real anger he came to her side, put his arm around her and led her away.

"Mi amor, what has happened?" he asked. "No, wait till we are in our room. Come."

Carolina was nearly blind with rage and fright.

"You fool," she hissed when they arrived upstairs. "Can you do nothing right? The assassin has not killed that woman. She still lives and can tell all."

Alfredo was worried. He had thought that the seaman would dispose of Lita at once.

"Perhaps he has had difficulty in getting her alone, or at least in a place where she would have no help," he said, trying to calm the nearly wild woman. "He is to come again late tonight for payment, but I will demand proof he has removed her." Alfredo was averse to saying "killed." It was perfectly correct to hire an assassin. Never again would he himself do the deed.

After lunch, Breed, Lita and the little girls went up to the rooms for a nap. Breed knew something had happened to Lita. When they were alone, she questioned her. Usually one of complete control, Lita broke down and wept. "Come, dear, what has happened?" Breed asked, putting her arms around her friend.

Lita took paper from the hotel desk and wrote, "The woman who killed my dear Dr. Costa-Nunez, who had me beaten and maimed, is here in the hotel and I am afraid."

Shocked, Breed put the paper down and said, "We'll tell John and he will call the sheriff."

Lita shook her head. "No, say nothing," she wrote. "Who will be believed? A wealthy woman or a former African slave? We must be very careful and not be alone."

That night, Alfredo was to meet El Toro in the alley behind the hotel at eleven o'clock. He had spent hours trying to calm Carolina, reassuring her that by the time he and the seaman met Lita would be truly silenced once and for all. As the hour approached, he brooded over his meeting with the assassin. How to be sure Lita was dead and how to be sure the seaman did not try to blackmail them and demand more money? He wondered if he should bring his small pistol just in case. He went to his bureau and reached under his cravats. Yes, it was loaded, ready should he need it.

Just then, Carolina entered and he closed the drawer. "Well, my dear, it's time," he said. "I will go and meet this man, pay him the rest of his wage and be back shortly." Alfredo patted Carolina's arm and, taking only his cloak, left the room. Beside herself, Carolina paced back and forth. Finally, she could stand the waiting no longer. She went to the bureau and searched through the drawer until she found the small gun. She slipped it into the pocket of her dressing gown and quietly followed her lover down the stairs to the back alley.

Alfredo did not have to wait long for El Toro, who seemed to slip from the darkened area like a shadow. His teeth flashed as he approached Alfredo. He put out his hand, palm up. "Good evening, sir, do you have the rest of my promised pay?" he asked.

"No pay until you give me some proof of the woman's death. I warned you. A tuft of hair. A finger. Some proof."

El Toro came very close to Alfredo and in a low voice said, "I want my pay. She is dead to you. You need no other proof. My pay, fool."

Alfredo jerked his head back as the other man's foul breath reached him. "It's you who is a fool. Do you think I will pay you more for what you may have failed to do?"

He did not see the huge knife slip from the seaman's coat sleeve and made only a small noise as the knife was jabbed into his chest. El Toro was over the dead man, and going through his pockets, as soon as he hit the ground.

Carolina came out and saw Alfredo lying motionless on the dirty cobbles. A rough-looking man, crouched behind him, was withdrawing a large knife from her lover's chest. Beside herself, she flew at El Toro and, hand in pocket, shot him at close range. Caught off guard, El Toro had dropped the pocketbook he had taken from the dead man. But just as Carolina fired he thrust the bloodied knife at her, catching her in the throat with a fatal wound.

Someone in the basement laundry was working late and, hearing the shot, rushed to the back entrance. He looked carefully out from behind the door and by the single lamp saw three bodies crumpled on the ground. Running to the front desk, he alerted the night manager.

It was midnight and the alley behind the hotel was alive with people. The sheriff and his deputies had been called from their homes, a doctor was there to certify the three deaths and many people who only surface after dark milled around.

The sheriff looked on while his men went through the gentlemen's coat pockets. The pocketbook removed by El Toro had fallen to the ground and one of the deputies brought it over to the sheriff. The hotel manager was in shock as he identified Sra. Carolina Costa-Nunez and her companion, Sr. Alfredo Ramos. The sheriff opened the pocketbook. Quite a bit of money was inside. In a secret pocket he found the diamond pendant that Alfredo had ripped from Elaine's neck after strangling her.

This is not a run-of-the-mill robbery, the sheriff thought. Why is the lady in her night clothes? And what dealing were they having with this villain?

In the morning, the hotel was agog with talk about the triple murder and the sheriff asked anyone who knew anything about the killings to come forward.

Earlier, before breakfast, Breed had told John about Carolina Costa-Nunez and her connection to Lita. John went to the front desk for a morning paper before joining his family at their table.

The manager could not wait to tell him of the night's horrific excitement. "They are all dead, you say?" John inquired.

"Yes, sir, and the sheriff is asking if anyone in town has any information." Nodding, John went to the dining room. Lighting a cheroot, he stopped and told the manager, "Send word to the sheriff that we may have something for him and ask if he'll join us here."

At the table, John seemed preoccupied. As soon as the little girls finished their breakfast he sent them to play in the hotel garden. When they were gone, he told Breed and Lita about the murders and that the sheriff was coming to talk to them. They were shocked and relieved. Awful as it was, Lita's nemesis was dead.

John arranged for a hotel maid to look after the girls while the sheriff interviewed Lita. He and Breed stayed to give her support. She wrote carefully of her past and of Carolina's cruelty. She knew Alfredo had most likely helped Carolina poison Dr. Costa-Nunez in Havana but doubted he was capable of murder on his own. When she had finished answering the sheriff's questions, he thanked her. Almost as an afterthought, he took out the diamond pendant that had been found in Alfredo's pocketbook. John was stunned. Taking it from the lawman, he said, "This was my late wife's. I gave it to her on our wedding day." Turning the clasp to the light, he showed the other man where his and Elaine's initials were inscribed.

"Well, by God, this is a strange turn of events," the sheriff said. "This Cuban must have murdered your wife, John!"

Everyone could only guess at such a connection and it was to forever remain a mystery.

Later in the morning, the family from Rancho Dos Aliso left for home. The day was overcast and Breed worried it would rain before they reached the rancho. The hours dragged by and John kept the little girls entertained by taking each in turn up in the saddle with him.

Breed and Lita spent most of the time going over the dreadful happenings of the past few days. When the party finally reached home, Blanca hurried them into the house and sat them down to large bowls of tortilla soup. After supper, while Lita and Breed put the exhausted little girls to bed, John told Blanca all they knew about the deaths at the Pico Hotel and the connection to Elaine's murder. The kind woman wept for the lost souls but thought to herself that his mother would approve of his new wife to be. She will make them all a happy family.

It had begun to rain. Exhausted from the trip to town, most went willingly to their beds. But John and Breed sat together before the fire, talking quietly about their wedding and the happenings of the past few days. He took her hand, kissed her palm and said, "I will always love you, now and forever."

Breed, tears in her eyes, leaned into his arms and whispered, "And I you."

THE END

❧ EPILOGUE ❧

From the Los Angeles morning paper on February 15, 1876:

Yesterday at the Mission Church, Miss Bridget Mary Seastrum of Boston, Mass., was united in marriage to Mr. John Loughlan of Rancho Dos Aliso. Madam Lita Costa-Nunez was matron of honor and Mr. Loughlan's daughters Annabelle, Marguerite and Nicole were bridesmaids. Mr. Huron Del Gado was best man. Following the ceremony a reception was held at the Pico Hotel.

From the court news of the London Times of May 20, 1876:

Lord and Lady Tiverton Holt announce the birth of a son, James George Francis Tiverton West.

From the Los Angeles morning paper: July 7, 1876:

Mr. and Mrs. John Loughlan of Rancho Dos Aliso announce the birth of twin sons: William Lars and Hugh Thomas on July 4th. They weighed 5 lbs. 8 oz. and 5 lbs. 9 oz. and are in excellent health. The Loughlans have three daughters.

From the Los Angeles morning paper: August 21, 1876:

Madam Lita Costa-Nunez announces the opening of her Salon of Design. Madam Lita has designed and created elegant attire for several of our social leaders. She promises fashions that will rival New York and Paris in style. Reception from 2 p.m. till 5 p.m.

CPSIA information can be obtained at www.ICGtesting.com
Printed in the USA
BVOW04*1937020515

398199BV00003B/63/P